YES, DADDY

YES, DADDY

JONATHAN PARKS-RAMAGE

Houghton Mifflin Harcourt
Boston   New York
2021

For information about permission to reproduce selections
from this book, write to trade.permissions@hmhco.com or to
Permissions, Houghton Mifflin Harcourt Publishing Company,
3 Park Avenue, 19th Floor, New York, New York 10016.

hmhbooks.com

Library of Congress Cataloging-in-Publication Data
Names: Parks-Ramage, Jonathan, author.
Title: Yes, Daddy / Jonathan Parks-Ramage.
Description: Boston : Houghton Mifflin Harcourt, 2021.
Identifiers: LCCN 2020039571 (print) | LCCN 2020039572 (ebook) |
ISBN 9780358447719 (hardcover) | ISBN 9780358447917 (ebook)
Classification: LCC PS3616.A75688 Y47 2021 (print) |
LCC PS3616.A75688 (ebook) | DDC 813/.6—dc23
LC record available at https://lccn.loc.gov/2020039571
LC ebook record available at https://lccn.loc.gov/2020039572

Book design by Emily Snyder

Printed in the United States of America
DOC 10 9 8 7 6 5 4 3 2 1

For Ryan

2011

PROLOGUE

YOU ASKED ME to be a witness in the trial.

I owed you my life and so I said yes.

What does one wear to a rape testimony? Your lawyer and I debated this endlessly. Nothing too tight, nothing too baggy, nothing too ratty, nothing too expensive, something sexless yet attractive, a suit jacket perhaps, but nothing flashy, a light navy was best, black was too morbid, too dark. I wanted to seem serious but not angry, definitely not vengeful; maybe glasses were a good idea, but the frames had to be simple, nothing flamboyant, nothing too gay, nothing that might trigger juror prejudice. Something to wear while the world decided if I had been raped.

Something that said: *Believe me.*

I dreaded our rehearsals for the witness stand. Your lawyer's endless questions. *What did the basement look like? How many men? What did they do to you?* I never slept, barely ate. Walked through the world a husk, disconnected from my body. Pain was the only thing that cut the numbness. I picked the skin around my fingernails with my teeth, tasting the blood on my tongue, repeating the process until all my digits were crusted in scabs.

Finally, the day of the trial arrived.

When I saw Richard in the courtroom, I snapped. He was a nightmare brought to life, sitting stone-faced with his team of defense attorneys. I recognized the fury in his eyes—I'd seen it before, of course—and I felt his rage burn a hole in my back as I walked up to take the stand. The courtroom shifted its attention toward me, expecting me to tell the story I'd told only three people—you, your lawyer, and my mother. Expecting me to explain my private hell in a public forum.

"When did you first meet Richard Shriver?" your lawyer asked when I was settled.

It was the simplest question of all, one we'd rehearsed and rehearsed during our months of prep. But staring at Richard, I suddenly forgot my lines. I clenched my fists and closed my eyes, praying that when I opened them, this would all be over, and the trial would dissipate like the edges of a bad acid trip. When my eyelids at last fluttered wide, I saw your lawyer's stricken face.

"Perhaps you didn't hear the question," he said, straining to keep an even tone. "I asked, when did you first meet Richard Shriver?"

My mouth refused to move.

"Jonah, do you need a minute?"

Nothing.

"Jonah, when did you first meet Richard Shriver?"

"In 2009," I finally managed, my voice dry and timid. Relief softened his expression. We had returned to our script.

"And what was the nature of your relationship?"

"I . . . I guess he was my boyfriend."

"But that relationship changed over time, did it not?"

Again, silence.

"Jonah?"

Panic lifted me out of my body. My consciousness floated by the ceiling fan. I clenched my fists tighter, clenched them until the scabs cracked and seeped blood. "I . . . don't know."

Your lawyer frowned. Richard's features shifted as well, assembling into a strange expression of pleasure. A familiar postcoital grin.

"But it *did* change, didn't it?"

"Richard . . ." I trailed off.

"Yes, Jonah?"

"Richard loved me," I blurted out, surprising everyone, including myself. Whispers rippled through the courtroom. Your lawyer returned to your side for a hushed consultation.

"No further questions, Your Honor," he said finally.

This is how I survive, I thought. *By withholding my story.*

How could anyone attempt to discredit a testimony that didn't exist? How could the press exploit the absence of a story? At worst, I would be cast as a malfunctioning witness, a minor character in the larger drama of the trial. A blip in Richard's history. A Wikipedia footnote.

Richard was now smiling in my direction. It was the same smile he'd used when he told me he loved me, the smile that kept me by his side, the smile that had once promised me a world beyond my own. Richard's attorney stood for cross-examination. His eyes shone with Christmas-morning joy. I was a gift ready to be torn open.

"You say you loved Richard?"

"Yes."

"And he was your boyfriend?"

"Yes."

"And did he abuse you?"

"No."

Even better than withholding my story: creating a new one. And I could, if I did enough Olympian-level mental gymnastics, believe it to be true. Here, with all these people as witnesses, I could say that Richard did not abuse me. And if a whole room of people believed it was true, then maybe the media would believe it as well, and if the media believed, then maybe the whole world would believe. And if the whole world believed that I had not been raped, then maybe that would be enough. Maybe that would make it true.

"Did he rape you?"

"No," I said, avoiding your gaze.

"Did he abuse anyone else during the course of your relationship?"

"No," I said, watching my answer register on the faces in the crowd.

"So you never witnessed Richard Shriver or anyone else rape, sexually assault, or abuse anyone."

"No," I said. Adrenaline stung my spine.

"Why, then, would your friend here accuse Richard of these horrific crimes?"

"For the money."

"How can you be sure?"

"Because he told me himself."

"No further questions, Your Honor."

That was it. I was left alone on the stand. Free to go. With my new truth. My new identity. No longer a victim. No longer a tragedy. I was Jonah, reborn.

Then I snuck a glance in your direction, saw you sobbing in your lawyer's arms. Suddenly, the entire lie collapsed as quickly as I had built it. I knew that what I'd done was irreversible, that justice had not been served, that I had ruined your life and my own. I hesitated, unable to pry my cracked fingertips from my chair. I wanted to rush toward you, explain everything. Beg for forgiveness.

But all I could do was stand and exit the courtroom.

2009

1

MAY 16, 2009. The day had been marked in my calendar for weeks. RICHARD was all it said, his name scrawled across the white box devoted to the sixteenth, the anxious loop of my *n* enclosing the date like a promise. Beneath his name, a time: 8:00 p.m. It was 7:15, and I was already late. Richard had no idea I was coming. He didn't even know who I was.

I couldn't find my tie. I scanned the cramped quarters of my apartment, my claustrophobia mounting. There were only two rooms — a kitchen and a bedroom — and it seemed impossible that I could lose anything in such a small space. The bathroom was down the hall, shared by other residents in a building that had been advertised on Craigslist as a "hip artist loft in the heart of Bushwick," although "gutter-trash shithole in the ass-crack of hell" seemed a more apt description. The apartment was a sublet, normally home to the lead singer of Ghost Dick, a minor indie band, but leased to me for the length of the group's seven-month dive-bar tour. The ad called the place "furnished," a rather generous word for a queen-size mattress occupying the majority of the splintered bedroom floor, a giant sound system crammed into the remaining square footage, and a single Ghost Dick poster featuring a crude rendering of a floating, phantom penis ejaculating over a crowded graveyard.

The rent was eleven hundred dollars a month, a sum I could barely afford and one that was currently sixteen days past due. Daily e-mails from Mr. Ghost Dick piled up in my in-box unanswered, their demands increasingly capitalized. WHERE THE FUCK IS MY MONEY, the subject line of today's missive shouted. IF I LOSE THIS APARTMENT, I WILL FUCKING KILL YOU, read yesterday's. I ignored them all. My anxiety grew exponentially. The truth was, I had spent my money for the month. Spent it on my plan for tonight.

Tonight. I ripped the mattress from the floor, desperate to locate my tie, losing valuable time. I'd been in the apartment for four months but still felt like an intruder in someone else's space, like a burglar who'd decided to spend the night. The only evidence of my existence was the bag I'd been living out of since moving to New York. Every day, I plucked my wardrobe from that massive duffel I'd carted all the way from grad school in Ohio; I couldn't use the bedroom's tiny closet because it was still stuffed with my sub-landlord's clothes. His kitchen was similarly unwelcoming. The photos he'd magneted to the fridge mocked me daily with scenes from an active social life—the rowdy keg party, the packed concerts, the kiss from a girlfriend or groupie or both—scenes that stood in stark contrast to my friendless existence as a recent transplant to the city. I'd developed an irrational attachment to my single piece of luggage—subtract it from the apartment, and I was erased.

I dumped the contents of my battered duffel onto the floor in the continued hunt for my tie. Everything I owned tumbled out and landed in a heavy pile. As I picked through the mess, my phone began to vibrate. I knew who it was—so few people had my number—and I debated whether to answer it. I was already late, and tonight was too important to miss. Still, this was one call I had to take.

I picked up the phone and braced myself for a familiar threat.

"Where's the money going, Jonah?"

"Hi, Mom." I sighed.

"Well?"

"New York is expensive."

"That doesn't answer my question," she snapped.

"What—am I supposed to have, like, an itemized statement for you?"

"Don't you make money waiting tables? Why do I get this same e-mail from you every two weeks asking me for five hundred bucks, sometimes a thousand? You don't even *call me* anymore, you just shoot off an *e-mail*."

"Mom, I have bills, I have rent, I have . . . groceries—"

"*Groceries?*" she spat. "How about *grad school*, Jonah? That's the bill *I'm* still stuck with on top of everything else. Why did I ever agree to let you go there? So you could become—what, a waiter?"

"Come on, Mom. Things take time. I've only been in New York for four months."

My mother knew exactly which punches would land. My very expensive master's degree in playwriting had paved the way for an illustrious career as a New York waiter. The job had been a blow to my delusional pride, but it paid at least a portion of my bills. My dream was to become a playwright, but I lacked the one thing most aspiring playwrights possess: rich parents.

"Jonah, just come home," she pleaded, her voice softening. "This New York lifestyle isn't healthy. You can live with me in Illinois, start going to church again—"

"Oh, because we all know how well church turned out for everyone the first time around," I sneered.

"If only your *father*—" She stopped midsentence, startled by the word we had tacitly banished from our conversations. The subject of our family's absent patriarch unearthed far too much hurt. Money was a much simpler fight.

"Please." I sighed. "Can you help me out a little?"

"*Do you know how much you've cost me?*" she snapped. "Fifty thousand dollars. Spent on you. You think *you're* in debt? What about *me*, Jonah? Where am I going to get *fifty thousand dollars?*"

Silence hung on the line. This was a new one. Never before had my mother calculated the cost of my existence and placed the blame squarely on my shoulders. Like I was a bad investment. Like I amounted to nothing more than the balance due on her credit card statement.

"Well, I'm sorry that I've come with such a hefty price tag. You sure you don't want to trade me in at Walmart for a cheaper model?"

"And you have the nerve to keep asking for money."

"*Stop it, Mom.* I can't keep doing this. I can't have a relationship with you if this is going to be the conversation every time."

"Jonah—wait. I—"

"No, Mom. I'm *done.* Don't call me again."

"Jonah!"

I hung up and threw my phone onto the mattress, then reached for my laptop, shaking. Praying. I opened the browser and went to my bank's website. My mother had access to my account, which allowed for the urgent, last-minute bailouts I needed far too frequently.

I exhaled in relief. The money had been deposited, as it always was, and would be available on Monday morning. The reward for fighting with my mother. Her apology, until our next argument. But this fight felt different, final in a way our others had not. I feared I'd never talk to my mother again simply because there was nothing left to say. I choked back tears as sudden panic seized my body; I felt like a skydiver with a faulty parachute looking over his shoulder to watch the thing that was supposed to save him flap uselessly in the wind, leaving nothing but the lonely hurtle toward death.

The ache in my heart turned into rage, strengthening my resolve. If I hurried, if the trains were on time, I could still make it. I grabbed my phone and shoved it in the pocket of my suit jacket. As I did, I felt something brush my knuckles.

My tie.

I lassoed the fabric around my neck as I made my way to the door.
I would not be late, not now.

Richard was waiting.

———

I was lucky—the L train was on time. I sat down, surprised by the
emptiness of the well-lit car. But then it hit me: the smell. An unholy cloud of sweat and trash and shit invaded my nostrils as the
doors closed, sentencing me to ride in the stench. My watering gaze
searched the car for the source and quickly landed on the only possible culprit.

He was homeless, of course—that was expected. But his age
shocked me. I struggled to make out his sleeping face, veiled by a curtain of long, oiled hair. He couldn't have been more than nineteen,
his cheeks still swollen by youthful fat, his forehead a blank slate
not yet creased by worry. The duffel bags piled at his feet seemed
new, their load ambitious. I wondered how long he'd been on the
streets, what tragedy had banished him from the world of the shel-
tered. Wondered what it would be like to let the city forget you, to
disappear in plain sight. Wondered—heart quickening in my chest
—where was his mother?

His eyes snapped open and caught mine in a hostile glare. I jerked
my head forward, focusing on the rushing tunnel outside the window,
suddenly eager to leave the car. Guilt kept me fixed to my seat. I
didn't want to join the countless others who'd already exited this
train car in horror, looks of disgust aimed back at his hunched figure.
I wanted to be kind, even if it meant holding my breath until the next
stop. The train shrieked against the track as we barreled through
darkness. I did my best to turn my thoughts to the task ahead.

I was on my way to Queer Film Voices, a cinema series in which
famous LGBTQ artists hosted screenings of historically important queer films. Two months prior, I'd come across an advertise-
ment for the event online and simply thought it might make for a

nice break from the nightly monotony of nursing microwaved burritos by myself. I had no real friends during those early days, and I possessed a fresh-off-the-bus desperation for any opportunities to ease the constant loneliness that plagued my new life in the city. My calendar became spotted with a pox of cultural happenings: free readings at the New York Public Library, free gallery openings in Chelsea, free concerts in McCarren Park—anything free, really. Free was all I could afford. Somewhere, maybe in the trampled grass as I suffered through a mediocre rock band's pro bono performance, I hoped to discover my "tribe," that group of fantasy friends who'd been waiting in the wings, ready to rush toward me with open arms and giddy laughter. It never happened; these events always had the opposite of the intended effect. I would feel my isolation harden into bitterness as I watched groups of people from afar, gawking as they clung to one another with baffling ease, jealous of the joy on their faces. I carried a flask whenever I went out—insurance against my dread—and it was inevitably drained by the end of each evening. At that point, I usually made my way to a nearby gay bar, where I knew that at least my body could be exploited for companionship, muscled arms and chiseled stomach exchanged for an hour in someone else's presence —a whole night if I was lucky. Rarely did my sexual encounters last much longer than that; my lovers always flinched at the subtle desperation that crept into my tone when I asked if we could "hang again soon." My loneliness was a disease no one wanted to catch.

And so it was without much hope that I first considered the prospect of attending the Queer Film Voices cinema series. I sat on my mattress distractedly perusing their website, wondering if the event was worth the trip into Manhattan. Many notable figures had passed through the series—the site featured photos of Gus Van Sant, John Waters, and Pedro Almodóvar—but the host for the upcoming evening was Richard Shriver, successful screenwriter, author, and playwright. I Googled Richard, my motives still unformed, and pored over the search results.

That's when I saw it. There, among the articles detailing his accolades and achievements, a photo caught my eye. I clicked to enlarge the image. It was Richard at a charity dinner or awards show or high-profile wedding, lightly sweating in a tux, his blissful expression tilted toward the young man sitting in his lap. Richard's age stood in stark contrast to that of his companion. Richard was a well-preserved fifty-five with a salt-and-pepper crew cut and a perfectly tailored jacket that almost hid his slight middle-aged paunch, while the man in his lap was probably my age—twenty-five—and possessed a cherubic smirk, dark eyes, and biceps that swelled beneath his suit jacket. I compared the boy's appearance to my own and felt a sudden, irrational jealousy. He had nothing on me, I told myself, taking solace in the caption that accompanied the photo: *Richard Shriver and guest.* As if the boy didn't even have a name.

Who this "guest" was didn't concern me much. What did light my interest was the sudden realization that I could, perhaps, become his replacement. In the photo, Richard's soft, yearning eyes betrayed a weakness, one I could harness for my own needs. His eyes were the portal to another world, the answer to my loneliness, and the minute they fell on me, I would make sure they stayed there. I would attend this event, walk up to Richard, and stare him down with the defiant confidence of someone with nothing left to lose.

"Fuck you, man," the homeless boy shouted suddenly, bringing my focus back to the subway car. I jumped in surprise but kept my nervous gaze trained forward. *"I know you can fucking hear me, you little bitch,"* he snarled.

I sat, sweating now, pretending that his earsplitting accusation had somehow failed to cross the six-foot distance between us. As if my insistence that he didn't exist could overpower his desire to be seen. As if I could make him vanish. Surprisingly, it worked, and silence returned to the car, thicker this time.

I'd studied Richard's plays when I was in grad school, though that curriculum failed to cover the personal topics I spent much of my free time researching in the months leading up to this evening. Things like the details of his privileged yet stifled upbringing as the son of a wealthy pharmaceutical executive, described in a 1994 *New York Times* profile. Things like his favorite restaurants, listed in the Broadway-themed issue of *Bon Appétit* from the previous December. Things like his affinity for Alice Munro, documented in the *New Yorker* essay he penned in 2004. Things like his difficult relationship with his mother and the screaming match they'd had outside a cancer benefit, as reported by Page Six on July 12, 2007. I'd sit on my mattress for hours picking at the vegetal debris of a four-dollar frozen dinner and scouring the internet for details of Richard's history, his tastes, his disposition. *How should a person be?* This was the question that plagued me in those early, isolated months. My research offered the answer: he should be like Richard Shriver.

I couldn't leave anything to chance. I cataloged all my discoveries in a document titled "Notes for Future Conversations," each entry a meticulous script for an eventual seduction. I imagined the lilt of my voice as I innocently suggested we dine at Odeon, a favorite downtown classic he'd mentioned in the pages of *Bon Appétit*. Pictured the moment I would drop a casual reference to "Runaway," his favorite Munro story. Dreamed of the day I would slyly offer up the details of my strained relationship with my mother in hopes it would inspire a similar confession from Richard. Of course, none of these planned encounters would ever come to fruition if I bungled the first impression. That was why tonight was so important. It was the way to Richard, the man who would save me from myself.

The subway car came to a sudden stop. The lights cut out. My heart pounded as the homeless boy let out a strange, forced laugh. *"Aha-ha-ha-ha-haaaaa,"* he roared, stomping both his feet in the dark.

"Sorry for the delay, folks, there's a slight problem on the tracks ahead. We hope to be moving shortly," the conductor announced over the speakers.

"Bet you can't see me now 'cause it's dark, right? *But you can still hear me, can't you, fucker,*" the boy yelled.

His silhouette charged toward me in the dark. I leaped from my seat and ran to the doors connecting our car to the next. Before I could escape, his hand gripped my arm. He yanked me back toward him. "You can hear me *now,* you little shit. *You can hear me now that I have you by your fucking arm,*" he screamed in my face, shaking me violently.

"*Yes,*" I yelled back, tears in my eyes. "Yes, I can fucking hear you."

Just like that, he let go. He lumbered back to his seat, humming tunelessly. The lights flickered on, and the train lurched into motion. Like nothing had ever happened. I glanced up at the clock—I'd still be on time.

Here, finally, was my plan: to make Richard Shriver love me.

I surfaced in the East Village and charged down First Avenue. The air that night was unusually cold for May, but my body still produced rivers of sweat, my shirt dampening more with each new tributary.

When I finally reached the brick exterior of the Anthology Film Archives, anxiety shortened my breath. For the first time since devising my plan, I allowed the possibility of failure to enter my mind. There was the embarrassing likelihood that I would leave the event without so much as a wink from the object of my obsession, crushed by yet another thwarted fantasy of companionship, and go back to the derelict confines of my sublet, the cold greeting of someone else's space.

I approached the box office, my Ferragamo loafers scraping the linoleum of the lobby. The shoes had cost me a week's worth of tips—five hundred and fifty dollars—a sum that also happened to be half the rent on Ghost Dick's crumbling lair, rent that was currently sixteen days late because of my decision to purchase the loafers. They had been an investment acquired specifically for this evening, as was the thousand-dollar blazer that swelled at my biceps, the two-hundred-dollar button-down that gripped my muscled chest, and the black jeans that hugged my ass as a tribute to the three hundred dollars I'd burned in their honor. Here was what my mother had sought on our call, the answer to the Mystery of Where Jonah's Money Went: my outfit. It had been months in the making. I'd purchased a new, expensive piece every other week, anxiously switching between dying Visas, slowly accumulating the perfect ensemble (and a proportionate amount of debt) for the night I hoped would change my life forever.

But now, faced with the reality of the lobby and its dim fluorescent lighting and stained walls and barred windows and nonprofit fundraising brochures lined up on a folding table next to the entrance, I realized I'd made a very expensive mistake. Everyone else wore ripped jeans and faded sweaters and yet somehow looked better than I did, or at least more confident. I was the sole idiot sweating in Paul Smith. No one was watching me, but my paranoia festered. I assumed—no, *knew it to be a fact*—that they all were laughing at me the moment I turned my back, ridiculing the loser who had spent two thousand dollars he didn't have to dress up for his wrong idea of the evening.

"Ten bucks," the box-office attendant said, barely glancing up from his copy of *Atlas Shrugged.*

Nausea gripped my stomach as I froze, paralyzed by the thought of spending even one more dollar on this night. I gaped dumbly, fixing my stare on the attendant's book cover. An illustration of Atlas stared back, his naked shoulders straining under the weight of the novel's title. I racked my brain for an appropriate response, but all I could think of was my credit card debt, my overdue rent, and the fifty-thousand-dollar price tag my mother had just placed on my life. I stood unmoving, my eyes on the novel, as the attendant squirmed uncomfortably, misinterpreting my stare as a judgment of his reading material. An insecure frown cracked his face.

"It's a joke," he said, dead serious, nodding to his book. "I'm reading it because it's, like, funny. I'm not actually buying into this shit."

I didn't care about his book, but seeing him flounder under my gaze righted something within me. My paranoia subsided, and I felt a renewed sense of power. I was no longer the outcast who had purchased a two-thousand-dollar ensemble only to realize he was overdressed for a screening of a vintage film; I was now the *driven motherfucker* who had *intentionally* purchased a two-thousand-dollar ensemble because I was the type of passionate person who would do what he needed to get what he wanted. "Here." I slapped a ten on the counter. He handed me a ticket.

I entered the theater and sank into a weathered velour chair. Vertigo crept at the edge of my consciousness, a new and recurring sensation in my life brought on by the constant combination of exhaustion and anxiety that roiled my body on a daily basis. All week, I'd worked doubles at my restaurant, picking up every shift I could to make extra cash, blowing coke in the bathroom to keep up. I'd come home around two a.m., pound four Miller Lites to quiet my brain, crash onto the mattress, and pray for sleep that never came. Instead, worried thoughts snowballed in my mind: the weight of my debt, my mother's anger, and Richard, Richard, Richard.

The movie started. Richard had selected *Entertaining Mr. Sloane,* a 1970s film adaptation of the notorious Joe Orton play in which a bisexual male hustler manipulates his way into the hearts of a middle-aged landlady and her homosexual brother, murders their father, and accepts incestuous sexual slavery as punishment for his crime. I enjoyed the campy mania and wicked humor of the movie. I hadn't known it was possible to laugh at such darkness, though clearly Richard had. It was, according to the program notes, his favorite film.

As the credits rolled, I felt a familiar panic—the moment I'd planned for had finally arrived. The lights powered on, and the faux-Randian box-office attendant took the stage. "Ladies and gentlemen, please welcome Richard Shriver," he announced into a cordless mic.

Richard walked out in front of the audience looking pretty much like he did in my favorite photo, though maybe a bit puffier. He sat on a black, busted folding chair that tipped when he shifted his weight to accept the microphone from the attendant. He was taller than I'd imagined he'd be, and pastier. His hair was thin but he wasn't quite balding, and his slight gut strained against the buttons of a soft gray shirt. His wardrobe was a master class in wealthy understatement—simple, but you could smell the money.

After a brief statement from Richard about his reasons for selecting the film, the floor was opened up for questions. My hand shot skyward, propelled by animal instinct. Richard scanned the crowd, paused for a moment to lock eyes with me and deliver an inscrutable grin, then called on the woman directly in front of me. The rest of the Q&A proceeded largely in the same manner—Richard teasing me with his gaze and then choosing someone else—until finally, after the moderator announced that there was time for one last question, Richard pointed at me.

It was a question I'd rehearsed many times. It had evolved over weeks of practice as I stood in front of the corroded mirror of the shared bathroom down the hall from my sublet. I'd say it over and over again, ignoring the pounding from neighbors waiting to shower, watching the shape of my mouth as I articulated the words, calculating the angle of my smirk to ensure that the subtext of my question was clear. I wanted Richard to pay attention, to know exactly what was on the table. Whenever I purchased another expensive piece of clothing, I'd put it on and rehearse my question anew, taking stock of the way my blazer looked when I raised my hand, the pop of my shirt buttons against my pecs, how my jeans bulged at my crotch.

Every time I went back to that mirror, the moment gained greater definition, and finally I could perform the question without thinking, like an actor on autopilot in a long-running play. My question —based on ideas outlined in a 2008 essay Richard had written on the life and work of Joe Orton—was this: *Do you think the misogyny inherent in Joe Orton's camp sensibility signals a sort of gay self-loathing born out of a shame surrounding his own femininity?*

But here's what I was really asking: *Wanna fuck?*

"Yes," Richard said, an answer to both questions. As he looked at me, his eyes softened and his mouth curved upward. It was the same dizzy expression I'd seen in the online photo of "Richard Shriver and guest," the image I'd worshipped with daily devotion.

At that moment, I knew I'd do anything to keep that smile on his face.

2

I WAITED FOR HIM.

I stood in the back of the auditorium watching as he finished a conversation with the organizers of the event—a short, wiry lesbian in a linen pantsuit and the disheveled gay academic who had founded the series. Richard towered over them, holding court. Their wide eyes betrayed an absolute submission to his charms; mechanical smiles appeared on their faces every time his booming laugh cut through the din of the exiting crowd. They were clearly no match for Richard, and I made a vow to avoid their fate. I couldn't be dismissed —I needed to be desired.

I tried to catch Richard's eye from my position in the back of the room. Even a small nod from him would have reassured me that my decision to wait was based on something other than fantasy, but he avoided my gaze. As the minutes passed and the auditorium emptied, my anxiety grew. Finally, Richard extracted himself from the conversation and made his way up the aisle.

Any doubt I'd had was quickly erased by Richard's impish expression as he approached. Smug dimples pierced his cheeks. "You waited!"

"Yes!" I replied dumbly.

"Well, what are you waiting *for?*" he inquired with a teasing lilt. I paused for just a second too long, embarrassed by the obvious answer. Richard loomed over me, even taller than he'd seemed from afar. He was six foot five to my six foot one, and he possessed a well-fed heft that worked on his massive frame. He wasn't fat—he was *substantial*. His face was fuller than it appeared in pictures, but it only made him more attractive. Flesh filled the small cracks that had previously marred his forehead, erasing the wrinkles I'd expected from my online research. He was, according to Wikipedia, fifty-five, though in person he could easily pass for ten years younger. He cocked a bushy eyebrow in my direction, and I worried that if I didn't say something soon, I'd receive the same tacit dismissal the event organizers had gotten just moments before.

"Well, um, I'm waiting for you," I said finally.

"Oh, dear, I hope I'm worth it." He said this with the ironic confidence of a man who knows he's worth a great deal. He spoke in a rapid-fire baritone, always anticipating the next sentence, searching for new topics before the old ones had a chance to get stale. "Hungry?" he asked.

"Starving."

"Well, it seems like we'll be forced to get dinner together, then." He sighed with mock resignation. "Where shall we go? Ladies' choice."

"How about Odeon?"

Richard's banter stopped for a beat, and he looked at me in surprise. "You're not only cute—it turns out you're psychic as well."

"What do you mean?" I asked, feigning innocence.

"How did you know that's my favorite restaurant?"

———

"I have to ask," Richard said, then paused briefly to down the last of his wine, his eyes teasing me from behind his upturned glass. "What does a handsome young man such as yourself want with a curmudgeon like me? I'm old enough to be your father."

"Are you trying to give me daddy issues?" I joked.

"Oh, I thought you already had them." He smirked. "Isn't that why we're here?"

"No, I'm here to inherit your vast fortune," I volleyed back.

Richard chuckled. "Honey, I'm a *playwright*. There's no gold in these hills."

"Why is it that rich people love to complain about being poor?"

"Would you rather we complained about the precocious twenty-five-year-olds who clamor for our affection?"

I laughed harder than his quip warranted. Our jokes were little pressure valves, each laugh releasing tension as we danced around the obvious: he was too old for me, too famous, too rich. By couching our circumstance in wry humor, we were able to dismiss May-December stereotypes and make space for something genuine to blossom. However calculated my efforts to ensnare Richard may have been, I *did* want something genuine to blossom.

I wanted love.

We sawed at our steaks, and an awkward silence descended on the table. We'd run out of small talk to kindle our connection, meaning we needed to throw bigger logs on the fire. I was too nervous to pry into Richard's backstory, so I tore at my meat anxiously, waiting for him to make the first move. Mischief danced across Richard's features; he seemed to enjoy the awkward quiet, to relish my discomfort, even, knowing that I longed for the conversation to continue but was too afraid to take the lead myself out of fear that I'd broach the wrong subject and offend my unlikely dining companion. This strange flirtation felt like a test—he was exerting his power, seeing if I'd submit.

"Are you close with your parents?" Richard asked finally. I issued a nearly audible sigh of relief. It was a standard first-date query, well within the socially acceptable bounds of our circumstances. Richard had no way of knowing about my fraught relationship with my small, fractured family. I paused, debating how much to divulge.

"Not exactly," I mumbled, staring down at my steak, watching as a pale lake of blood pooled beneath my french fries.

I had a choice. I could share my painful history or I could deflect with an evasive response. Thus far, our date had been a frothy affair marked by candlelit flirting and an avoidance of weightier subjects. Yet I could tell that he wanted more of me, more depth, more substance, and he wanted it *now*.

And wasn't this what I wanted as well? The very discussion I'd planned for in my "Notes for Future Conversations"? Hadn't I dreamed of the moment I would offer up my story in hopes that we could bond over our battle scars?

I told him the story of my childhood in Lake Bluff, Illinois. Told him of my auspicious beginnings, when I was delivered into the loving arms of two doting parents, the only child of a powerful megachurch minister and his loyal wife. Would my father, in an ideal world, have preferred a few more strapping young boys (or, in a pinch, some delicate little girls) to round out the picture of his perfect Christian family? Probably. But God—in conjunction with a string of defeated fertility specialists—worked in His notoriously mysterious ways. Did my father, despite his faith in God's plan, nurse some resentment against my mother for denying him the family of his dreams? Most likely. But any tension that bubbled in their marriage was always tempered by my existence, the one child God had granted them. Their little "miracle boy."

Before I could even talk, I became the foundation of my family, its sole stabilizing force and living proof of the Lord's grace. My parents showered me with attention and were rewarded with the perfect pious son who sang in the church choir, made muffins for youth-group bake sales, and attended a Reputable Christian University. The son who could do no wrong.

Until he did.

"We love you deeply, Jonah." Those were the first words out of my father's mouth when he discovered a chat-room window I'd forgotten to close. This was during my senior year at Wheaton College, when I was still living at home with my parents, still dependent on them for shelter and money and support. There, glowing on our family's shared desktop computer, was my discussion with Papa4DirtyBois, a graphic dialogue that explored the ways in which I hoped to choke on my internet suitor's *big daddy dick*. "And God will save you from this lifestyle," my father continued, frowning at our Dell.

Our family prayed. We went to church. We put on brave faces. We told no one about my shameful secret, now our family's shameful secret. No one, that is, except "Doctor" Jim, the ex-gay counselor my father hired to cure me of my homosexuality. Doctor Jim's "treatments" only amplified the misery and shame that constricted my lungs. I began to wonder if my panic attacks were, in fact, the side effects of exorcism, Satan's desperate claws around my rib cage.

I wanted to die.

The irony haunts me to this day: my father's love, the very force that should've saved our family, was ultimately the thing to destroy it.

I told Richard all this, fighting back sobs in the dreamy glow of Odeon. I offered it up like a question, one I hoped he could answer. How could I solve the riddle of my past, the problem of my father's love? Despite Richard's relative silence throughout my monologue, I was encouraged by his warm expression, the buzz of the wine, and my confidence that this older and wiser and brilliant and beautiful man would have the answer to buttress my collapsing sense of hope. I wanted to believe in love. And so I believed in Richard.

"Your courage is remarkable," he said once I'd finished.

"Oh, I don't know about that."

"No, really. Even as your entire world crumbled, you maintained your strength. You stayed true to who you are. It's so moving."

"I hope I haven't scared you away with all my born-again horror stories. I swear I'm actually fun when I'm not unearthing my deepest trauma."

"Oh, please, I'm happy to listen. How are things with your family now?"

"Not great. My mom hates the idea of me living in New York, hates to think of my 'lifestyle' here, but I still lean on her for money" —I paused, emotion bubbling in my throat— "which hasn't worked out well. I recently, *very* recently, in fact, stopped speaking to her."

"I'm so sorry," he said, placing a hand on my knee.

"What about you?" I pivoted, eager to redirect the conversation. "Are you close with your mom?"

"That's a story that'll take a lot longer than dessert." He laughed bitterly. "We talk, but in the purely literal sense of the term. I call her on the phone, noises come out of my mouth, noises come out of her mouth. But we don't really *say* anything."

"Why not?"

"Because if I were to say one honest thing to my mother, I would have to say them all." Richard sighed. "And even if I were brutally candid about the pain she's caused me over the years, she wouldn't hear it. Denial is my mother's superpower."

"Have you ever tried to articulate the issue? Even write it down for yourself? It sounds cheesy, but sometimes journaling really helps me."

Richard issued a weary chuckle. "Oh, honey, there's no money in journaling. But if you're really that curious, you could come to the opening of my new play, which will give you a pretty good idea of where I've landed with my mommy issues."

I stopped for a moment to gauge the sincerity of his invitation. It hit me by surprise, as it was hidden in the rhythm of our sarcastic repartee.

"I mean, if —if you're serious, I'd love to," I sputtered.

"I'm very serious," Richard cooed. He got out of his chair and joined me at my seat on the banquette. He put his arm around me and we kissed for the first time, his mouth hungry for mine. I felt a surge of happiness in his embrace, became giddy with the possibility that after months of hell, filled with the pain of inventing an identity in an unforgiving metropolis, I might have finally found hope. Richard was the first person in the city with whom I felt a real connection, and our date marked the only conversation of substance I'd had with anyone since moving to New York. I couldn't talk to my mother for obvious reasons, and the idea of therapy—even the legitimate, non-conversion variety—was far too terrifying. My only acquaintances were the waiters at my restaurant, and though we would go out for drinks after our shifts and do bumps of cocaine together in the bathrooms of gay bars, my fellow servers were not the types of people I could open up to.

But I could talk to Richard.

"What about your father?" Richard asked. "Do you two still talk?"

I stalled, anxiously wiping my mouth with my napkin. "He's . . . he's dead," I lied. "Brain cancer."

"I'm so sorry."

It was a lie I'd told for years every time someone asked about my father. A cover story, much easier than telling the truth.

————

"So tell me, Jonah, what is it you *do* for a living?"

We cuddled over a devastated crème brûlée, our spoons abandoned. My cheeks flushed. I had avoided this subject all evening, rerouting the conversation every time I felt it moving toward the topic of my employment.

"I'm a waiter," I murmured.

"But what is it you *really* do?" Richard said, squeezing my knee. "Surely a charming, intelligent, and handsome person such as yourself must have greater aspirations than simply being a waiter."

"Well, I'm also a writer. Or, I mean, I *want* to be one. A playwright."

"*Two* writers in the marriage?" Richard teased with theatrical flourish. "Oh, dear, this is a recipe for *disaster.*"

"It'll probably end in flames," I said dryly, returning to the comforting rhythms of our earlier banter.

Richard laughed and I relaxed. He rubbed my shoulders as he continued. "I'd love to read your work sometime."

"I . . . I'd like that," I said, though the idea of offering up my work to a man like Richard was unbelievably intimidating.

"Maybe I can help put an end to your career as a waiter."

"Trust me, I'd love nothing more—"

"Your bill, sir," the waiter interrupted, offering the check to Richard in an act of presumption that seemed designed to insult me. I watched as Richard opened the thin, black folder and panicked when I saw the total at the bottom of the bill: $325.00. The idyllic bubble of our date popped, and the cost of dinner brought reality crashing in. All my credit cards were maxed out, and until my mother's electronic deposit into my checking account cleared the twenty-four-hour holding period, I had only fifty-six dollars to my name. A sum that would not cover even half the dinner.

Richard looked over the bill in silence. I watched, dread mounting. I had to offer to split it with him, at least. It was the bare minimum of social grace that the moment required, though I feared if he accepted my offer, our relationship would end with the waiter's announcement that my card had been declined.

"Should we split it?" I croaked finally. Richard looked up from the check, frowning. He held my gaze for an excruciating ten seconds. I felt a sudden, inexplicable pang of longing for my parents, a strange desire to see my mother's name appear on my cell phone's caller ID. A yearning for my father's ghost to darken Odeon's doorway.

"Don't be silly," Richard finally said, laughing. He was just fucking with me.

"Thank you," I replied, an embarrassing amount of gratitude gushing into my tone.

"Don't even think about it. I'm writing this off. Business dinner with a talented young writer."

"I'll get the next one," I promised unconvincingly.

"Oh, please, it's silly for you to pay. I have the money. Tonight you get a free dinner."

I beamed in relief, too young and dumb to know that there was no such thing.

————

Later, we spilled into the darkened sprawl of Richard's massive West Village loft, not bothering with the lights, eager to bring our evening to its climax. We stumbled into the bedroom, ham-fisted at first, attempting to find, in the words of the Diane Warren dance track, the rhythm of the night. But a consistent tempo eluded us; it was all offbeat kisses and ill-timed elbows. We ripped off our clothes and floundered onto the bed. Richard fumbled my legs into the air, pressing his hard cock against my ass. We stopped for a beat, catching our breath, recalibrating. Richard leaned forward, gave me a tentative kiss. It felt like an admission of defeat, something I refused to accept.

So I punched him. Right in the chest.

Richard's jaw dropped, and his hot breath rushed at my face. His mouth twisted—challenge accepted. I struck him again. He slapped my face, gripped my jaw, pried it open with two fingers, and spit in my mouth. I lunged forward and latched onto his lips with my teeth. He pressed the full weight of his body into mine, pinned my hands to the mattress. With my legs in the air, I raised my ass to meet his cock, hungry to have him inside me, a desire he refused to satisfy, opting instead to shove me off the mattress and onto the floor.

I caught my breath, kneeling on the hardwood. Suddenly, I felt

Richard's foot on my back, a cold pressure that sent a shudder through my body and a pulse of blood to my dick.

"Open the bottom drawer," he ordered in an unfamiliar voice, pointing toward the dresser in front of me. I grabbed for the drawer, but Richard kicked my hand.

"Slower," he demanded.

"Yes," I gasped.

"Yes *what?*"

"Yes, Daddy." I reached for the drawer, slower this time, pulled the handle with care, and produced a thick leather dog collar attached to a long metal chain.

"Put it on."

"Yes, Daddy," I moaned, clasping the collar around my throat.

The leather was cold and tight. Richard took the metal chain in his fist and knelt behind me. He gave the leash a playful tug, teasing my ass with his spit-slicked cock, pulling my head back at random intervals.

Then he thrust his dick inside me at a speed that gutted me, left me breathless. With the air in my lungs fully expelled, he tugged at my dog-noose with new force, constricting my airway. The longer he prevented me from breathing, the stiffer my cock grew, until finally he let go. I gasped, choking on air, as he rammed my ass with increased speed until he roared in release, shuddering inside me, and my dick spurted hot liquid and my mind went blank and my vision went black and I collapsed onto the floor.

Tears spilled from my eyes onto the stained wood—something inside me had been purged. When I was in Richard's bedroom, my helplessness was eroticized, transformed into a source of power. I was most alive here, close to death, panting on the floor with a collar around my throat.

That night, I felt at peace. Richard and I tumbled into bed, exhausted, blissful. His lips brushed my forehead as I drifted to sleep on his handcrafted Swedish mattress, under a massive, low-burning pendant lamp, in his stunning West Village loft, miles away from my own crumbling apartment deep in the bowels of Brooklyn where no amount of reading or television or masturbation could distract me from the persistent thrum of anxiety brought on by my friendless isolation, soul-crushing job, familial trauma, and overwhelming financial debt. But that night as Richard held me in his arms, something swelled within me, a feeling that stuck in my throat and pushed tears from my eyes, a feeling that was difficult to place but could perhaps best be described as relief. I felt protected in Richard's embrace. Nothing could touch me here in this beautiful downtown palace.

I was safe, at least for now.

3

I NEVER SET out to write a play about Richard.

It was more like I realized I was already writing one.

The morning after our first date, Richard cooked me a massive breakfast before sending me out into the bright West Village streets. I shielded my eyes from the sun as I stumbled out of his building. Despite my stale suit and unwashed hair, I felt incredible, buoyed by the promise of new romance. It was a stunning spring morning, one of those rare New York days when the weather is so idyllic that it washes away all memories of previous meteorological abuse.

My radiant mood even survived reentry into my scuzzy apartment. I ripped off the previous night's clothes, slipped into a pair of gym shorts, and plopped onto my mattress. I pried open my laptop, planning to waste a few hours on the internet before I had to change for work. There on my computer screen, in a window I'd neglected to close the previous night, was my "Notes for Future Conversations" document.

I scrolled through it idly and came across the section where I'd imagined the moment I'd bring up my estrangement from my mother with the goal of triggering a similar confession from Richard. I studied my work, noting the discrepancies between my fantasy and the reality. *Why not make a few corrections?* I thought, and I plunged into the document and began revising. I fixed the dialogue

to more accurately reflect our conversation, added a few embellish-
ments, and noted the particulars of the setting. After an hour, I sat
back to reread my work. That's when it hit me: what I had on the
page was a scene.

I was writing a play.

The more I thought about it, the more it made sense. All the plays
I'd written in grad school were inaccessibly experimental—long on
bizarre, esoteric ideas and short on relatable human experience. I'd
always felt like nothing much had *happened* to me in my life (other
than my familial trauma, a wound too raw to write about), and as
a result, I was unable to produce the "deeply personal works" that
garnered praise for my MFA classmates.

But now, life was happening to me—*Richard* was happening to
me. I realized that Richard could not only be a source of love and
stability but also an excellent source of material. I continued writing
into the afternoon, riding the wave of inspiration, invigorated by my
work in a way I'd never been before.

And at the center of it all: Richard. Before I met Richard, fate was
a concept to which I'd never given much credence. After I'd abandoned God in the wake of my family's ruination, chaos had seemed
to be the best explanation for the arbitrary machinations of an in-
different universe. But that afternoon as I pounded at my keyboard,
filled with hope, I was gripped by a newfound belief in destiny. Little
in my life was certain, but of this much I was sure: Richard Shriver
was my future.

———

"Have you seen Rashad?" I yelled to Derek, the bartender on shift
that evening. Derek shook his head as he poured a nuclear-green
substance into a sugar-rimmed martini glass and garnished it with
a cherry.

"Not in the last twenty minutes." He frowned at the cocktail in front of him. "How any grown man can drink these with a straight face is a true mystery."

I was the most recent hire at Perdition, a "new-American eatery" in Chelsea, and my lack of seniority meant that I received the worst schedule of the entire staff. Weekend nights were the most lucrative and therefore reserved for employees who had been there the longest. Lately, I'd been begging for shifts from the other waiters, occasionally even scoring a Friday or Saturday. I desperately needed the money, and though I wasn't particularly close with any of my co-workers, most were sympathetic to the familiar plight of the impoverished New York transplant. For a while, I'd managed to float on the generosity of my fellow servers, but it was becoming clear that their charity had an expiration date. I got the sense that the others felt it was time I got my shit together.

I'd just paid my rent to Ghost Dick, twenty days late, which meant I had an eleven-day period in which to replenish my zeroed-out bank account. During that eleven-day stretch, I was scheduled to work only four slow weeknight shifts. I needed to pick up at least one weekend shift to make next month's rent, but so far every waiter had turned me down. The only person I'd yet to ask was Rashad, because he'd already let me take his Friday for the past two weeks and I didn't want to push my luck. But now I had no choice. I scanned the restaurant for his face, praying he might bail me out one last time.

Suddenly, I felt a hand grope my ass. I turned to discover one of Perdition's regulars, an overtanned, leather-faced fashion executive, holding an empty wineglass. "Jonah, babe," the man slurred, "can I get a refill on my chardonnay?"

"Of course," I said, forcing a smile.

"I think your ass has gotten tighter since the last time I was in." The man grinned and slapped my butt. His dining companion—an equally decrepit fashion-Gollum—laughed loudly. I suppressed my disgust, issued a strained chuckle, and turned from the table.

Unfortunately, I'd gotten accustomed to the unsolicited affections of lecherous diners during my brief tenure at Perdition. The restaurant catered to a clientele that was primarily gay, wealthy, and white, and it was the type of establishment where PR gurus and real estate kingpins and Broadway producers all paid top dollar for mediocre food and a chance to grab a handful of ass. Although we were usually called "boys" by our customers, the servers were all homogeneously muscular gay men between the ages of twenty-one and thirty-two. The differences between Perdition and Hooters were few —the sex of the waitstaff (male versus female) and the price of the food (expensive versus cheap). I looked around the dining room— which featured a blinding-white interior with white minimalist tables, white modernist dining chairs, a white marble bar, and walls that the owner insisted were *not* white but "bone"—hoping to locate Rashad.

I found him behind the waiters' station, hiding from a table of obnoxious gay entertainment lawyers celebrating the birthday of their handsy senior partner. "Table twenty-three is *murdering* my buzz," Rashad said. He moaned, lifted a coke-piled house key to his nostril, and snorted. "Mama needs a break." Rashad peered out into the dining room and then discreetly palmed the small bag of cocaine into my hand. I shoved it in my pocket, saving it for later.

Out of all the waiters at Perdition, I liked Rashad best. He was one of the few Black men employed by our horror-show boss, Brett, who otherwise maintained a lily-white waitstaff that matched the color of both the restaurant's interior and its clientele. But Rashad's beauty had somehow trumped the noxious prejudices of our employer. Rashad's face was thin and feminine; he had deep brown eyes set above high cheekbones. He was tall with long, muscled limbs that he'd once utilized in his former career as a dancer. A severe ankle injury had forced him into early retirement from Alvin Ailey and brought him limping to Perdition's doorstep. He had the air of a fallen prince and the wit of a drag queen. Our relationship didn't extend beyond the requisite postwork partying at neighborhood gay bars, but he was the closest thing I had to a friend in the city. He'd taken me under his wing at Perdition, and I hoped today would not mark the end of his benevolence.

"Oh my God, how is it *this slow* on a Thursday," I complained. "I've had only two tables all night."

"Well, hopefully the cast of *Gay Law and Order* leaves a hefty tip. So far they've had approximately twelve gallons of Appletinis each. Whoever started the myth that gay men have great taste has clearly never been to this fucking restaurant."

I laughed and steeled myself to ask for the favor I desperately needed. "So, I was wondering . . . if maybe you wanted Friday night off . . . I could, uh, cover for you?"

Rashad shot me a withering look. "Bitch—I have thrown you my last two Fridays. And as much as I love *not* coming to work in this shithole, I love paying my rent more."

"I just thought—"

"Sorry, honey. You're gonna have to ask someone else."

Anxiety scrambled my brain. I struggled to muster a *Don't worry about it,* but my mouth felt frozen. I stood there dumbly, my face blanching. Rashad frowned.

"Hey—is everything okay?"

"Oh, yeah, sorry. I just, uh, was thinking about something else."

"I mean, look—you've been working your ass off recently. It would probably do you good to have a little break."

"Totally," I said, distracted. I took my cell phone from my pocket and pulled up the text thread with my mother. It killed me, but I had no choice. I needed her to rescue me.

Can we talk? I typed.

"Put that thing away," Rashad whispered as I sent the text. "If Mommy sees you on your phone, he will fucking kill you. He's looking for a fight tonight."

"Mommy" was the nickname we'd given to the owner, Brett, a

gay, coked-out zombie who possessed all the maternal instinct of Joan Crawford clutching a coat hanger. If Mommy was in a good mood, he'd grab your dick through your pants and whisper in your ear about how he wanted to fuck you, or he'd make you kiss one of Perdition's investors "as a joke" after the restaurant closed for the evening. If Mommy was in a bad mood, he'd circle your tables, hunting for a misplaced dessert fork or an improperly folded napkin, and scream at you when he finally found an excuse. Tonight, as Rashad and I discovered when Mommy barreled into the waiters' station, it was the latter.

"What the fuck are you doing on your phone?" Brett snapped.

"I just—"

"You know what? I don't even want to know. Because any excuse is a bad one. The level of disrespect I get from you guys is *unbelievable*."

"Brett, I'm sorry—"

"You see this?" Brett barked, holding up an empty wineglass. "Your table is *desperate* for a simple glass of chardonnay. Get *out* there."

I rushed out of the waiters' station and bellied up to the marble bar for a glass of chardonnay. As I waited for the bartender, I felt a buzz in my pocket: a text. I abandoned my mission and rushed into the bathroom to check my phone, anxious for my mother's response, praying we could mend the rift between us before the first of the month. Praying I wouldn't lose my apartment. I locked the door behind me and yanked my cell from my pocket.

It was Richard: *Miss you already ;)*

A fresh wave of adrenaline washed over me, though this time it was not accompanied by dread. I felt a surge of hope. I pushed thoughts of my rent aside, allowing myself to bask in the glow of Richard's text. *Miss you too*, I typed. *Hang again soon?*

I sent the message and instantly regretted it. Was *Hang again soon* too forward? Would it turn him off? I pulled the bag of cocaine out of my pocket, deciding to cut my agitation with a quick bump. I scooped a small pile of white onto a key and brought it to my nose. I hesitated, catching my bloodshot gaze in the bathroom mirror. *I need a break,* I thought, studying the purple bags beneath my eyes. I snorted and a familiar shame flooded my mind. I imagined my mother's judgmental stare, my father's righteous disappointment. Cocaine was just another wicked facet of my sinful homosexual lifestyle, proof that I'd succumbed to the unholy impulses that lay at the end of the slippery gay slope my conversion therapist had warned us about. And yet I found myself unable to resist. One bump stung my brain with enough confidence to erase all guilty feelings that preceded my consumption of the drug. Just a sprinkle of the white powder was sufficient to fill the void, to lend my spirit the illusion of wholeness.

My phone buzzed again.

Would love to. What are you doing tomorrow night?

Nothing, I replied.

My heartbeat quickened. I was unsure whom to thank for my accelerated pulse — Richard or the cocaine. It was then I realized: Daddy could be my new drug.

The first weeks of my courtship with Richard were thrilling. To describe our initial encounters as "dates" would be a comical understatement — they were quite literally *events*. Richard's life was a hurricane of astonishing appointments, his wealth and status affording him access to a never-ending series of high-profile cultural happenings. There were the house seats to the revival of *A Little Night Music,* followed by a backstage visit to Richard's "good friend" Stephen Sondheim, an encounter during which I remained bashfully mute. There was the New York premiere of *Whatever Works,* that year's tepid Woody Allen offering, where Richard pulled me onto the red carpet and I found myself awkwardly sandwiched between him and

Patricia Clarkson. There was the evening we turned down dinner with Barbra Streisand ("Oh, honey—I've attended that particular dog-and-pony show one too many times," Richard had grumbled) for an opening-night table at a new Mario Batali restaurant. There was even a private tour of MoMA, an exclusive preview of the Cindy Sherman retrospective, arranged thanks to a dinner-party promise made by curator Klaus Biesenbach.

My Paul Smith suit—the source of so much anxiety on the night I'd met Richard—proved a prudent investment; though it may have been overkill at the Anthology Film Archives, it was the perfect costume for life on the town with Richard.

Of course, we always did what Richard wanted, always deferred to his calendar, his life. This was fine with me, as both my calendar and life were empty. Richard presented a ready-made identity, and I was glad to adopt it, even if it was an imperfect fit. Underneath the giddy euphoria of our early romance, I felt a nascent unease; I feared that I hadn't *earned* my place at the party, that I'd entered through an unseemly loophole. That's why during our MoMA visit, for example, when Klaus Biesenbach stared me down underneath a grotesque Cindy Sherman clown portrait and asked me what I did for a living, I froze.

"He's a writer too," Richard snapped when it became clear I would not summon a response in an acceptable amount of time.

"Oh, how lovely," Klaus replied flatly, not bothering to feign even the slightest enthusiasm. He asked me nothing for the remainder of our museum tour, and I was relieved to recede into the background and claim the social posture of the silent, stunning arm candy.

Afterward, on the hot Midtown pavement, Richard asked why I had been so quiet.

"I *hate* Cindy Sherman," I said, defensive.

"I wish I'd known—we could've avoided a whole afternoon with Klaus. I find him to be a dreadful *bore,* don't you?" The dig at

Klaus was Richard's little olive branch—we could make fun of him together. I opted to sulk instead.

"Though I'm sure he would've liked to hear your opinion on Sherman. He's usually up for a friendly debate."

"I just . . . wasn't in the mood," I mumbled. I felt as though I had failed some test, and Richard was offering a subtle critique of my performance. "It was awkward when he asked what I did. I'm a fucking waiter."

"You're a *writer*." Richard sighed. "And I'm sure you're a good one. Not that I'd know, since you won't let me read any of your work."

"You know I'm nervous about sharing my stuff with you."

I'd been fending off Richard's requests to read my work for weeks. I harbored a secret fear that he would hate my writing and I would be thrust back into my old life, revealed as a fraud, a Talentless Mr. Ripley who'd failed to rise above his station. Complicating this feeling was the fact that my work in progress was about Richard himself—a detail I'd concealed in all our conversations surrounding my new play. My coyness was a cover for my anxiety regarding the autobiographical element of my work and the likelihood of Richard's objection to the subject matter. The only thing I feared more than failure was success, the possibility that my work was *too* good, that I'd captured a truth about our dynamic that, once articulated, would destroy the giddy spell of our relationship—like a magician who'd explained his secrets.

"Oh God—*get over it*," Richard snapped. "Just *send* me something already. If you really want to get ahead, you can't be such a pussy. You're dating a famous playwright, for fuck's sake, *take advantage of the moment*."

Richard's outburst stunned me into silence. He stormed to the curb to hail a cab. I hung back, embarrassed. Thus far, I had consciously avoided taking advantage of the moment. I didn't want

Richard to feel that there was an implicit, transactional nature to our relationship. I wanted to believe that, although both of us might have had ulterior motives at the outset, we'd transcended those impulses and discovered something pure and honest. I wanted to believe that my place in his world was rightful, that no one was getting anything out of this.

I wanted Richard to love me.

Here, then, was the worst-case scenario of showing him my play: it would reveal my misguided conception of our relationship, a one-sided fantasy that would make Richard wince at my naïveté and banish me from his life.

"Greenwich and Jane Street, please," Richard instructed the cabbie once we were installed in the back seat.

We rode in silence until Richard broke the tension with a sigh. "I'm sorry. I shouldn't have snapped at you. I just care about you and want to see you succeed. I'm trying to *help* you."

"I know," I mumbled. "And I *am* going to send you my play once it's finished. I promise."

"Good." Richard placed his hand on my knee and kissed my cheek.

My phone buzzed in my pocket. I pulled it out, hoping it was my mother. She had yet to respond to the text I'd sent from Perdition three weeks prior, and as a result, I'd yet to pay my rent. It was now June 7, meaning my payment was, once again, dangerously late. I looked at my screen, disappointed to find a string of furious texts from Ghost Dick.

What the fuck, dude.

You're late on rent again . . . AS FUCKING USUAL.

I'm serious, I can't keep doing this.

You better fucking pay me by tomorrow or I'm kicking you out.

And I'm NOT fucking around this time.

"Who is it?" Richard asked.

Nausea roiled my gut as our cab jerked over rocky West Village cobblestones. I prayed that my sub-landlord was merely bluffing, but I didn't have the luxury to call him on it. I hated that shitty apartment down to the marrow of my bones, but it was all that stood between me and homelessness.

"The guy I'm subletting from." I sighed. "Things have been really slow at the restaurant recently. I'm late on rent this month."

"What about your mom?"

"We're still not speaking."

"Well, why don't I help you out?"

"I don't know . . ." I trailed off nervously. Richard always picked up the check whenever we were out together, but this felt different. Never had he supported me so directly. Still, I'd be lying if I said the thought hadn't crossed my mind.

"It's like, what, a thousand bucks? That's nothing."

"Are you sure? That's so generous of you but . . . you really don't have to."

"Oh, don't be ridiculous. I'm happy to give you the cash." Richard slapped my thigh to close the deal. "Consider it my apology for being such an asshole today."

"Thank you so much," I managed. I was struck with overwhelming guilt, but I had to accept his offer. I needed that money. "I know it's a lot to ask."

He tweaked my nipple. "I'm sure you'll figure out a way to make it up to me."

4

"BITCH — WHEN ARE YOU gonna let us meet your man?" Rashad teased, threatening me with a ketchup bottle in the waiters' station of Perdition.

"We've only been dating, like, two months," I said defensively.

"And how's the sex?"

"It's actually *amazing.*"

"Whatever you say, Anna Nicole. As long as he leaves you the country house."

I laughed and gave Rashad a playful shove, accustomed by now to this line of questioning. People always asked what "attracted" me to Richard, the not-so-subtle implication being that I was young and muscular, he old and paunchy, and this physical inequity surely meant I was compromising my desire in the bedroom, ensnaring a powerful man with insincere fellatio. This assumption felt boring, puritanical, and unimaginative to me. Perhaps tedious, lube-thrust-repeat sex was predicated on both parties being physically well matched, but real sex—the kind that keeps you screaming—was about power.

"Are we not chic enough to hang with your daddy?" Rashad said, pulling me into a headlock. I wriggled away, wondering if the hint of jealousy in his tone was real or imagined. Our banter had grown flirtatious in recent weeks, and despite my devotion to Richard, I found myself captivated by Rashad when I was around him.

"I haven't introduced him to anyone because it's still so new. And he's not my 'daddy.'"

"Whatever you need to tell yourself. Just make sure he buys you Balenciaga." I laughed, but then Rashad's eyebrows raised in alarm. "Watch out—Mommy's coming in hot."

"Jonah! Have you been to table seventeen?" Brett yelled, storming into the waiters' station, his bloated face gleaming with coke sweat.

"They *just* sat down."

"So I'll take that as a no. Is that a no?"

"I was just about to go over—"

"Really? Because to me, it seems like you were chatting away with Rashad like you didn't have a table that just sat down and desperately needs some drinks."

"Jesus, I'll go out there. Something tells me it's gonna be okay—"

"Oh, it is? *Thank you* for your reassurance. That makes me feel *so much better.* I guess it's *completely okay* for *paying customers* in *my restaurant* to go without food or drink or anything remotely resembling good fucking service."

"Well, I can't give them good fucking service when you're back here wasting my time."

"I'll waste your fucking time if I feel like it. Now get out there and get that table some drinks, you worthless piece of shit."

I burst into the dining room, suppressing my rage as I approached table seventeen. There sat a well-preserved man in his late fifties with a shock of expertly trimmed, bright white hair and a similarly blinding beard. He looked like a wealthy, slender Santa Claus—as if Saint Nick had dropped fifty pounds, moved to Miami, and bought a new wardrobe at Neiman Marcus. Across from him sat a pale and muscular man in his mid-forties with a handsome-craggy face; he wore a tight black T-shirt that stretched across Equinoxed pectorals. Their conversation seemed oddly one-sided; the pale man maintained a glum and immobile frown while South Beach Santa gesticulated with abandon.

"Hi, guys. I'm Jonah and I'll be your server tonight," I interrupted. "Can I start you off with something to drink?"

"So *this* is where he's been hiding you," South Beach Santa said flirtatiously.

"Excuse me?" I replied, caught off guard.

"Richard. He has been *determined* to keep you his little secret, but I have, at last, found you!"

"Um . . . yes, I'm dating Richard. And you are . . ."

"Charles Moore." He extended his hand. "I'm Richard's ex."

"Oh! Well . . . uh . . ." I stammered in surprise.

Charles laughed. "Don't worry, darling. I haven't come to chew you out in a jealous fury. On the contrary, I just wanted to say hello. Richard and I are still the best of friends."

My initial shock subsided, and my mind raced to catch up. Richard had mentioned Charles in passing a few times and I realized I'd also come across him in my research of Richard's past. Charles Moore was, of course, the famous Broadway producer. He and Richard began their relationship in the early 1990s when Charles financed *The Plague,* Richard's critically acclaimed off-Broadway debut. The gutting AIDS drama put both men on the cultural map and served as the foundation for their triumphant careers. Even after their romantic separation in 2001, they remained professionally linked. Charles produced all of Richard's plays because Richard insisted that Charles was the only producer he could trust with his work. I assumed that Richard had told Charles where I waited tables, though it seemed strange that Charles would take enough of an interest to track me down.

"It's . . . it's lovely to meet you," I stuttered. My gaze shifted to Charles's dining companion, who maintained an air of cold indifference.

"Oh, how rude of me!" Charles exclaimed. "This is Sandro, one of our closest friends."

"Nice to meet you," I chirped. Sandro said nothing but extended his limp hand. We exchanged a tepid shake.

"I hope we'll be seeing you this weekend?" Charles inquired.

"This weekend . . ." I trailed off before remembering my plans. "Oh, yes! At the opening of Richard's play. I'm so excited."

"And I assume you'll be joining us in the Hamptons the following week?"

I paused, and panic roiled my stomach. Richard hadn't mentioned a trip to the Hamptons. Had I done something wrong? Was he still angry about our fight outside MoMA? My cheeks flushed. I didn't want to admit that I hadn't been invited, but I couldn't lie either, as Charles would inevitably discover the truth.

At that moment, I felt Brett's hovering presence over my shoulder. I turned, and for once, I was happy to see his damp, swollen face.

"Everything all right here, guys?" Brett asked with feigned cheerfulness. "So sorry for the delay in getting your drink order. The first round's on us."

"Oh, that's so kind of you," Charles responded. "Although I assure you, there was no issue to begin with."

"Still, I insist," Brett said. "Is Jonah taking good care of you?"

"Yes. In fact, Jonah's the very reason we came in tonight."

I lanced Brett with a smug, vengeful look. *They came for* me, *motherfucker,* I said with my stare. *Maybe I'm not a worthless piece of shit after all.*

"Oh, really?" Brett said. "He's one of our best servers." I could barely suppress my laughter. There was nothing more satisfying than watching Brett grovel before wealthy customers he wished to impress, especially when I was the reason for his groveling.

"Well, he also happens to be dating my best friend," Charles said. Brett raised his eyebrows.

"Yes." I smirked. "I'm dating Richard Shriver."

"Oh," Brett said, rocking back on his feet. If there was one thing that impressed him more than money, it was fame. "Well, why were you keeping it a secret from me? So sneaky, Jonah. You should bring your boyfriend for dinner one night!"

He smacked my ass, and even though my stomach sank in shame, I let out the usual, well-rehearsed laugh I employed when Mommy spanked me in public. Brett walked off and I turned to my table, eager to move on from this portion of the evening. "What can I get you boys to drink?"

"We'll take two Campari sodas," Charles announced.

"The drink of the summer!" I blurted with excessive gusto. "At least, that's what I read somewhere. The *Times,* maybe."

"I'm sure you did, dear," Charles replied with a teasing wink.

I turned from the table, embarrassed. *The drink of the summer!* What an inane thing to say; I sounded like a dead-eyed trend reporter for the local news getting the *scoop on this season's hottest cocktails.* It had all been going so well, but I now feared that I'd irrevocably humiliated myself with my stupid comment. Charles would surely gossip about my idiocy at dinner parties across Manhattan, eliciting derisive laughter as he lampooned Richard's latest boy-toy.

I walked away slowly, attempting to overhear Charles and Sandro's conversation, convinced they would mock me the minute my back was turned. Much to my surprise, the opposite seemed to be true.

"I think he'll make quite a nice addition to the group, don't you?" Charles said.

"Yes," Sandro replied. "A perfect fit."

———

Later that night, as I stood polishing silverware in the waiters' station, I felt the stiff insistence of Brett's cock on my ass. He pressed his body against mine, massaging my shoulders.

"Nice work out there tonight, Jonah," he whispered.

"I'm not in the mood for a massage."

"Excuse me?"

I turned and saw a storm gathering in his eyes, the sign he was about to snap from horny to angry. The line separating Brett's two moods was tenuous. "I don't think Richard would appreciate your . . . behavior."

For the first time in the history of my employment at Perdition, Brett backed off. "You know, you should have your boyfriend come dine with us some night."

"I'm not sure this is his *scene*."

That was the final knockout punch, the one that sent Mommy slinking out of the waiters' station, his sweaty hands definitively denied. Now that I had Richard in my court, Mommy could no longer call me a worthless piece of shit. Thanks to my new boyfriend, I was actually worth something, and I could wield his status as a weapon. I felt a rare sense of confidence. Richard Shriver—*the* Richard Shriver—liked me, maybe even loved me.

So why wasn't I invited to the Hamptons?

And with that, my newfound strength vanished.

———

"We need to get out of that restaurant." I sighed.

"We *are* getting out." Rashad gracefully navigated his kitchen as he fixed our third margaritas of the night. Plants sprouted on every available surface in his Bed-Stuy apartment—vines spilled from clay pots on the counter, bamboo stood sentinel by the entryway, orchids bloomed on end tables. I sat on a vintage butterfly chair, its frayed edges masked by a beige throw. The small two-bedroom was not much bigger than my apartment, but where my sublet felt hopelessly transient, Rashad had created a *home*. A place where he belonged, a place that belonged to him.

"We're too talented to die in that graveyard of dreams," he continued. "Which is why I'm currently busting my ass around the clock."

"How are rehearsals going for your show?"

After his career-ending injury at Alvin Ailey, Rashad had decided that if he couldn't dance, he would choreograph. For the past year, he'd toiled away at the restaurant while simultaneously creating a series of well-reviewed pieces at various avant-garde performance venues. PS 122 had recently commissioned a new work that Rashad described as an autobiography told through voguing in which he recounted the story of growing up in New York's ballroom scene. The score had been created by indie rapper Petra, his childhood best friend and current roommate, who'd acquired a small but growing fan base by releasing music on her MySpace page. I envied Rashad's talent for collaboration, his confidence in his own vision. Rashad knew he was brilliant—he was just waiting for the rest of the world to figure it out.

"They're going well. I think it's gonna be pretty fierce. But I'm working with another nonexistent budget. Experimental performance pieces don't exactly pay fuck-you money. Or any money, really."

"Maybe you should sell out and start choreographing Shania Twain videos."

"Maybe I should get a sugar daddy like you."

"I don't know how much longer my situation is gonna last." My anxiety spiked at the thought of Richard. "There's a Hamptons trip and I haven't been invited."

"Oh."

"I'm worried he's going to dump me."

"I mean . . ." Rashad hesitated. "Would that be the worst thing?"

"But I—I need him."

"*Need* him? I think you'd be better off without him." We locked eyes. His lips twisted into a teasing smirk, his gaze an invitation. Possibility swelled in the silence.

Then came the rumble of the cocktail shaker. "Another margarita?"

"Sure."

He poured my drink. A drop of syrupy liquid spilled onto my wrist. Rashad wiped it with his thumb. He lingered on my pulse, let it pound beneath his grip. Goose bumps rippled my skin.

"Oh, I almost forgot." He released my hand, licked the sugar from his finger. "You have to hear Petra's latest track. The one I'm using in my new piece."

He crossed to the sound system and pressed Play. An urgent house beat throbbed through the apartment, shaking the floor. Petra's voice soared above a synth bass.

"It pays to have a roommate who's a musical genius," he said.

"It's so fucking good."

"If it's that fucking good, why aren't you dancing?" Rashad swayed his hips. Challenged me with his stare.

I stood and danced toward him. "So, do I get a spot in your piece?"

"Honey, if this is your audition, we're in trouble."

"Fuck you." I laughed and pushed him.

He caught my hand. Pressed it to his chest. His heart drummed against my palm. "I'm sorry," he whispered in my ear.

"Apology accepted," I murmured. Our bodies drifted together, merged to the beat. His forehead touched mine. An alternate future unfolded in my thoughts. One where I settled into a life here, with Rashad, in the warmth of his home. Our home.

His hands slid down my back.

Suddenly, the front door swung open. We jumped apart.

"You guys better thank me. I just majorly splurged on Patrón." It was Petra, back from a liquor-store run.

"I . . . I should actually get going," I stammered, collecting my things. I felt dizzy, adrenalized. Like I'd been roused from sleepwalking only to realize I was standing at the edge of a cliff. I couldn't afford to give up on Richard — he was my foundation, my fire, the key to everything I'd ever wanted.

Also, he was paying my rent.

5

I SAT WITH RICHARD in the back of a cab, sweating. Eighth
Avenue was a parking lot and we were late to the opening of his play.
Our tardiness was not my fault—an accident ahead had created
the gridlock—but that didn't stop Richard from issuing a passive-
aggressive sigh, as though I'd engineered the collision to spite him.

"It's the opening of *your* play," I said. "They can't start without
you."

Richard shot me a scathing look before returning his gaze to the
traffic outside.

"I met Charles, by the way," I continued with labored enthusiasm.
"He visited me at my restaurant." I thought this might be a natural
segue to the matter of the Hamptons trip. Richard still had not extended an invitation to me, and I hoped that if I hinted enough, he
would realize his error of omission. *Oh my God—of course you're
invited,* Richard gushed in my fantasies. *It's crazy—you've become
such an integral part of my life, I simply assumed you were coming.
How stupid of me to forget to actually ask you.*

"I know—he told me." Richard grunted. My hopes were crushed
by his scowl.

"Oh . . . you didn't mention that he told you."

"Well, I'm mentioning it now," Richard snarled and then went
quiet, restoring the cab to a stuffy silence. The windows fogged

against the cool night air. I scoured my brain for new topics, anything to lift the weight of Richard's agitation.

"I e-mailed you some of my work, you know." After our fight outside the MoMA, I'd decided to share a draft of my play with Richard. It seemed a necessary concession if we were to continue our relationship. Despite his assurances otherwise, I feared that he still nursed some resentment from the episode.

"I haven't had a chance to read it yet."

"Oh, I mean, obviously you've been busy. I wasn't—"

"Can we ride in silence for *one second*?" Richard snapped.

"Of course. I'm sorry. I didn't—"

"What the *fuck* is going on out there?" Richard yelled to the driver, pounding on the partition for emphasis.

"Nothing I can do, buddy," the cabbie said, shrugging.

Richard reeled back in anger. Suddenly, he slammed his fist against his door. I jumped.

"What the fuck, man?" the cabbie yelled.

"That's it. I'm walking. It's only seven blocks." Richard yanked open his door.

"Wait—" I pleaded, unwilling to surrender our ride just yet.

"I said, *I'm walking.* I don't know what *you're* doing. But *I'm* going to walk the seven blocks to get to the Broadway opening of my play *on fucking time*," he yelled and took off. I fumbled with my wallet, shoved a couple of twenties at the cabbie.

By the time I emerged onto the street, Richard was half a block ahead. I ran to catch up, hoping he would glance back to confirm that I was following. Maybe he'd even stop, soften his expression, and wait for me. Maybe he'd hold out his hand, let the foot traffic swarm around him, and stand sentinel until my palm was firmly in his grip.

Much to my dismay, he did no such thing. Richard's gaze remained fixed on the sidewalk in front of him, his shoulders hunched and stiff, his gait steady. I chased him up Eighth Avenue, dodging

dumbstruck tourists, fighting back tears, desperate for any acknowl-
edgment from the hurrying figure ahead.

At that moment, it hit me: I loved Richard Shriver. Maybe that's
why it hurt so much when, minutes later, after I finally caught up, he
slapped me across the face.

————

Richard's play was entitled *Flesh and Blood,* and the story goes like
this: Royce and Amelia Laughton are cofounders of a successful Wall
Street firm, an invincible empire that keeps them flush with enough
cash to buy second, third, and fourth homes. The aging couple has
only one child, a gay son named Stephen, whom they'd placed in a
top executive role at their firm once he was of age and possessed the
requisite business degrees. The blissful ecosystem of their family is
destroyed when Stephen discovers that his parents have been using
the firm to operate a massive Ponzi scheme. Soon, the FBI makes
similar discoveries, and the couple is arrested. Key to his parents'
defense is the testimony of their son, but during prep for the trial, a
dark family secret comes to the surface: Since he was fourteen years
old, Stephen has been engaged in an ongoing incestuous relationship with his mother. It is this admission, not the federal investigation, that finally shatters the family. Still, despite the horrific revela-
tions preceding the trial, Stephen promises to testify in defense of his
parents, displaying a twisted sense of familial loyalty. But when he
gets on the stand, Stephen makes a spontaneous decision to sabotage
the trial, testify against his parents, and ensure that they spend their
lives in prison. The final scene of the play features Stephen visiting
his mother in jail, unable to surrender his sick love for the woman
who both gave him life and destroyed it. As the stage lights dim, the
weeping son kisses the partition separating him from his mother and
whispers: *"I love you."*

The play was brilliant and devastating. Early in the evening, an
astonished silence fell over the audience as we surrendered to the

eerie pull of Richard's dark vision. The singular holdout was Richard's own mother, who sat one row in front of me, an unimpressed frown fixed to her taut, surgery-sculpted face. She wore a tasteful strand of pearls and an impeccable Chanel suit and sported a severe, white-blond bob that bore a striking resemblance to the wig of the actress playing the mother. It could have been a coincidence of costuming, although, given Richard's previous admission that *Flesh and Blood* was all about his "mommy issues," I wondered if the hairstyle was a blatant *Fuck you* to his own mother. During the curtain call, the audience stirred from its shocked stupor and rose for a thunderous standing ovation—everyone but Richard's mother, who remained planted in her seat issuing little more than a limp golf clap, as though her son had fumbled through a workmanlike game on the putting green instead of creating a transcendent work of drama.

The applause lasted for nearly five minutes, the assembled theatergoers unwilling to break the spell of the production and return to the reality of the evening. I, for one, was all too eager to remain in the safety of a darkened theater, dreading the Social Olympics of the impending opening-night party and the inevitable stares that would greet me when it was discovered that I was Richard's significantly younger, poorer, not-famous boyfriend.

I glanced at the empty aisle seat to my left. Richard had abandoned it early in the first act, preferring instead to pace at the back of the theater—his nervous, opening-night tradition. Our earlier fight remained unresolved; after slapping me on the street corner, Richard had paused for only a moment, eyes widening suddenly as if he were waking from a dream, then plowed ahead wordlessly, resuming his rush to the theater as if nothing had happened. I hung back, reeling from the slap, already racking my brain for ways to forgive the man I loved: *He's a genius, he's under pressure, the monumental stress of this evening caused him to resort to uncharacteristic expressions of anxiety. Besides, it barely hurt.* When we reached the theater, it was time for the play to begin. I issued a hurried apology as we ran down the aisle to find our seats. What I'd done to be sorry *for* was still unclear to me, but I was so desperate to resolve the tension between us that I accepted total responsibility for Richard's foul mood and his act of violence. He gave me a vague "Don't worry about it" as the lights dimmed and then disappeared a few minutes later to take his place at the back of the auditorium.

Now, as I waded through the crowds in the aisle, I tried to locate Richard. I saw him trapped in conversation with his mother, his mouth pursed tight. Richard shot me a warning look; I had been cautioned about his mother and forbidden to speak to her. "My mother has never been particularly *enthused* about my romantic life," Richard had told me earlier, "and you do *not* want to be on the receiving end of her disdain."

I remained at a safe distance as she gave Richard a distracted hug, smoothed her Chanel, and trotted into the night. Once her bouncing white bob had disappeared, I approached Richard.

"That was brilliant," I gushed. "Truly moving. Everyone *loved* it."

"That's nice, but the only review I really care about is the *Times*," Richard intoned with a forced irony that did little to mask his anxiety about the impending critical reaction. "Hopefully they'll be kinder than my mother."

"She didn't like it?"

"*I don't understand why you insist on writing such nasty things,*" he cried in a grotesque falsetto imitation of his mother. "*You've lived a blessed life. Why don't you write about* that?"

"She was probably just angry that it was about her."

Shock contorted Richard's face. "Excuse me?"

"I mean—that's . . . that's what you said, right? On our first date?" I backpedaled in a frantic attempt to jog Richard's memory.

"I don't recall that discussion."

"You said that this play was really about your . . ." I trailed off. A red fury flushed Richard's face, one that seemed to betray a deeper anguish.

Did Richard's mother actually molest him? I wondered.

"Let's go to the party," he snapped, then pressed forward, once again leaving me to follow in his wake.

————

"There's my agent," Richard said, scanning the crowd at Cipriani minutes after we arrived. "You'll be okay if I jet off for a second to say hi," he continued, more statement than question.

"Of course." I was eager to appear confident, but terror stiffened my spine as I watched Richard vanish into the crush of bodies. I loitered by the bar, desperate to delay my inevitable awkward immersion in a roomful of strangers. As the bartender handed me my first martini of the evening, a scream sliced through the thrum of small talk. I whirled around, surprised to discover the shriek was directed at me.

"Ahhh! It's *so* good to see you again," gushed a woman I'd never met. She was a stunning blonde in her early forties with filler-plumped cheeks. Her rail-thin frame was squeezed into a red floor-length gown that she hiked up absently while skittering toward me. I stood dumbfounded as she swept me into a warm, aggressive hug that literally left me breathless. Our bodies pressed together, and the sequins on her gown pushed through the fabric of my shirt, stinging like nettles.

"It's been *too* long. I haven't seen you and Richard, in, what— like a year?" The timbre of her voice sounded oddly familiar. At that moment, I realized that she was none other than Kristen Sloan, the Academy Award–winning actress who'd starred in a feature-film adaptation of one of Richard's early works. "It was the St. Bart's trip for Richard's birthday, right?"

She clearly thought I was someone else, but I was reluctant to correct her mistake, partly because I was intimidated by her presence and partly because she was the most famous person in the room. If we formed an alliance, her power would be conferred on me by proxy. I could cease being seen as Richard's arm candy and become, instead, a mysterious friend to the famous actress.

"How *are* you?" I replied, avoiding her question.

"Absolutely *devastated*," she said dramatically, gripping my hand and tossing back her head. "Wasn't the play just *gutting?* I cried all the way to the party. You've got *quite* the talented boyfriend."

And there it was. She thought I was someone else, but she also knew I was Richard's boyfriend. Perhaps she'd mistaken me for the boy from the photo of "Richard Shriver and guest" that I'd studied for so long. My jealous thoughts drifted to Richard's previous conquests. I hoped that I was the final stop on his promiscuous journey through the land of twinks.

"I know, I'm so lucky," I murmured.

Despite the mistake she'd made, I quite liked Kristen (or "Krissie," as she insisted I call her, a privilege she bestowed on those in her inner circle. If you *really* knew her, you'd *never* call her Kristen). She stayed by my side for a generous amount of time and became my party life raft. The warmth of her attention felt good, even if it was intended for someone else.

"By the way, I'm *so* excited to head out to the Hamptons tomorrow," she said. My stomach dropped at the mention of the trip. "I'll see you there?"

"Yes," I blurted out, then instantly regretted the lie.

"*Perfect.* Well, I'll stop monopolizing you. We'll have *plenty* of time to catch up this week!" She administered a brisk hug before screaming in the direction of another acquaintance and diving into the sea of bodies.

I stayed behind, reeling from the encounter. Why had I lied about the Hamptons? I'd truly fucked myself now. I would have to either bring it up with Richard this evening in a Hail Mary attempt to get an invite or wait for my lie to expose itself on the trip when Charles or Krissie inquired about my absence and discovered that I was never meant to be there. Asking Richard about the trip seemed the best course, but I couldn't muster the courage to confront him. I feared the omission was intentional, and acknowledging this reality would force me to accept its implication: that Richard and I were over.

I spent the rest of the evening avoiding him. I floated through the party, largely unnoticed, like a horror-film ghost that only the cursed few can see. Friends of Richard's who did recognize me either ignored my presence or offered a tired greeting before moving on. Fran Lebowitz mistook me for a waiter. I eventually took refuge in my cracked iPhone screen, pretending to text friends I didn't have.

Toward the end of the night, an urgent murmur rippled through the crowd. *The* review, the only one that mattered, was in. Phones lit up like fireflies at dusk, dotting the room with their glow. Guests huddled around their screens, eager to read the verdict in the *Times*. I located Richard in the crowd; he stood in a concerned conference with Charles, their eyes locked on the same iPhone. I watched their smiles grow in tandem and knew without reading a word that it was a rave. Photographers circled as Richard hooked Charles in a playful headlock and landed a fat kiss on his cheek.

I caught Charles's eye through the blaze of flashbulbs. He waved me over to the chaotic corner he occupied with Richard. As I approached, Charles whispered something in his ear, eliciting a laugh from my giddy boyfriend.

"We're a hit," Richard said with drunken warmth as he pulled me into his arms.

"Congratulations," I said and kissed him, tasting the sting of bourbon on his breath.

"I'm sorry. I've been a total asshole-nightmare person tonight."

"Oh, it's *fine*." I relaxed in Richard's embrace. The slap suddenly felt like a distant memory, something we'd laugh about, a funny little footnote in our love story.

"No, it's not. I've been a monster. I'm always a wreck at openings."

"It's true. Trust me, I know," Charles chimed in, laughing. "But now *you're* the lucky one who gets to deal with it."

"By the way, are you all packed for tomorrow?" Richard asked.

"Tomorrow . . ."

"For the Hamptons? Please tell me you haven't forgotten."

I felt dizzy with relief. I didn't care if Richard truly believed that he'd invited me or if he knew he hadn't and this was simply a tactic to save face. Regardless, my anxiety evaporated like a nightmare banished by the morning, dream logic rendered absurd in the daylight.

"Oh, the Hamptons! Of course I haven't forgotten," I said, swooning deeper into Richard's arms.

"So you're still coming?"

"Absolutely."

6

"WAS IT JUST ME, or did brunch suck *extra* today?" I collapsed against the wall in the waiters' station. It was the morning after Richard's opening, and I'd just finished slogging through my Sunday shift despite a massive hangover.

"I had some prissy fag send his shrimp and grits back to the kitchen *three times*," Rashad complained. "Said they were too 'shrimpy-tasting.' I was like, 'What do you expect when you order *shrimp and motherfucking grits*?'"

"Thank *God* it's over." I stripped off my sweaty shirt. Rashad gave me a sly smirk.

"You know, I've been thinking a lot about your audition from the other night."

"Oh, really." I laughed as I pulled on a fresh white tee. "Do I get the part?"

"You get a callback," Rashad teased. "But I need to see more. What if we went dancing tonight? There's a party at China Chalet."

"Oh, I would love that—"

"Just the two of us. We could grab dinner before."

"—but I'm actually going to the Hamptons with Richard today."

The conversation stopped for a beat. I fought the urge to wince. Disappointment flashed across Rashad's face. "Oh," he said, forcing a smile. "You scored an invite after all."

"Yeah," I replied, trying to sound casual. "Turns out Richard just forgot to mention it."

"*That's* why you hauled that big-ass suitcase in here today." Rashad motioned to the corner of the waiters' station where I'd stashed my duffel bag.

"It contains literally all my earthly possessions."

"You need Daddy to buy you some more clothes," he quipped half-heartedly.

"Sorry—I don't know why I didn't say something earlier," I lied. I'd purposely avoided Rashad the whole shift. I couldn't believe I'd almost cheated on Richard. Guilt burned like acid in my stomach. And yet the sight of Rashad sparked an unresolved longing, a memory of that night. The pressure of his hands against my back. The honeyed tang of his sweat.

"Have a great time," Rashad said with a sweetness that crushed me.

I had the sudden impulse to ditch the entire Hamptons trip, stay behind with Rashad, and get stoned with him in my cramped sublet, eating cheap street pizza and laughing about the idiots we waited on at the restaurant. Maybe he'd get drunk and spend the night curled up next to me on my shabby queen mattress, not caring that it was on the floor. And maybe later, deep in the dark, we'd awake, legs tangled together, lips almost touching, our breath mingling as I closed the gap between us and kissed his kind, moonlit face. Suddenly, this seemed 100 percent preferable to spending a stilted week in the country with a group of wealthy, middle-aged capitalists, playing the part of the poor outsider, jockeying for approval. But no, I couldn't back out. These were just last-minute jitters, I told myself—this week would be *fun*. I was going to the beach with Richard. The man who loved me, even if he hadn't said it yet.

But he's going to, I thought. *He has to.*

Rashad gave me a warm hug goodbye. "Don't get into too much trouble." He grinned. "Unless that's what you're looking for."

Richard drove us out in his zippy BMW. We snacked on cherries during the ride and spat the pits onto the road and laughed when one got stuck on my cheek. It was a sweltering late-June morning, and hot wind from the open windows cut the blast of the car's AC.

Eventually we came to a stretch of farmland in Sagaponack, the small village in Southampton where Richard had his summer home. Rolling green gave way to a tall iron wall, a Serra-esque structure that looked incongruous with the beachy architecture of the surrounding neighborhood. We followed the wall for about a mile, speeding through its shadow, before arriving at a large gate. Richard's BMW crawled onto the gravel driveway, stones popping under his wheels.

"Home sweet home," Richard sang as he punched numbers into an intercom system. The gate swung open, and a massive, modernist house appeared in the distance, planted in the middle of an artfully overgrown field that burst with wildflowers. It was the sort of home I'd seen only in architectural-porno mags: a towering, minimalist rectangle with a gray metal skeleton and giant windows for walls.

"'What a dump,'" I said, doing Elizabeth Taylor doing Bette Davis.

"Total shithole," Richard deadpanned. "But don't worry — that shack belongs to Charles. Wait until you see mine."

We sailed through the gate onto a long stretch of driveway; tall grasses shivered as we roared past. As Richard had explained on the car ride, his summer home was one of four residences on the vast compound he shared with his closest friends, each house a massive glass box like the one we'd just passed.

"The neighbors pitched a fucking fit when we started building," Richard boasted wickedly. "Said we were ruining the aesthetic of the neighborhood."

"They were probably just pissed they couldn't afford your architect," I said despite the fact that I'd never met an architect in my life.

"They couldn't stop me," Richard declared with self-satisfied aggression. "No one can."

The whole setup had been Richard's idea. He'd bought the land as a present to himself after the seventh and final season of *Greed*, his wildly successful television drama about the inner workings of a corrupt hedge fund. The experience had been harrowing for Richard; he hated ceding control to idiotic television executives, preferring the unfettered autonomy bestowed on Broadway playwrights in their natural habitat, the theater. Richard fought the network's notes on every line of every script, and the more he resisted their demands, the greater their demands grew, and so began a seven-year pissing contest that left both sides considerably drained. Over time, Richard's anger spread to every corner of the production, ensuring the misery of each writer, costume designer, and assistant in his employ. Richard emerged from the experience exhausted, bitter, and determined to put the miserable millions he'd accrued to therapeutic use, and so he'd purchased a vast plot of land in the middle of Southampton, erected an iron wall to enclose his curative splurge, and invited his closest friends to build summer homes on the grounds. Richard's only request was that they use his architect, and the chosen few agreed, trusting Richard's impeccable taste and—unlike the beleaguered Hollywood executives—knowing better than to challenge his creative control.

After Richard, Charles was the next to build a home on the property. Sandro—who Richard informed me was none other than Sandro Rüegg, the Swiss film director who'd been doing esoteric art films in his native country before Richard enlisted him to direct what turned out to be an Oscar-winning adaptation of one of his stage plays—had followed shortly thereafter. Ira and Ethel, an elderly couple I'd yet to meet, built the fourth and final home. Ira Stapleton was a legendary Broadway costume designer whom Richard and Charles hired for all their productions. Ira's wife, Ethel, was an accomplished seamstress who'd worked in some of the top New York fashion houses before retiring to play housewife (and occasional creative consultant) to her husband. With Ira and Ethel installed, Richard's vision was complete. It was the Compound That Richard's Ego Built, and all roads literally led to his residence at the far end of the estate.

"Here we are," Richard said as his home came into view. It was larger than the rest, though its cold gray exterior matched the other structures we'd passed. We pulled into his driveway and sat for a moment surveying the wildflower field and the perfect arrangement of sleek, modern monoliths. The smell of honeysuckle drifted in through the open windows. I was overwhelmed with happiness.

Bang.

Something hit the trunk of the car. I shrieked.

"Don't worry. It's just Evan, my butler." Richard laughed.

I turned to the back windshield. *Butler* was an absurd term for the person smiling at us through the pollen-pocked glass. He was around twenty-two, twenty-four max, with bleached hair and a mean face. He wore short jean cutoffs, a loose, ratty tank top that barely covered his muscular chest, and giant, ugly, gold-framed glasses that made him look like he'd been miscast as the too-handsome child molester in a 1980s Lifetime movie. A closer inspection of his eyewear revealed that the frames were empty. His feet were sausaged into Nike shower sandals, and he sported a pair of pink knee socks stretched over meaty, bulbous calves. He wore his bad clothes with the ironic arrogance of someone who knew that even the most hideous garments couldn't rob him of his indestructible sex appeal. I was intimidated, and, judging by the look on Evan's face, this was the exact response he'd been hoping to elicit.

Richard leaped out of the car, leaving me behind in the passenger seat.

"Mrs. Danvers!" Richard squealed as he smacked Evan's ass.

"*Maxim!*" Evan cried as he kissed Richard's cheek. "And this must be the new Rebecca?"

Richard kept his hand on Evan's butt, and my heart dropped. There was a familiarity between the two that filled me with jealous dread. Evan's gushing performance seemed designed to exclude me while exhibiting a closeness to Richard that was meant to rival my own. They spoke in a language beyond my comprehension; I didn't know what it meant to be "the new Rebecca," though I doubted it meant anything good.

Evan wriggled out of Richard's arms and opened my car door. "Welcome," he sang with simulated cheer. "Richard told me all about you."

Evan made a big show of helping me with my bag as we walked toward Richard's glass box, but his enthusiasm felt forced, almost threatening. His face seemed familiar, and as we walked together, I developed a growing suspicion that we'd met before, although where, I wasn't quite certain.

"I rescued Evan from an internship at *Artforum* last year," Richard said with mock gallantry. "I told him he'd learn much more here."

"I'm on track for a very lucrative career as a professional butler-slash-twink," Evan said, a strange tension creeping into his voice.

"It's better than the track you were on before," Richard snapped with a harshness that halted the conversation.

I stayed silent and walked behind them. Their banter devolved into the stilted rhythms of an embittered married couple; their coded jabs filled the air with tension. Evan dropped my bag near the glass-walled entrance to Richard's house, punctuating his efforts with a passive-aggressive grunt. He took off the fake glasses to wipe his sweating brow, momentarily revealing his bare face.

I realized how I knew him.

After I'd studied his image for so long, the "guest" from the online photo of "Richard Shriver and guest" finally had a name: Evan. A rush of vertigo hit my brain.

"Oh, shit, I forgot the gate," Richard said.

"I'll get it." Evan rolled his eyes as he picked up a dusty bike from the side of the road. The unfettered joy I'd felt moments before was replaced with nausea — what was *he* doing here?

"Thanks, love," Richard called as Evan pedaled off and disappeared in a cloud of up-kicked dirt. His use of the word *love* stung me. How carelessly he tossed it at Evan when I'd been hoping to hear it directed at me for weeks. I caught Richard's eye, then snapped away.

"Don't mind Evan," he said. "He seems like a brat, but it's just an act. He's actually sweet once you deactivate the bitch-shield."

Richard put his arms around me, kissed the top of my head. He smelled like deodorant and sweat and Tom Ford Tobacco. It seemed like a heavy scent for summer, but something about it calmed me. I eased in his embrace and he spoke with his lips in my hair. "It's just you and me now." His voice vibrated through my scalp. In the distance, the sounds of clanging metal echoed across the property.

It was Evan, closing the gate.

————

Our first night in the compound was a quiet one. Richard and I stayed in and decided to make a simple pasta with fresh tomatoes, mozzarella, and basil that we'd procured at the local farmers' market. The house was huge and open with twenty-foot ceilings and tall, white walls covered with mismatched and beautiful art pieces. My favorite was a small watercolor of Batman and Robin jerking each other off, their gloved arms blurred with effort.

"I finally read the play you sent me," Richard called from the counter, where he was preparing to blanch tomatoes for our sauce. He took each red globe in his hands and cut a shallow X on the bottom. I straightened up in my seat at his glass-topped dining table, knife in hand, momentarily abandoning a half-sliced mozzarella wedge.

"Oh, you did?"

I was terrified. Though my play was not an exact reflection of my relationship with Richard (if anything, it ended up being a sort of nightmarish refraction of reality that explored my underlying anxieties about our affair), there were certain autobiographical details that had no doubt raised Richard's shaggy eyebrows. It followed the life of an ambitious young waiter struggling to become a writer who dates an older, successful playwright. Eventually, thanks to the benefits of socializing with people in the playwright's circle, the younger man becomes famous. But as his success grows, his relationship crumbles, and he realizes that he has mistaken ambition for love. By the end of the play, his romance has grown so toxic and his career so tainted that he kills himself.

"When did you write this? Before you met me?" Richard prodded, placing the tomatoes in a pot of boiling water.

"Yes," I muttered. If you counted my "Notes for Future Conversations" document as an early draft, my response was technically correct. Any version of the truth was embarrassing, though this seemed like the least incriminating explanation.

"Well, what an incredible coincidence," Richard teased. "That your imagination conjured such a close facsimile of the man you would eventually date in real life. Or perhaps you'd been looking for someone like me for quite some time. I can only assume, based on your work, that I'm your *type*."

"I know what it looks like, but it's not about us."

"Oh, I never thought it was." Richard shrugged, nonchalant. "It's clearly about *you*."

"I—I suppose most fiction has an ounce of autobiography," I said, deflecting.

"Though I don't think you have to be so terribly hard on yourself. It's not a crime to be ambitious."

"I never said it was."

"But your play seems to suggest otherwise. You quite literally give yourself a death sentence for pursuing your goals."

"That's not me, that's the character."

"Right. Well, regardless, I just think your *character* needs more dimension and defining qualities beyond his ambition."

"Okay . . ." I murmured, giving up any attempt at defense. My worst fears overtook my thoughts—I was a fraud, I was untalented, I had not earned my place at Richard's glass-topped dining table. I felt the sudden urge to run into the night, away from Richard, away from my failure. But I had nowhere to go, no choice but to sit there and listen as he decimated my work.

"And the suicide is quite overwrought." Richard removed the tomatoes from the boiling pot and put them in ice water. "He can still be destroyed by his ambition in the end, but there are subtler punishments than a noose."

"So you thought it was terrible."

"Not exactly." Richard plucked a tomato from the ice bath. "There were some good ideas. With a little finessing, you could say something very powerful about desire."

"And what's that?"

Richard paused to skin the blanched tomato, a pulpy orb bleeding in his fist.

"The things we worship eat us alive."

The things we worship eat us alive. The line would've worked in one of Richard's plays, but it clunked there in his real-life kitchen. It felt like he was trying something out on me, a snip of dialogue he'd use in his work later. I thought his delivery was too dramatic as well, and his pretension made me feel superior. I felt relief; the power balance had tilted in my favor. But it tilted back when I realized that this was precisely what I was trying to say with my work: *The things we worship eat us alive.* He'd arrived at the central motif in a few minutes right here in the kitchen while I had spent countless drafts failing to articulate that simple idea.

"So I should just throw the whole thing away," I said, wiping moisture from my eye.

"Don't be absurd." Richard sighed. "I think you should revise it. You're very talented."

And just like that, hope soared again in my heart: *Richard Shriver thinks I'm talented*.

Desire places people in dangerous positions. This was a fact I'd yet to learn and something Richard knew all too well.

The real reason Richard invited me to the Hamptons?

To play games he knew I'd lose.

7

I JERKED AWAKE to the sound of someone in the kitchen.
It took me a moment to orient myself to my new surroundings,
as strange sunlight illuminated a foreign bedroom. Richard was
beached on the opposite coast of his king-size mattress, snoring
loudly, in no position to tackle an intruder. I shivered as I grabbed
my bathrobe off the cold concrete floor and made my way to the
kitchen.

It was just Evan. He stood by the sink, wearing nothing but a pair
of tight briefs that contoured his cock with alarming precision. He
shot me a lazy grin as he pulled a case of eggs from the refrigerator.

"Morning," he said, cracking an egg in a bowl.

"What are you doing?"

"Making breakfast for you guys." He tossed a shell into the sink.

"I'll do it."

"But Richard asked me to —"

"I *said,* I'll do it," I snapped.

Evan shrugged. "Suit yourself. He likes his eggs fluffy with just
a little sprinkle of shaved cheddar on top. And whatever you do,
don't add chives." He laughed bitterly but failed to let me in on the
joke.

"Don't worry, I won't."

"You *sure* you can handle him on your own?" he asked, clutching his chest in a parody of concern. He shot me the same smug stare I'd seen in that society-page photo. Jealousy constricted my breath.

"Yes," I grumbled.

"Loosen up." He swatted at me playfully. "I'm only offering a little help."

"Next time, keep your mouth shut unless I ask you to open it," I grumbled just loud enough for him to hear. Evan's eyebrows lifted in surprise. A tense silence swelled between us.

Suddenly, he exploded into laughter. His rapid squeals echoed through the kitchen like a strange, strangled alarm. "Oh, honey, I don't think *that's* how you want to play this."

"Sorry, that came out wrong." Embarrassment flushed my cheeks. "I'm just—"

"Trust me," he snapped, his smile flattening. "You want me as your friend."

———

"Where's Evan?" Richard barked. I wheeled around to discover him frowning in his bathrobe. "I *told* him we wanted breakfast this morning."

"Relax. I said he could go. *I* want to make breakfast for you."

"Did he tell you about my chive thing?" Richard asked with a wary, childish whine.

"Yes. I've got this."

Richard loosened a little, though clearly the change of plans bothered him. He was not one to relinquish control lightly, even when it came to eggs.

But if there was one thing I knew how to make, it was breakfast. Growing up, I spent every Saturday morning in the kitchen with my mother cooking a pancake feast while my father worked on his sermon in the study. That was love—standing above the mixing bowl with my mother's arms around me, both our hands clasping the wooden spoon as we stirred together, a pile of freshly washed blueberries glistening beside us. She always smelled like detergent. We'd stir the batter to the rhythm of laundry in the dryer, a gentle cadence to underscore our perfect, tender ritual.

I cooked that same meal for Richard, hoping to replicate the familial intimacy, hoping I was still worthy of love. I loaded the table with an unending supply of pancakes and eggs and hash browns and grits. The sting of coffee cut through the smell of butter in the air. Richard devoured everything I placed in front of him. After my work was done, I joined him, sweaty from the stove, bursting with affection.

"Dear Lord, that was good!" He slapped his belly in surrender and nuzzled me close. "You're incredible."

"No, *you're* incredible." I planted a kiss on his cheek.

"All right, I have dish duty."

"No, you don't have to—"

"*Of course* I do. You made our gorgeous feast, I get to clean it up."

Richard cleared the table and I retired to the couch with my laptop. My cursor hovered over the file containing my play. I felt inspired to begin my revisions, encouraged by my discussion with Richard the night before. A concentrated silence fell over the house as Richard rinsed dishes and I settled into my work.

After about thirty minutes, Richard came hunting for me, dishrag over his shoulder. "What are you *doing*," he whimpered playfully. "I *miss* you."

"I'm working. Someone's gotta make the money around here."

"*Fine.* I'll just go back to being the houseboy." Richard threw his dishrag at me and tackled me with kisses. "You know, Charles is coming out this weekend. I'm sure he'd be willing to read your play once it's finished. He's looking for up-and-coming playwrights for this new programming initiative he's working on for Lincoln Center. Might be a good fit."

"Okay, cool. That sounds good." I tried my best to sound unimpressed, but my voice wavered with excitement.

"He gets in tonight with everyone else. We're all having dinner together."

———

I showered before dinner, guts in a twist. These were Richard's closest friends. My performance mattered. I toweled off and changed into a crisp Marc Jacobs button-down. Richard, still in his boxer-briefs, frowned at me.

"Where do you think you're going? Le Cirque?" he snapped. "It's just dinner at Ira and Ethel's."

"I'll change," I sputtered, embarrassed.

Richard shook his head and put on a loose beige T-shirt. "We're at the beach." He sighed. "Relax."

I changed into a T-shirt. Richard laughed off the exchange, but a tense silence fell as we walked along the stone path that connected his house to Ira and Ethel's. Dusk settled onto the field. Ira and Ethel's glass-walled home appeared on the horizon, a sharp square of light cut into the encroaching darkness.

"You must be Richard's new beau," Ethel gushed when she opened the door. She swept me into a warm hug. "It's *so* nice to finally meet you."

Ira followed Ethel's greeting with a more formal handshake, and the couple invited us into their home. Ethel was in her early seventies, though she could've passed for an eerie fifty-five, her face gored flat by the knives of well-paid surgeons. She wore a casual white linen pantsuit on her thin frame and a simple gold necklace dotted with four small diamonds. Ira was shorter than his wife—he couldn't have been more than five six—and flitted about neurotically, adjusting his horn-rimmed glasses with compulsive regularity. He wore a loose Hawaiian shirt, khaki shorts, and tight gray ankle socks.

"If you don't mind taking off your shoes . . ." Ira said, eyes widening as I approached the white shag carpet.

"Oh, of course." I jumped back like the rug had bitten me.

"Thank you, dear," Ethel said as she handed me a cocktail. "Campari and soda?"

"We guzzle them like water around here," Ira chimed in with a conspiratorial grin aimed my way. "It's the drink of the summer."

The drink of the summer. It was the exact wording of my inane assessment of Charles's beverage at Perdition earlier that week. Had Charles gossiped about our encounter? Was Ira's comment merely coincidence, or was he mocking me? My thoughts became a muddled cocktail of anxiety, paranoia, and Campari. I downed my drink with a speed that led Ethel to raise her expertly plucked eyebrows.

"Someone's thirsty," Ethel remarked, pulling me away from Ira and Richard. "Shall I give you the grand tour while you still have the ability to remember it?"

"Sure." I laughed. "I didn't mean to down this so fast, it's just *delicious*. I swear I'm not a budding alcoholic."

"You'd be in good company if you were. Just wait until Charles shows up."

Ethel guided me away as Ira and Richard huddled in the corner, deep in conversation. The house was a modern open concept with smooth concrete floors and the same lofted ceilings as Richard's. A ten-foot-long table made of reclaimed wood and supported by thin iron legs stretched across the dining area. It was set with charming mismatched china, linen napkins, polished silver, and wineglasses. A marble island marked the beginning of the kitchen. Evan was hunched by the stainless-steel stove, laboring over crab cakes. He caught my stare and gave me a sarcastic thumbs-up.

I hated him.

"I hope you like crab cakes, dear," Ethel trilled.

"They're my favorite," I lied. It seemed far too late to mention my crab allergy.

Ethel's phone buzzed, and she excused herself. I lingered by the kitchen island, afraid to enter Richard and Ira's discussion. They wore concerned expressions, frowning into their Camparis. Ethel paced outside, iPhone glued to her ear. An irrational fear gripped me: *Everyone is talking about me.*

Suddenly, Evan dropped a plate of crab cakes. The room fell silent as he crouched over a mess of broken china and chunks of fried meat.

"*Help me,*" he snarled.

I pretended not to hear him.

———

The remainder of the guests soon drifted in from their various corners of the compound. Charles arrived drunk, carrying a cocktail transported from his own property. Sandro was next to appear, accompanied by Kristen Sloan ("It's *Krissie,*" she scolded me with an impatient smile when I accidentally greeted her with a full-blown "Kristen"). She was staying in Sandro's guest room for the night but flying to Portugal via private plane tomorrow.

Several waiters appeared from nowhere and joined Evan in serving the guests. The waiters were all gay males in their early twenties and wore matching black T-shirts that accentuated their muscled torsos. They said nothing and circulated around the room with Campari sodas on metal trays. There seemed to be three of them, though it was possible there were four; their clean, pretty faces were difficult to differentiate. The staff-to-guest ratio seemed excessive, but lewd stares from Sandro, Charles, and Richard explained the superfluous manpower. I didn't know any of the waiters personally, but I knew the type. In my parallel life, I was one of them.

But not tonight. Tonight, I was miles from Perdition, and I felt superior to the hired beef. I made a point to frown at each waiter as he approached with his tray and triceps and perfect teeth. *I am not one of you,* my nasty squint implied. I prayed the rest of the room thought the same.

When Richard and I were in New York, meals with his friends

went one of two ways: good or bad. A Good Dinner meant that our dining companions asked me questions and took me seriously as a person. A Bad Dinner meant I sat in silence, unable to find an entry into the conversation, cast in the role of mute bimbo. Jokes would be made about my age, my silence, my appearance. If people were cruel, Richard would compensate with performative kindness afterward—he bought me ice cream, he bought me books, he bought me sweaters from Dries Van Noten. I almost came to enjoy the Bad Dinners; the dread I felt during them was cut with a Pavlovian anticipation of gifts. But tonight we were miles from the nearest Bloomingdale's—if things went badly, my humiliation would go unrewarded.

Ethel clapped her hands, silencing the small talk. "Shall we take our seats?"

––––––––

My throat was on fire. Failing to disclose my crab allergy had been a critical error; the single, polite mouthful I'd consumed had triggered a reaction. I chugged the water in my glass, hoping to cool my burning esophagus. Panic shortened my breath, making it difficult to distinguish anxiety from anaphylaxis.

Do I need a doctor? I wondered.

"You've barely touched your crab cake, dear," Ethel cooed from across the table. "I thought they were your favorite."

"Just . . . savoring . . ." I coughed.

Evan stood sentinel in a corner of the room, supposedly at our service. I motioned for him to refill my water glass. He stayed put, choosing instead to look directly through me. With no other recourse, I downed an entire Campari soda. The alcohol hit my oxygen-deprived brain with surprising speed. The room spun as I caught kaleidoscopic flashes of my dining companions: Richard's lips greased with tartar sauce, Ethel's dentures caked in succotash, the food jammed beneath Ira's yellowed fingernails, the meat spilling off Sandro's plate. Nausea roiled my gut as their piggish symphony crescendoed; everyone scooped and chewed and chugged until finally Richard interrupted.

"I have a bit of news," he announced from his seat to my left. "Amy Pascal wants to adapt *Flesh and Blood* at Sony."

"That's great if you want Satan's midwife to fuck your script to death," Charles barked, gnawing on a crab cake as he spoke.

"She tears *everyone's* work apart," Sandro concurred. "Unless you're Aaron Sorkin."

"But aren't I basically Aaron Sorkin?" Richard whined.

"Um, no?" Charles laughed. Meteors of crab meat rained onto his shirt, collecting in a greasy constellation on his chest.

"You know what I mean. I'm worth Aaron money. I deserve Aaron respect."

A smear of tartar sauce hung from Richard's waxen jowls. Sweat cascaded down my forehead as I assessed the mass of dried mayonnaise, weighted perilously by a green-gray caper. Was it *my* responsibility to say something? My throat constricted further at the thought of interrupting the conversation.

"Do you not *like* it?" Ethel whispered, glaring at my uneaten food like it was a dead rat. "I would hate to think our cuisine isn't up to your . . . *standards.*"

"No! No . . . it's delicious," I wheezed, eyes watering.

"Then eat up," she snapped. My heart pounded in protest as I placed another bite in my mouth.

"Well, I say you do it if Amy backs up the money truck," Ira said to Richard.

"*Beep, beep, beep!*" Charles screeched, a string of saliva stretching between his lips.

"It's more like a money minivan." Richard sighed.

I discreetly spit the mouthful of crab into my napkin. It was too late, however; a fresh inferno blazed through my mouth. I felt dizzy, strangled anew. I turned to look for a waiter. And there was Evan again. Staring at me. I motioned for water as he approached my seat. He placed another crab cake on my plate instead. Murder crossed my mind.

"No . . . I . . . need water," I whispered. But he just floated back to his corner.

"How much are they offering?" Krissie inquired, pushing uneaten chunks of congealed meat around her plate. Her fork issued small, spine-tingling shrieks as it grated the china.

"Eight hundred and fifty thousand." Richard pouted.

"Holy shit." I coughed, almost involuntarily. Everyone turned to me in shock, as if a houseplant had spoken. "That's a lot . . . right?"

The room burst into laughter. Shame flushed my already burning face. My neck blistered. Fire ants crawled beneath my flesh. Where was the nearest hospital?

"How do you think Richard puts crab cakes on the table, darling?" Charles gesticulated with his Campari soda, spilling some on his shirt in the process. "He makes *money*."

"Aaron Sorkin got two point five *million* for *The Social Network,* you know," Richard grumbled. "Just for the script fee. Now he gets *another* million because it's getting made."

"Oh, honey, I'm so, so sorry," Krissie said as if someone had died. "You're a living genius."

"Oh, stop."

"You deserve *so* much more."

My vision blurred; adrenaline raced through my system. Yes, I needed a doctor. But the thought of interrupting dinner to announce my medical emergency was almost as anxiety-producing as the emergency itself. Suddenly, a bowl of tartar sauce appeared in front of me. Perhaps a spoonful could quell the fire in my throat. A whiff of eggy vinegar stung my nostrils. My stomach churned.

"You're right, Krissie," Richard said. As he spoke, the chunk of crusted tartar sauce was dislodged from his jowl and plummeted into the sauce in front of me. I nearly retched but still forced a heaping spoonful into my mouth. The tepid dose did the trick; my windpipe began to cool as my panic receded.

I closed my eyes. Relief at last.

"Ladies and gentlemen, we seem to be putting our poor guest to sleep!"

My eyes snapped open. Charles aimed a bitchy grin in my direction. A hunk of meat glistened in the greasy tangle of his beard.

"Oh, no, I was just—"

"I'm *so* sorry, my friends are *unbelievably* tedious," Charles slurred, a trace of acid in his tone. "Tell us, Jonah, what do *you* think about your poor boyfriend's paltry script fee?"

Everyone looked in my direction. I coughed. "I mean . . . eight hundred and fifty thousand . . . it's, like, not enough?"

Charles clutched his chest in mock horror. "Not *enough?* But it's almost *one million dollars,* Jonah! That's *so* much money."

"But, I mean, everyone just said it wasn't enou—"

"How could you be such a *greedy* little boy?" Charles roared, slamming the table with sudden, inexplicable violence.

"I . . . I'm not," I stuttered, staring at my plate, clenching my jaw, determined not to cry.

An awful silence descended as the room waited for Charles to respond. But he refused, opting to snatch his tumbler and down the rest of his drink instead. We were all his hostages, forced to watch as he tilted his head back and chugged, his neck constricting like a snake's stomach, his Adam's apple the bobbing prey.

"Oh, leave him alone, Charles," Richard snapped, coming to my rescue.

"I'm just teasing, Jonah." Charles smiled suddenly, as if his outburst had never occurred. "You've been a *delightful* addition to the conversation."

There was no doubt: This was a Bad Dinner. A Very Bad Dinner.

"I hope everyone saved room for dessert," Ethel chirped.

"No one responded to my e-mail, by the way," Richard complained later that evening. There was a brief pause as all the guests glared at their rhubarb crisp.

"Oh, this is about that GLSEN benefit thing?" Ira inquired innocently.

"Yes. I didn't shell out a hundred thousand dollars for a table so I could eat alone."

"Oh, *my*, that's about one-eighth of a Richard Shriver screenplay," Charles quipped with feigned alarm.

"Shut up, Charles." Richard rolled his eyes. "You guys said you would come."

"What's it for again?" Sandro asked, bored.

"Homeless gay youth." Richard pouted.

"Don't you do enough in that arena as is?" Charles cocked his head toward me. Everyone let out an astonished chuckle. Each jab from Charles sent me spiraling further; the more he humiliated me, the greater my desperation for his approval. This was Richard's best friend, his former partner, the man who could dramatically alter the trajectory of my career. Self-hatred raged through my mind: *Say something, you idiot. You deserve a seat at this table, so fucking prove it.*

"Richard gave *me* only a thousand bucks for rent," I deadpanned. "Do you love these *other* homeless kids more?" I turned to Richard with a mock-pitiful look and everyone erupted in laughter.

"Richard, why so cheap?" Charles followed up, and they howled louder.

Victory. It was Richard's turn to blush now. I felt a surge of relief as approving faces beamed in my direction. I was a gay phoenix, rising from the ashes of a Very Bad Dinner.

"Well, well." Charles smirked, impressed. "Look who came to hang with the grown-ups."

"Really, I admire the homeless for their sense of style," I continued, on a roll. "I mean, actual garbage bags are preferable to the trash Rick Owens debuted at Paris Fashion Week this spring."

As I said this, I had the disconcerting experience of hearing my own voice from outside my skull, as if my consciousness were separate from the strange machine of my body. The cumulative stress of the evening—the adrenaline and the booze and the shame and those poison crab cakes, that wretched meal—felt like a rush of helium. I was floating high above the room, hanging from the rafters, watching the group of people below. I made more jokes about homeless gay youth, and I wondered who this callous person talking was, this stranger who bore an uncanny resemblance to Jonah Keller. How quickly he threw those homeless kids under the metaphorical bus when recent events had left him precariously close to a similar fate. How easy it was for him to throw empathy out the window. What would his parents think? His mother would be disgusted. Her son had succumbed to the wicked homosexual lifestyle. And his father? His father would be unsurprised. He knew firsthand the evil of which Jonah was capable. His son was beyond hope, beyond the grasp of God's grace.

His son was unworthy of love.

As this spell of dissociation grew stronger, panic coursed through my body, and I fixated on a memory of my father—that Sunday before church when he gripped my shoulders and shook my body as if he could exorcise my gayness with abuse, a one-punch cure, and then slapped my face and slammed me against the wall of framed photos in our foyer, knocking my third-grade school picture to the ground. I heard the glass shatter and felt my father's hands on my shoulders; I was in Ira and Ethel's home in Southampton but I could hear that glass shatter and I could feel my father's hands on my shoulders. I fell silent and the conversation moved on and pain shot down my spine and suddenly Charles appeared, tumbler in hand.

"For you," he barked, shoving a Campari soda in my face. "I like you."

I grabbed it like a life jacket and let the cool glass float me back to the room and my body. I was very drunk but downed the bitter liquid anyway. Anything to stop the flashbacks.

"Sorry about before." He giggled mischievously. "I can be a bit of a tease."

"You can tease me all you want, baby," I flirted drunkenly. Now that I had his approval, I was desperate to keep it.

"Be careful what you wish for." Charles laughed as he pulled up a seat next to me. "Richard tells me you're a playwright. A good one."

"I am," I slurred. "Well, I'm a playwright. I don't know about the *good* part."

"I'd love to read some of your stuff," he said, placing a hand on my knee. "Richard says you're revising a play?"

He massaged my thigh. A web of veins covered his fist. I looked down for a beat too long and came back up, blushing.

"I can definitely, um, send you the draft when it's done," I said dumbly.

"I'd like that." Charles stared at me with an unnerving focus, moving his hand toward my crotch. My cock stiffened.

"Come on, I want to show you something," Charles said, rising from his chair.

I paused for a moment, then followed him. I glanced back to locate Richard, who had moved to a couch with Sandro and Krissie. He laughed at something Krissie said, gave me a little wave, then returned to his conversation.

Charles was already out the sliding glass door, not even checking to see if I'd follow. I slipped out behind him and was suddenly hit by a hot cloud of honeysuckle air. I slid the door shut and caught Evan's eye through the glass. He frowned and whispered something to one of the waiters.

I rushed to catch Charles in the darkness.

The rest of the night happened in sick fragments separated by stretches of black. It was like watching a movie while fighting sleep; I kept nodding off, unable to track the plot.

I was on the stone path several paces behind Charles. Small spotlights on the trail hit his feet as he jerked past them, drunk. Tall grasses scratched my legs.

Black.

Then: I was in the wildflower field. Charles was gripping my forearm, dragging me through dark brush. I tripped, but he didn't slow or loosen his grasp. I stumbled behind as he marched faster, his nails digging into my flesh.

Black.

Then: We were outside a small, windowless building with steel siding that was dwarfed by the tall iron wall behind it. We must have been somewhere on the edge of the property. Charles stood several feet in front of me, sifting through keys in the dark. Another waft of honeysuckle hit my nostrils, but this time the smell was too sweet. I felt the sting of rejected Campari rise in my throat and I bent at my middle and vomited on the grass. Charles looked up from his keys, frowned, and stumbled toward me. I collapsed in the grass and let the earth cool my face as my eyes shut. I did not want to enter that building.

Black.

Then: Evan's voice above me, arguing with Charles. Their feet planted on the grass directly in front of my face. *"Don't,"* Evan insisted; the rest of his plea faded with my consciousness.

Black.

Then: my body floating through darkness, buoyed up by strong, male hands.

8

I WOKE UP alone in Richard's bed. I looked down at my naked body. There was a scrape on my shin, a bruise on my left hip, and a thin red line that stretched across my forearm, glistening wet in the sunlight.

I turned and stared out the window, my mind empty, a throbbing pain in my skull. A red speck flitted in the distance, darting through the tall grass of the wildflower field. I stood slowly and approached the window for a closer look.

It was a cardinal.

Suddenly the bird changed course and shot directly toward me. I watched helplessly as the small animal hurled itself toward death. It hit the large glass window at full speed and dropped like an anchor. I peered down at the dead bird in the grass, its neck bent at an impossible ninety-degree angle.

Out of nowhere, a Doberman pinscher galloped into the frame and snatched the fallen cardinal in its jaws. The dog's stride was uneven, and as I watched it disappear into the grass, I realized why: it had only three legs.

"That's Scamp, Sandro's dog." Richard's voice surprised me. I wheeled around.

"Jesus, you scared me," I said, clutching my temple. "How long have you been standing there?"

"Long enough to realize that your ass is the finest in all of South-ampton." Richard smacked my butt. I winced and craned my neck to kiss him.

"You had quite the wild night last night," Richard teased. "Charles said he found you passed out in the field."

That's an interesting interpretation, I thought, but I said nothing. After all, I was just a guest. I didn't want to ruin anyone's good time.

———

Krissie wanted just one dip in the pool before her jet left for Por-tugal. Sandro called around to let everyone know they'd be swim-ming at noon. Evan would make Campari sodas for interested par-ties. Even the mention of last night's drink made my stomach churn, but a swim sounded refreshing. I slipped into a black Speedo without showering, and Richard donned his aqua trunks.

We were the last to arrive. The pool was a sharp blue rectangle cut into immaculate white concrete, slightly raised from the earth, not connected to any home. Krissie swam laps as Sandro idly flipped through a damp *New Yorker.* Ira and Ethel sunned themselves side by side on ivory pool chairs. Charles stood by the bar cart, where Evan cracked open a bottle of Campari. My stomach roiled again as Charles turned to greet us. I scanned his face for any tacit acknowl-edgment of the night before, but none appeared.

"How are you?" I managed to say as Charles approached, drink in hand.

"Oh, *I'm* lovely. The real question is: How are *you?* You're lucky I found you in the field. This is a dangerous neighborhood, honey," Charles said, gesturing toward the surrounding compound. Richard laughed.

I felt insane. Charles's nonchalance was unnerving; I began to distrust my own memory of the night before. My head hurt and I didn't have the energy to spar with Richard and Charles, so I turned to the bar cart. "Pellegrino, please," I mumbled. Evan fixed my drink wordlessly. In the distance behind him, I saw the windowless, steel structure from the previous night. That much had been real. A light breeze sent shivers through my body. I needed sun before I hit the pool.

I found a chair, and Richard sat beside me. Krissie emerged from the water, grabbed a towel, and took a seat next to Sandro. Charles peeled off his shirt, revealing a patch of white chest hair, and perched on the edge of the pool, dangling his feet in the water. The sun hovered directly overhead, and we all baked in silence for a moment.

"Don't make me go to Portugal," Krissie whined from under her striped Missoni sun hat.

"Just stay," Sandro said after a lazy beat. Scamp, the three-legged Doberman, trotted up between his owner and the actress. Krissie took the dog's head in her hands and let him lick her face.

"Cancel the plane, Scamp," she cooed. "Tell them I'm staying forever."

"How long are *you* staying?" Charles asked, turning toward my chair.

"I leave tomorrow," I said coolly. "Gotta get back to work."

"I don't like the idea of you going back to that awful restaurant," Richard mused. "You should stay the summer."

"Believe me, I'd love that." I laughed. "But my sublet ends next week, and Mama's gotta find a new place to live."

"All the more reason to simply stay *here*," Charles insisted playfully.

"Anyway, I can't miss all that work," I continued. "Spending the summer here would be a dream, but there's no way I could afford it."

"But *I* could," Richard said.

I looked at him and realized he was serious. The offer took me by surprise.

Charles chimed in before I could formulate a response. "Think of it as an artist's residency," he said. "Take the time to work on your play."

"Exactly," Richard agreed.

"I—I don't know," I replied, trying to think of good reasons to return to the city. None came. I shot an insecure glance toward Evan, but he wasn't looking at me. He sat hunched on a folding chair behind the bar, staring at nothing, looking depressed.

"Oh, you should!" Krissie gushed. "What a fun idea."

"After all, you still owe me a draft of your play," Charles said. "And I'm sure Sandro would take a look as well."

"No, I won't," Sandro intoned dryly. "I've made a vow to read nothing but magazines for the summer."

"Well, Ethel and I would be delighted if you stayed," Ira said. "Wouldn't we, Ethel?"

Ethel, half asleep, murmured a vague affirmation from behind the *New York Review of Books*.

"It's settled, then," Richard said. "You're staying!"

Just like that, my fate was decided for me. I didn't say no because there was never an opportunity to do so. My mind raced to catch up. Maybe it *was* a good idea to stay. I would have to quit my job, a prospect that thrilled me. I could take the time to revise my play and share it with Charles and Richard when a new draft was ready. If Charles liked it, there was a strong possibility he'd select me for his Lincoln Center program, which could lead to a reading, a workshop, or even a full production of my work. I could see my future career unfold before me, a fantasy of success rooted in this one pivotal moment, and suddenly, it seemed like staying the summer was the most important decision I'd ever made. Or, rather, the most important decision ever made *for* me.

My thoughts were interrupted by Paul McCartney's voice coming over the pool's sound system. The song was from a recent solo album, a limp and sterile imitation of his earlier, more successful work. As Paul's lame warble echoed across the oasis, Sandro dropped his *New Yorker*.

"Ugh, who chose this?" Sandro spat.

"It's Paul McCartney!" Ira said defensively. "You can't criticize a living god."

"I abhor late-career Paul McCartney," Sandro complained.

"Pure trash," I agreed, hoping to impress Sandro, who remained cold toward me. "It sounds so Starbucks-y."

A strange silence fell over the pool.

"What do you mean by *Starbucks-y?*" Krissie asked coyly.

"Like, it sounds generic and corporate and lame but clearly has pretensions of depth and quality—like something that's stupid enough to be played at Starbucks, aka the maw of corporate hell," I replied. "Didn't Paul McCartney even, like, sign a record deal to distribute an album exclusively at Starbucks? I mean, *kill me now.*"

Krissie let out a loud laugh, but it didn't feel like a response to my statement. Others at the pool also chuckled, clearly in on a different joke. Evan sighed in his seat.

"I feel like I'm missing something," I said.

"I'm flying to Portugal to vacation with Howard Schultz and his family," Krissie explained.

"Howard Schultz . . ." I still didn't understand.

Evan swooped in to refresh my Pellegrino. "He's the CEO of Starbucks." He sighed, looking at me with pity. I blushed and everyone laughed.

"It's gonna be a loooong summer," Charles teased, swatting my leg.

"Oh, shut up, Charles," Evan snapped.

Charles whipped his head around to Evan, a furious smile stretched across his face. "Anything for you, sweetie," Charles cooed in a menacing singsong. "Our employee of the fucking month."

Suddenly, I needed to vomit.

———

I wiped the puke from my mouth and looked in the bathroom mirror. I froze, transfixed by my appearance. The longer I stared, the less I recognized myself, and gradually my face dissolved into an assortment of detached shapes. My stomach heaved again. I bowed over the toilet, but there was nothing left inside me.

I brushed my teeth twice, eager to scrub any stench from my tongue before I returned to the pool. I didn't want to betray the reason for my sudden exit. I placed my toothbrush back in the small clay jar on the sink and hurried out of the bathroom. The cold concrete of Richard's floor numbed my bare feet.

I stepped out of the house and onto the sharp gravel of the driveway. The pain felt good on my toes; it brought me back down to earth. I stood for a moment, collecting myself, then turned and shut the door. When I turned back, I was shocked to discover Evan standing there. Watching me.

"Don't stay," he said flatly. "You don't belong here."

It was my worst fear articulated, but before I could muster a response, Charles swooped in and grabbed Evan's arm.

"Evan, can I steal you for a second?" He smelled like Campari. Evan remained silent as Charles dragged him into the wildflower field. "Don't worry, I'll bring him right back," Charles said, laughing.

I never saw Evan again.

———

By the time I got back to the pool, the party was breaking up—Krissie had to pack and get to her jet. Richard and I returned to his house and showered together. He felt horny as we toweled off, so I knelt on the bathroom floor and let him fuck my mouth.

"When are you quitting your job?" Richard asked as I wiped his semen off my face.

"Right now, I guess," I said with a smirk and tugged his dick.

I wrapped a towel around my waist and walked to the bedroom. As I grabbed my phone from the nightstand, a seed of apprehension planted itself in my thoughts. I considered the impact this decision would have on my life. This was a bridge I had long dreamed of burning, but when faced with the prospect of incinerating my only source of income, I hesitated to light the match. I stared at Brett's number in my phone, daring myself to dial it. *Richard will support you,* I assured myself. *It would be insane to pass this up.*

"I'm quitting," I said as soon as Brett answered.

"Jonah?"

"I'm *quitting.*"

"Did you finally find a better pimp?"

"No, I finally realized that working for a coke addict who abuses his staff was not the best move for my mental health."

"Lemme guess: the big city scared you, so you're moving back to whatever shithole small town you crawled out of."

"No, actually. I'm quitting to focus on my writing."

"Your *writing?*" Brett laughed. "You sure you don't wanna pursue something a bit more within your wheelhouse? Like being a porn star, perhaps?"

"You have no idea what I'm capable of." My anger mounted.

"I know you're capable of sucking Richard Shriver's dick for cash."

I had fantasized about this exchange many times before. In my mind, the conversation always looked the same: I would keep the upper hand by maintaining my composure. I would not stoop to red-faced fury. I would not give him the satisfaction of seeing the hurt he'd inflicted on me. I would restore my dignity with two simple words: *I quit.* But now I couldn't stick to the plan. I felt my temperature rise. A long-festering hatred surged through my body, desperate for release.

"Don't you get it?" I snapped. "I don't fucking work for you anymore, *so fuck off, you worthless piece of shit.*"

I hung up and hurled my phone at the bed, where it landed with a soft thump. Adrenaline coursed through my body, throbbing in my veins. A sudden, elated mania seized me. So this was freedom, this

was it, this was the first day of the rest of my life and the last day of
my shitty day job; this was the day that would lead to better days,
which would lead to better years, which would lead to a better lifetime, a perfect existence with the career and the husband and the
money, with the homes and the awards and the attention—yes, today was the day that would lead to an avalanche of brilliant tomor-
rows, a future so full and bright that it would threaten to burn and
flatten my nerves, but I would not crumble, I could handle it all, this
was my destiny.

I'd gotten what I wanted.

So why couldn't I stop pacing? Why was I gnawing my fingertips?
Ripping the skin with my teeth? Why did the pain bring a rush of
relief?

The promise of my new life suddenly felt more like a threat. What
if I failed? Failed myself, failed to live up to my own expectations.
Failed Richard. I had no safety net, no home to return to, no family
to fall back on for support.

I needed this to work.

I looked up at the ceiling, squeezing my bloody thumb. My breath
came in short, panicked intervals. Vertigo flooded my senses and the
room spun and I gripped the small wooden desk in the corner of
Richard's bedroom, desperate for balance. I needed something to
ease the pressure constricting my rib cage. An antidote to this terror.

My laptop. It sat on Richard's desk like an answer. I could channel
this energy into my work. Yes, the anxiety and uncertainty and this
strange, new fear could be sublimated into my work, my play, the
deeply personal story that would grant me catharsis and impress my
new inner circle. The play was, after all, autobiographical. I could
literally write my way into a wonderful new life. Control the narrative. Make more "Notes for Future Conversations." Hadn't I written
my way into this situation to begin with? My words had power, and
if they had power, then so did I. I'd revise this play and share it with

Richard, he'd offer his critiques, and I'd shape it accordingly. Together we'd create the story of us; we'd create a beautiful script for
our beautiful life. A script that erased my painful family history. No,
I didn't need the story of Mom or Dad or God or Jesus—I had the
story of Richard and Jonah. And that story would be enough to save
me, to rectify my past and usher me into the world of artistic success
I'd long dreamed of joining.

My breath settled. The vertigo stopped. It wasn't so frightening
now that I'd broken it down. Step by step. First, I would revise my
play, then I'd seek the mentorship of Richard and Charles.

Charles.

As I edited my script, I also revised my memories of the previous
evening. I decided that I'd been very drunk and therefore could not
trust my recollection of my encounter with Charles. A calm settled
over me as I composed a new narrative of the night and adapted it
into a scene for my play.

The scene was quite funny, a sort of midsummer night's romp.
It was possible that Charles hadn't pulled me through the field, and
perhaps I'd fallen on my own. Perhaps I'd chased him. Yes, that was
it. I'd pursued him in the dark, too drunk to know what I was doing.
How hilarious, chasing such a well-known man across his property,
then passing out right in front of him. How kind of him to laugh it
off and help me back to my bed. How sweet of him to look past this
whole embarrassing evening and offer his mentorship the following
morning by the pool. What generosity. It all made perfect sense; the
scene practically wrote itself.

There was still the problem of the steel structure. And the jangle
of Charles's keys.

A gardening shed. A big one, but a gardening shed. That's what
it was.

But who gardens at night?

It wasn't a gardening shed, then. But what was it?

A wine cellar. A storage unit. None of my business.

My phone buzzed. I looked at it, noticing the time—5:00 p.m. Three hours had vanished. A text message from Rashad appeared on the screen. I felt a low-grade enthusiasm when I thought of him; he was someone I knew by circumstance, a circumstance that no longer applied to my life.

I glanced at his message: *You quit?!!?!??!!?*

Ya, I replied.

Bitch, gimme the tea . . . what happened???

Just got tired of that fucking place

Ummm me too but u don't see me pulling a fucking jerry maguire and telling Brett to go fuck himself . . . did u get another job or something?

I didn't respond. The conversation already felt like an artifact from my former existence. I shut my phone off and returned to the glow of my computer screen. In the distance, I heard a faint commotion. It was coming from Charles's home.

Was that Evan, shouting for help?

No, it couldn't be. Just the dog, probably.

The distant uproar faded.

Dinner that night was at Charles's. His home shared the same cold and modern design as Richard's and Sandro's and Ira and Ethel's. It seemed strange that people with such powerful egos had no desire to distinguish their homes from the others. There were, of course, minor differences. For Charles, it was a massive Richard Prince canvas that hung above the dining table, a photo collage of four vintage porn models blown up to life-size proportions, one with her breasts heaving skyward, one slapping her own ass, one curled in a fetal position, one shyly blocking her vagina. Black holes were painted over their features—their faces gouged by the artist.

I sat opposite the painting, losing my appetite.

The waiters were back again tonight. Evan was not. I was glad he was gone; I felt more relaxed without his presence. I was unsure how much of my Evan-related discomfort had been a result of Evan's actual disdain for me and how much was projection, but it didn't matter now. I was curious about his sudden disappearance from the compound, but no one else seemed concerned and I didn't want to broach the subject. How they chose to manage their staff wasn't my business, and I didn't wish to offend my hosts by questioning them on such a gauche topic.

Krissie was also gone, off to Portugal to join the Starbucks family vacation. Without her, Ethel was the sole woman present. Dinner was grilled swordfish, which the waiters distributed while dodging Charles's drunk hands.

"Sandro—is your *boyfriend* coming this evening?" Charles slurred in falsetto. It was only seven o'clock, but Charles was already obliterated. Sandro rolled his eyes and said nothing.

"Well, I, for one, hope he is," Richard said, encouraging Charles. "He was so *charming* the last time he visited."

I didn't like the smirk on Richard's face.

"A memorable visit, certainly," Ira remarked. Ethel stiffened.

"Ethel just *hates* it when Sandro's boyfriend visits," Charles said and grabbed my leg. I flinched slightly. Richard didn't seem to notice.

"Don't you, Ethel," Charles persisted while massaging my thigh. "Don't you just *hate* it?"

Ethel said nothing. She stood from the table and cleared away her untouched swordfish.

"Yes, he'll be here," Sandro said finally. "He's coming from that thing at Alec Baldwin's but he's joining us for drinks later."

"You didn't touch your swordfish," Ira said to Ethel.

"Because I can't fucking *stand* swordfish," Ethel shouted and slammed her plate into Charles's sink. It shattered, and the crash echoed. Flecks of porcelain flew and landed on the floor. No one moved. Ethel thrust her jaw forward, her eyes watering, daring anyone to speak.

"I didn't think the swordfish was *that* bad," Charles joked. No one laughed.

"I'm going to bed," Ethel snapped. "Coming, Ira?"

Ira hunched over his plate, looking sheepish.

"That's what I thought," Ethel spat. Shards of china crunched under her heels as she marched out.

"What just happened?" I asked.

Suddenly, Charles burst into laughter. His laughter gained momentum and increased in volume. It infected Ira and Sandro and soon the three of them were in tears, gasping for breath between each howl. The more they laughed, the more my chest constricted. I realized that no one knew where I was or why I was here. I was alone among relative strangers.

Why were they laughing?

I fought vertigo. Attempted to breathe normally. Their laughter became shrill, violent. I looked to Richard, who gave my back a reassuring rub. He wasn't laughing, a comforting fact. I told myself that it would all be okay as long as Richard didn't join the crescendo of hysteria.

But then he broke. His lips quivered, his mouth opened, and an awful sound burst out.

9

YOU WERE SIXTEEN years old at the time. You were Sandro's boyfriend, the mysterious person who had elicited such venom from Ethel. You arrived drunk after that awful swordfish dinner. Charles was cutting lines of cocaine on his glass-topped Herman Miller coffee table. I recognized you immediately. Your sexuality had been the subject of much gossip at Perdition when the restaurant was slow and we lounged in the waiters' station, debating which celebrities were closeted. Rashad had always defended you, saying that your sensitivity was a testament to your talent and not an indication of your sexuality. I held the opposing view, eager to align you with the likes of Jackman and Cruise and Travolta, men whom our waitstaff had unanimously concluded were closeted. I suddenly wished Rashad was at the compound with me. I yearned for the warmth of his smile, the sharp staccato of his laugh. I wanted to run from this room, run off the property, run the length of Long Island to return to Rashad's comforting embrace. Instead, I sat on the rug by Charles's coffee table and drank my sixth Campari soda, attempting to hide my shock as you made your entrance.

You were Mace Miller, the child actor who had risen to fame thanks to an incredible performance in Sandro's Academy Award–winning film version of *The Plague,* which had been produced by Charles, costumed by Ira, and adapted from his own stage play by Richard. You were on every list that year, every "Thirty Under Thirty" and "Twenty Under Twenty." The press was eager to highlight your precocious abilities, your poise, and that fabulous behind-the-scenes wit. Sandro and Richard and Ira and Charles—your famous mentors who'd recognized your talents and championed your career—were a footnote in every article. "I owe them everything," you insisted in the *Times* profile that had run earlier that year, a breathless work of journalistic fellatio that praised your performance in a highly anticipated Sundance indie and broke the news about your starring role in Sandro's yet-to-be-filmed superhero blockbuster. You were, according to the cultural consensus of the day, unstoppable.

You were also kind of a dick.

"Save some for me, you whores," you said in a lilting tenor, giving Charles a gentle kick as he railed another line from his seat on the white shag. Charles snatched your ankle and yanked you to the floor.

"Mean boys don't deserve treats," Charles growled as he violently wrestled you.

"Get *off* me," you said, groaning.

"*I win,*" Charles shouted as he pinned you to the floor with brutal force. Tense laughter rippled through the room. Everyone chuckled except Sandro, whose eyes softened in lust as you disentangled yourself from the brawl and nestled in his sinewy embrace. Your smooth, pale face was ruddy from the fight. You gave Sandro a kiss, your plump lips consuming his thin grimace. The room fell silent, all of us watching as you climbed on top of him and straddled his lap. Your massive six-foot-four frame eclipsed Sandro's, your body swollen with precocious muscle that felt incongruous with your cherubic and underage countenance. Your body was an adult's, your face a child's. On camera, it made sense. But in person, you were a jumble of incompatible parts.

You gyrated against Sandro, and the energy in the room shifted. Charles shuffled closer to me on the carpet. Richard pulled a waiter onto the couch. Ira's hand stroked the crotch of his jeans. There was an inevitability in the air, a tension you cut by pointing at me.

"Who's *she*," you snarled.

"Jonah's my new friend," Richard said, massaging his waiter's shoulders. "He's staying with us for the summer."

My head spun as you extended your hand. I was still sober enough to shake it but drunk enough to know that if I opened my mouth, my slurred speech would betray an embarrassing level of intoxication.

"Lovely to meet you," you said unconvincingly and turned to Charles. "Where'd you find this one?"

"A gutter somewhere." Charles laughed as he bellied up to the coffee table and snorted another line of cocaine. I felt sick. I gripped the shag's soft tendrils, attempting to stop the room from spinning.

"Well, I hope she holds up."

"Be nice," Sandro snapped. "Only nice boys get to be superheroes, and your contract isn't finalized yet."

"I *am* being nice," you mumbled, bravado deflated, acting—for the first time since arriving—like the teenager you were. Sandro leered as you shrank, and I understood the true reason Sandro had intervened on my behalf. He didn't care if you were mean to me. He wanted to rob you of your adult pretensions. Expose the child underneath.

"Where's Mrs. Danvers?" you said, pouting.

"She's been let go," Richard said, stone-faced. "We were worried she'd set the manor on fire."

"But we've already found a potential replacement." Charles grinned as he slapped me on the back. The slap took me by surprise —my muscles failed to respond in time, my body flew forward, and my head hit the corner of the coffee table.

"Are you all right?" Richard said with more annoyance than concern.

I nodded and the room went black.

———

Then: I was back, awake again, but the room was different. The three waiters circulated among us, wearing nothing but briefs, their tan physiques interchangeable. My body felt heavy; I was anchored to the shag, afraid to move. You ripped off your shirt, grabbed a small glass bottle from the marble kitchen island, poured a few drops into your drink, then passed the bottle to Richard, who sat on the couch stroking the bare thigh of a waiter. Richard took the bottle, dribbled the substance into his drink and the waiter's, then passed it to Sandro, who, I suddenly realized, was crouched on the rug next to me, fully naked and wiping cocaine from his nostrils. He took the glass dropper, turned to me, and said, "G?" Before I could answer, a clear trickle of it hit the red surface of my drink and sank downward, sliding against half-melted ice cubes. Sandro took the glass and pressed it against my lips and poured the liquid into my mouth.

Black.

Then: Cold night air hit my naked body. I was standing over the pool. I didn't remember taking my clothes off. I watched as Richard and the same waiter kissed in the pool and Sandro stood by the bar cart as you knelt in front of him and sucked his cock while another waiter ate his ass and Charles sat on the pool's edge and masturbated. I couldn't locate Ira. I stumbled back, fell onto a pool chair. I sat motionless for a minute, attempting to orient myself. A dripping penis hit my face. I looked up, and Ira forced himself in my mouth. Chlorine stung my throat.

Black.

Then: The jangle of Charles's keys as the entire party stood naked and dripping outside the windowless steel structure.

Black.

Then: Inside. Concrete floors. Two sets of bunk beds. Three of the beds were disheveled, sheets carelessly mangled. The fourth was perfectly made, with severe hospital corners. Our nine naked bodies crushed together in the small space. In the center of the floor, there was a large metal hatch with a thick iron ring attached. A waiter grabbed the ring and lifted the hatch, his eyes dead, muscles straining. One by one, I watched as bodies sank into the floor.

I hesitated. You stayed behind, Mace, observing me with a kind stare.

"It's okay," you whispered. Your secret, childlike tenderness surfaced. "It's a little strange at first. But it gets easier."

You stroked my back with a cold, wet hand. I could barely stand, let alone speak. I swayed above the portal to the basement, unable to stop my eyes from rolling backward. In an instant, your expression snapped from kind to annoyed, and your demeanor returned to its guarded, condescending default.

"C'mon," you snarled. "You knew what you signed up for."

With you at my back, I made my way down the hatch. The cold metal stairs stung my feet. As I descended, I caught a glimpse of a single Nike shower sandal under the impeccably made bed.

It was Evan's.

One of the shoes he'd worn every day. The sight of it made my stomach turn; I wondered where one could go and how far one could get wearing just a single shoe.

Black.

Then: A massive basement lit only by a dim red bulb. The men became silhouettes, difficult to distinguish from one another. Outlines of strange structures loomed in the dark.

Black.

Then: I was on my stomach, arms tied behind me, face against the cold concrete. You were in the same position next to me. My eye caught yours, but you were somewhere else. Tears slid down your expressionless face. The men took their turns.

Black.

Then: Someone carried me through the basement. My feet were numb, worthless. A scream sliced the air, stifled by thick, padded walls.

Black.

Then: I was floating, arms and legs looped through straps suspended from the ceiling, my back digging into a leather sling. Fear shot through me and I froze, my eyes fixed to the ceiling. Hands stroked my body, my dick, my face. I tasted the grime on their grips as they pried my mouth open and stuck their fingers inside, tasted the tang of sweat and chlorine and lube and sex and blood. I spat, suddenly wide awake, adrenaline hammering my temples.

"Stop," I screamed but a hand flew over my mouth. Someone thrust himself inside me. A sharp pain ripped through my insides and I screamed again. My consciousness escaped my body, became one with my howl, and I was pure sound, echoing off the walls of the basement, rushing through the thick stench, soaring over the crush of bodies below. I was noise, I was air, I was nothing. I watched myself from above as men took turns in the dark. Their figures dissolved and divided until the room was a jumble of shadows. All I could think was, *This isn't happening,* and that phrase lodged in my brain, *This isn't happening,* and repeated, *This-isn't-happening-this-isn't-happening-this-isn't-happening,* until it became a drone of meaningless syllables. I needed to leave this room and so I screamed again and rode my scream to the sky. My body was in that basement but I was up in space. I became a star, long dead but burning bright, searing through time toward oblivion, toward blackness, toward God. Yes, this was surely God's work — but was He punishing me or saving me? Was He in the basement or in the sky? Or was He everywhere all at once? Was He the terror that surged through my body, the paralyzing awe? Was He death, was this death, was this when I would slip away forever into His embrace, the promise of love I stopped believing in when my father destroyed my faith, a faith that roared to life in this moment so that finally I found myself praying to God, praying He would deliver me from this horror?

I prayed for my life.

Then: He answered.

A stabbing pain brought my mind crashing back into my body. I was in the basement again. I looked up to see Charles thrusting into me, mania contorting his face. I struggled with my straps, slipped loose, and kicked him in the stomach. He gasped, stumbled, fell to the ground.

Time stopped.

Then: I ran. I ran as their hands clawed at my body. I ran to the stairs, climbed out of the basement and into the waiters' quarters, and slammed the hatch behind me, catching someone's fingers with a sick crack. I stumbled through the stuffy, windowless structure, opened its iron door, and burst into the wildflower field. It was dawn. A wet fog sent a shiver through my naked body. A strange sob bubbled in my throat and I began laughing and crying all at once.

I ran through the field, past the pool, along the gravel drive. As I ran, I thought of my parents, yearned for their embrace, longed for their love. I ran toward my memory of home, the place where I was safe from nightmares, where my mother tucked my VeggieTales quilt under my chin and banished the monsters from my room, offering an extra prayer to God as I drifted back to sleep. I would run until I reached home, until I could tell my mother that I'd seen God, that all my father's fire and brimstone had been bullshit, that the Lord had not abandoned me because of my sexuality, that He had just saved my life. I would tell my mother that the Lord loved me. My beating heart was the only proof I needed.

And so I ran. I ran toward my mother, anticipating the moment we could reunite, rejoice, share the Good News of Christ's love. She would take me in, heal my wounds, make me whole.

I ran. Coarse grass sliced my thighs, stones cut my feet, but I welcomed the pain. It was through this pain that I would emerge on the other side, safe. Resurrected. I reached the massive gate and leaned against the call box, bursting with relief.

And then I realized: I didn't know the code.

Black.

10

I LAY NAKED in the dirt next to the gravel drive. My eyes fluttered open as Scamp sidled up against me. His three legs quivered while he licked my face. I was covered in sweat, skin hot from the morning sun. It was then I realized that I'd spent the night outside. Unconscious, naked, alone.

Richard's BMW appeared on the driveway in the distance. Scamp sprinted into the brush. I stayed motionless in the dirt. The engine's purr quieted. Richard stepped out.

"Are you all right?" he asked, helping me to my feet. His index and middle finger were tied together in a splint.

I felt sick.

"I was so worried about you," he gushed, clearing a strand of oiled hair from my face. "No one could find you last night. You just vanished."

"I . . . I . . ." I was exhausted, disoriented, unable to make sense of Richard's effusive concern. Why this sudden kindness?

"Let's get you back inside, get some clothes on you."

"*No.*" I recoiled. "I'm not going back inside."

"Jonah, you're not making sense," Richard said, concerned. "You've been lying out here all night. It's not healthy."

"Open the gate."

"You're scaring me, Jonah."

"I said, *open the gate*."

"But you're not wearing clo—"

"Just *open* it."

Richard punched the code into the box. The iron gate shuddered to life. "No one's keeping you here, Jonah. If you don't want to stay the summer . . ." Richard trailed off, his gaze shifting to the road beyond the compound.

I looked out at the empty lot across the street. Its summer-scorched desolation stood in contrast to the lush wildflower fields behind Richard's iron walls. Earlier in the week, Richard mentioned that a developer had been sitting on the plot of land for over two years, her plans for it thwarted by the 2008 recession. Ground had been broken and left abandoned; weeds now sprang from the churned soil. My gaze extended farther, about half a mile down the road, where the lot gave way to a thick forest. There, among the trees, stood a quaint home, a Hamptons classic, with gray shingled siding and a screened front porch.

A light flickered on in the living room. Someone inside.

My legs stiffened, ready to run.

I felt like I was in the third act of a horror film, the part where the final girl emerges from the clutches of the monster and stumbles toward freedom, toward that house on the horizon, toward the strangers who will aid her escape, who will put an end to this nightmare, who will give her shelter and dress her wounds and call the police and wait for the sirens to wail.

The end.

Except it wasn't. I put myself in the final girl's blood-caked Keds. After the credits rolled, where would I go? Back to the city? In just two days, Ghost Dick would return and I would be forced to find a new sublet, an undertaking made nearly impossible by the fact that I had fifty-six dollars in my checking account. I would have to earn money, but how? I'd need a job, but the idea of procuring employment in four days in New York City seemed highly unlikely. Even if a miracle occurred and I found a job immediately, I would still need to work there long enough to accrue sufficient funds for the first month's rent plus, possibly, a security deposit. There was the option of finding a street corner or a park bench—it was summer, after all; I wouldn't freeze, and I had just one duffel bag, a light load to carry for a few nights. But what if those few nights turned into a whole string of nights, which turned into a month, which turned into permanent homelessness?

My mother. If I could just get her on the phone. Get her to send money. If I could somehow repair the torched bridge between us, build something new from the ashes. But that too was a risk. My every attempt at communication had been thwarted by her impenetrable silence. I could perhaps grab her attention with the truth, recount the awful events of the summer via text message, but then I would be forced to confront something more dreadful than her silence: her judgment. Surely it was my sin, the shameful fact of my sexuality, that led me to the exact place promised in the ex-gay books we'd read together as a family. It always started with gay sex, these Christian authors warned, and soon devolved into rape and bondage and pedophilia and bestiality. She would demand that I return to Illinois, stay with her, attend conversion-therapy sessions. Maybe we'd even try that camp she'd heard about; maybe she'd send me away until I was finally fixed, until the sin had been beaten out of me once and for all. Suddenly, my fantasies of reuniting with my family, the manic surge of hope I'd experienced while running for my life the previous night, seemed preposterous. My mother would never change.

And my father was a ghost. Because of what I'd done to him.

The sun vanished, blocked by a cloud. I shivered, remembering my nakedness. I would, what—show up on this random Hamptons doorstep wearing nothing, coated with dirt and blood, and practically scare an innocent family to death? They'd more likely call the cops *on* me, not *for* me. *There's a naked man trying to break into our house!* the father would shout into his phone as his young daughter cried on the couch and I pounded on their front door. *Send someone quick, Officer. He seems dangerous.*

I stared out at the open field.

Richard's voice brought me back. He'd been speaking, though I hadn't heard what he'd said.

"What?" I managed dumbly.

"I said I'm sorry."

I turned, was shocked to see him crying.

"I . . . I thought you'd have fun. I thought you liked it rough."

"That wasn't rough, that was . . ." I stopped myself, afraid to say something I would be unable to retract. I took in the stunning expanse behind Richard. "Our little slice of gay heaven" he'd called it while cradling me in his arms during our first night here, his embrace a promise of protection. *Gay* and *heaven* were two words I'd never believed could exist in the same sentence, but anything felt possible in this magical setting. Healing felt possible. As I looked at Richard now, it seemed inconceivable that I'd been raped here, among the wildflowers, surrounded by people I trusted, my new family. I couldn't say *rape* because naming it would make it real; Richard and I would never return from that word. I'd be banished forever from this compound, from the man I adored.

"Jonah, I would never hurt you," Richard whispered, stepping closer. "I . . . I love you."

His words made my head spin, as competing realities fought for space in my brain. Richard wouldn't rape me. Richard *loved* me. The words I'd wished for all summer.

"I love you too," I murmured, collapsing into his arms. It was a phrase I'd never uttered to any man but my father.

"So you'll stay?"

"Yes, I'll stay."

Gay heaven again. That night, Richard made spaghetti alla Norma with fresh eggplant from his own garden, a sauce he'd learned to make under the tutelage of a private chef at the Italian villa of one of his friends, an eccentric baroness he'd known for ages who often hosted famous authors and screenwriters and movie stars at her crumbling Tuscan paradise, and *Oh, we should travel there this fall,* Richard insisted as the pasta boiled, *fall is the best time to visit Italy, the time when the crowds vanish and the temperature cools and the grapes are ready for harvest, yes, that's it, Italy in September and then somewhere tropical for Thanksgiving, maybe St. Barts, and then of course we'll do Paris for New Year's, it'll be fucking freezing and the crowds will be a nightmare, but, oh, Paris at New Year's is worth it, we'll stay at the Hôtel Plaza Athénée, but any of these plans can be altered should you finish your play and should Charles select you for his Lincoln Center workshop—which he almost certainly will—and we'll simply adjust our vacation plans accordingly.* I listened to Richard and swooned, so glad I'd stayed, giddy at the prospect of our life together. The events in the basement seemed so distant, so impossible, so foggy, like a long-forgotten night terror.

"I have a surprise for you," Richard said the following morning, grinning from the driver's seat of his BMW as we sped down Montauk Highway.

You sat in the back seat, Mace, silent next to Sandro.

What were you thinking that morning? Did you know about my night spent outside? Had Richard told Sandro of my attempted escape? I have so many questions, questions I didn't dare ask that morning. I chose to interpret your presence as proof that what happened was normal. There you were in the back seat, smiling at the green expanse speeding past your window. Unfazed. Content, even. You'd been to the basement before and you'd emerged unscathed. You were happy to be here, and if you could be happy, then why shouldn't I be happy? I remembered the words you'd offered as you

opened the basement hatch that night: *It's a little strange at first.*
That's all it was, *strange*. A strange little episode.

"Here we are!" Richard exclaimed as he pulled into a parking lot.

It was a church. A small brick building with a steeple and a cir-
cular stained-glass window above its wrought-iron doors. My pulse
quickened. I had not stepped into a church since leaving Illinois,
since destroying my family. I did not want to enter one now.

"A church?" I asked. Richard turned to me, registered my frown.

"Oh, honey, no." Richard laughed. "My poor little ex-ex-gay.
This is a *former* church and a *current* clothing store. We're treating
you boys to a little Sunday shopping spree."

The interior had been converted into a stunning boutique, the
pews removed and replaced with racks of high-end clothing. The
stained-glass windows were preserved, with the stations of the cross
illuminating a new crop of saints: McQueen, Gaultier, Prada. I was
filled with relief. It was as if religion had been rendered powerless by
commerce — holy shrines removed by enterprising architects and replaced with rows and rows of new things to worship. Things to buy.
Things much easier to obtain than God's forgiveness.

I loaded my arms with jeans and T-shirts and button-downs
and floated toward the fitting room. *You have no power over me,*
I screamed to God in my mind. Our Father failed to retaliate — no
plague of locusts descended on Southampton. I didn't turn into a
pillar of salt. Proof that I was free from the wrath of His judgment.
Free to do whatever I wanted with Richard.

"I'll wait by the register," Richard announced after I'd modeled
my final look.

"Hey," you said minutes later, stopping me as I emerged from my
fitting room. "That stuff looked great on you."

"Oh, thanks," I replied. I was surprised by your warmth, given
how cold you'd been toward me. "You too."

"Just wanted to make sure you're . . . okay." Your voice dimin-
ished to a faint whisper.

"Yeah . . ." I hesitated. "Why wouldn't I be?"

We paused, both afraid to summon memories from the basement.

"Sandro is so good to me," you said abruptly, an answer to a question no one had asked. We watched him from afar as he dug through a pile of T-shirts. "I'd be no one without him. I mean, he's the one who got me the role in his superhero movie. And it's not just Sandro —everyone on the compound is so generous."

"I know, Richard's been wonderful," I agreed. This was a much safer topic: the sugar our daddies supplied. All that uncomplicated sweetness.

"You're a part of the family now." You said *family* with surprising warmth, like you wanted this just as much as I did. "Wanna be my big brother?"

"Sure." I laughed.

"We're so lucky."

"So lucky," I echoed, grateful to have you as my mirror. You provided a reflection that was easy to look at, a reality I wanted to believe in.

I've found my new family, I thought. *And they'll keep me safe forever.*

———

"That'll be three thousand, four hundred, and sixty-seven dollars," the cashier said after ringing up my purchases. I looked to Richard, worried he would berate me for the shocking sum. But he just smiled and swiped his credit card.

"How about that total!" He chuckled. "We did some *serious* damage."

"All sales are final," the cashier continued. "Our summer-clearance items can't be returned."

"Oh, not to worry, these are definite keepers. Keepers for my keeper." Richard planted a kiss on my forehead.

I turned and looked back to where you stood with Sandro, the two of you locked in hushed disagreement behind a rack of leather jackets. You shoved the rack in anger, the punctuation to a furious whisper. The jackets crashed to the floor. You stormed out, and Sandro followed. I turned to Richard, who just rolled his eyes and laughed.

"It's always something with those two," he said.

———————

Later, I unwrapped my bounty in Richard's bedroom. Torn tissue paper sat in a delicate dome on the mattress. I shuttled back and forth from the bedroom to the walk-in closet, where, thirty minutes earlier, Richard had cleared a vast swath of space for my — really, his — purchases. "Your own little section," he'd cooed as he tossed an armful of his dress shirts to the ground. "In *our* closet."

He watched from the bed as I ripped the last item from its swaddling: a simple black Alexander Wang T-shirt that cost $270.

"It's too much," I'd said, reexamining the price tag.

"No, it's just enough," he said, watching me wriggle into the shirt. "It's gorgeous."

Buzz. Buzz. Buzz. It was my phone, buried beneath the tissue paper.

"Someone's eager to get hold of you," Richard muttered, tension creeping into his tone.

"I have no idea who it could be."

"Maybe your other boyfriend, coming to rescue you from my clutches." He forced an edgy laugh.

"I'm sure that's it," I joked flatly.

"Let's find out."

Richard brushed the paper onto the floor. He picked up my phone, frowning.

"'Dad'?" he said, reading the caller ID, then holding it out for me to see.

"I . . . I . . . that can't be . . ." My mind spiraled into oblivion.

What could my father possibly want? I stared at my phone. Its glow was menacing.

"I thought you said your father was dead. Brain cancer?"

"I . . . I lied."

Richard pressed Decline. "Perhaps you should explain yourself."

11

I DIDN'T KILL my father, but his loss felt as irreversible as an execution. I often wonder whether my actions were born out of a confused survival instinct or if something darker was at play. I first started lying about my father's death in grad school as a way to dodge the inquiries of classmates, teachers, dates, and anyone else who attempted to unearth my personal history in casual conversation. Over the years, it had become rote. At times, I forgot my father was actually alive. At times, I forgot the truth.

I got my first erection in Sunday school. "He is risen!" my Adventure Bible exclaimed. It was a caption to a cartoon of Jesus exiting the tomb, though on that sweaty summer morning, it felt like a mocking description of the situation inside my elastic-waist Levi's. The teacher, Dottie Tripplehorn, disturbed by the pained expression of the preacher's son (especially when we were discussing a matter so profoundly joyous as the resurrection of Jesus Christ), shot me a chilly, McMansion Mom smile and asked if everything was okay.

I replied that everything was, in fact, okay, despite my growing fear that God was somehow punishing me, that the stiffness in my pants was divine penalty. How else was I, at eleven years old, supposed to interpret this? My body, which belonged to Christ, was no longer under my control. The Father must be disciplining me for my sinful thoughts about His Son, the olive-skinned Savior whose muscles strained under the white robe that cloaked His perfect frame, strained as He stepped from the tomb, radiant, blue-eyed, flaxen-haired, strong. I wanted His arms wrapped around me, I wanted to taste His lips, I wanted to tear off those white robes and see what lay underneath, to touch the body of Christ. I wanted him inside me the way Amy Grant described in "Fill Me with Your Love," my mother's favorite song, the one she'd play on Friday afternoons. "Let's dance before Dad gets home," she'd coo. We'd sway and twirl and listen to Amy sing about how she wanted our Savior to enter her body, to fill her with His love.

I wanted Jesus to take me in His arms like in the song my father sang from the stage on Sundays, the band rocking steadily behind him, the lights dimmed so he was just a silhouette of my father, barely recognizable except for the sound of his booming tenor, the lyrics to "Draw Me Close" soaring through space, putting words to my agonizing desire. I wanted the Lord's warm embrace, and if I squinted hard enough, let my eyes soften in the darkness, I could imagine that my father's silhouette was actually that of Jesus, the fixture of my daydreams, the hero who would step down from that pulpit, take me in his arms, fulfill my every need. And as my fantasy continued, I always felt myself stiffen.

Each erection terrified me more than the last.

I took to masturbating in the bathroom at church. It was the only way to rid my body of God's punishment. I would stroke myself in the stall until my mind went blank with pleasure and I collapsed on the toilet seat. And then, with my dick softening in my hands, the shame would come flooding back. What I'd done was surely the worst sin of all, and I knew that God would soon inflict another erection on me, and the cycle would begin again.

I started a journal. A place to purge my anxiety. I ripped up a portion of the carpet in my closet and stuffed the thin notebook underneath, threw my old Nikes on top. I dug it out only in the middle of the night. When my parents were sleeping but I couldn't. I'd record the fears that kept me awake, indent the pages with my heavy scribbles. Writing was the only path to rest. My way of surviving the night.

When I was twelve, my father gave a sermon titled "Sexual Brokenness." Spit flew from his mouth as he quoted Leviticus 20:13. "If a man lies with a male as with a woman, both of them have committed an abomination; they shall surely be put to death; their blood is upon them." I sat in a puddle of my own sweat. My tailbone chafed against the unforgiving pew. My mother squeezed my hand, oblivious to my shame. I realized: *Dad's talking about me.*

Dad wants me dead.

Later, in high school, I would think of Jesus while stretched across Trent's mattress, a hand tied to each post of the twin bed in his dorm room, as I had requested. Think of the pain Jesus must have felt, splayed out like that, forsaken by His Father on the cross. I was seventeen. Trent was twenty, a college student at a state university miles away from my hometown, but even so, it was not enough distance to keep the image of my father's raging face from burning on the backs of my eyelids, reminding me of my place in hell. I demanded Trent call himself "Daddy," a trick I'd learned watching gay porn on the family computer in the furnished basement of my parents' house, my toes curling on the wall-to-wall carpeting while my father led Bible study upstairs. The word allowed me to access a private fantasy in which I was Jesus and Trent was God. He was punishing me but also relieving me, every slap across my bound body a reckoning that filled me with shame and sent blood racing to my cock.

Trent got boring. I turned to chat rooms in search of new frontiers. I lied and said I was twenty-one. The men were sometimes skeptical of my upper-lip peach fuzz when they met me, but no one turned me away. I was hotandhorny21 and I was looking for "a daddy who knew how to punish his boy." They were more than happy to comply. They would punish me in the backs of their minivans while their wives slept at home; they would punish me in the Best Western ten miles outside of town; they would punish me in the woods next to the highway, my arms pinned to the nettles that blanketed the forest floor. They were thirty-four, then forty-three, then fifty-six. They were the subjects of guilt-ridden stories in my journal. They were my father, they were the Father, and I was always, in my mind, the son. I loved each of them as I was unable to love my own father.

Attending a Christian university was expected of me. I lived at home and commuted to Wheaton College, where I signed a community covenant that asserted immoral, homosexual relationships were against God's will and would result in expulsion. I chose theater as my minor, hoping (but failing) to find other secret "sexual deviants" in our production of *The Importance of Being Earnest*. Oscar Wilde's gayness was never mentioned during the course of rehearsals, but that didn't prevent me from doing my own research. What started with Wilde continued with my exploration of Williams, Albee, Baldwin, Kushner, Lorca. I stopped writing in my journal and began penning plays instead. My amateur dramas were awful— esoteric dialogues between a character named Jonah and long-dead queer artists. But they made me feel less lonely. I confessed my desires to James Baldwin, shared my shame with Tennessee Williams, and they became part of my imaginary community, the source of what little strength I had.

Sometimes I wrote plays about my father, short one-acts that ended in my confession, his forgiveness. A fantasy, to be sure. I knew he would hate me for what I was.

I lived in fear of his hate.

But it was love that inspired him to put me through conversion therapy. After my father discovered my sinful chat-room habit— before I graduated from Wheaton College, when I was twenty-one and still living with my parents—he hired an ex-gay counselor, Doctor Jim. He was "our kind of Christian," which meant that he had attended a Prestigious Evangelical University and was well versed in traditional fundamentalist theology. Whether he was an actual doctor was of less concern to my parents than his religious schooling and the fact that he was a specialist in dealing with "this kind of issue." It was—as my father repeatedly explained to Doctor Jim—of the utmost importance that my treatment remain confidential.

In a particularly cruel twist of fate, the man charged with "curing" me of my homosexuality was, to put it crudely, hot as fuck. Doctor Jim possessed a muscular, corn-fed heft, a quarterback's shoulders, and a movie star's cheekbones. He favored tight, asscontouring khakis and crisp button-downs, undone to showcase a tuft of dark chest hair that matched the perfect stubble outlining his jaw. A photo sat on the desk in his office: Doctor Jim beaming on a stretch of bright green lawn, clutching his cheery Christian bride, swarmed by four young daughters in pastel dresses gripping baskets that brimmed with colored eggs. Someone in an unintentionally menacing Easter Bunny costume lurked in the background of the photo, casting an incongruous dread over an otherwise idyllic Midwestern scene.

"God loves you, Jonah," he said during our first session, placing his hand on my knee. A rush of heat and shame and desire shot through my body. "And with His guidance, we *will* heal you."

We began our weekly sessions. Doctor Jim was determined to unearth the "root cause of my homosexuality," a process that involved delving into my family's past. Doctor Jim seemed eager, at first, to blame my mother. *Is your mother overbearing? Does she prevent you from connecting with your father? Has she pushed the positive male role model from your life?* Much to Doctor Jim's consternation, the answer to all these questions was an emphatic *no*. Far from being overbearing, my mother was expert at fading into the background, ever the obedient servant to her husband the pastor, keen to conform to the submissive role assigned to her by the church's patriarchal theology. She never spoke up, never questioned my father, always had a casserole at the ready. With his theories about my mother debunked, Doctor Jim had no choice but to move on to my father. *Is your father absent from family life? Does his busy work schedule prevent you from seeing him regularly? Did you lack a masculine role model in the home?* Once again, Doctor Jim's theories failed to hold up. My father worked, yes, but always made it home in time for dinner. My relationship with Dad had been the picture of heteronormativity, complete with playing catch on the front lawn and father-son fishing expeditions. If anything, it was my mother who had been absent, pushed toward the edge of our family's frame, like the grotesque Easter Bunny in Doctor Jim's photo, a portrait my gaze often turned to in these moments of interrogation. I wished I could transport myself into the honey-lit normality of their Midwestern family.

At the end of every session we prayed to God that we would find a solution to the problem of my sexuality, that He would deliver me from this life of sin. And yet I felt nothing. Nothing except the sting of failure. God had abandoned me in my time of need. Maybe God hated me; maybe I hated God; maybe I hated myself.

I definitely hated myself.

Worse than the sessions was the reception I got from my parents afterward. Every week it was the same. I'd open the door to the smell of my mother's macaroni and cheese baking in the oven. It was my favorite dish from childhood, a homemade casserole with four types of cheese and a crust that crackled when my mother sliced it. We'd sit at the table and I'd stare at my plate, desperate to avoid the hopeful smiles of my parents, the looks that said: *Maybe this week it worked. Maybe God has shown our family grace. Maybe this nightmare is finally over.* They never pried—it was always assumed I would volunteer news of my progress. Every week, I was filled with shame as I mumbled, "We're still working through things." Their faces would fall, and my mother would turn the conversation to the weather, or the Bible, or the boring details of her day.

Doctor Jim assigned me homework. I played football with my classmates, I purchased more masculine attire at the Army/Navy surplus store, I asked girls out on dates. Nothing worked. Doctor Jim supplied me with a Victoria's Secret catalog one week, and when that failed, we moved on to harder stuff — *Playboy, Penthouse, Hustler.* Doctor Jim was careful to mention that the use of pornography was typically a sin but that God would make an exception in this case. We needed to employ drastic measures. I was forbidden to masturbate to these magazines — that would also be a sin — but was told to monitor my levels of arousal when I looked at the naked women. An erection meant that I was finally letting God into my heart, that I was eliminating my wretched "same-sex attraction." And so, as I'd done before in childhood, I once again offered my cock to the Lord. This time, locked in my bedroom with a copy of *Penthouse,* I hoped that the blood of Christ would surge to my dick. Still nothing. Soon, I defied Doctor Jim's orders and attempted to rouse my penis by stroking it, begging for God's forgiveness as I touched myself, praying that He would pardon this lesser sin in light of the fact that I was attempting to rid myself of a greater one. I would clutch the magazine in my left hand while failing to get off with my right; I tugged at my flaccid penis until it chafed, then threw the magazine against the wall, buried my face in my pillow, and screamed until my throat was sore. I'd then cry softly to myself, attempting to conjure the magazine women in my mind, hoping that perhaps my studious appraisal of this pornography had cured me, as Doctor Jim promised it would. Maybe those images just needed a moment to soak in. My fantasies usually returned to the blond woman bound up in my *Hustler,* her mouth gagged with a white bandanna, her eyes wide with terror, her arms and legs tied to the posts of a rusty bed on a set resembling a torture chamber. I'd begin to stroke myself again, but as I did, I would always imagine myself in her position, ready to be punished, ready to be filled by the hard cock lurking at the edge of the frame.

I wanted to die.

After a year of treatment, Doctor Jim had still not discovered the root of my homosexuality. My parents' patience wore thin. The macaroni casseroles were replaced with frozen dinners nuked by my depressed mother. My father, unable to contain his disappointment, began skipping family meals, taking his hot plastic tray directly from the microwave to his study, where he would eat while poring over the Bible. Once, my mother made the mistake of suggesting that it would be "good for the family" if my father joined us at the table.

"Don't *you* tell me what's good for this family," he snapped.

"Doctor Jim says it's important for the father to . . ." My mother trailed off, fearful of his seething expression.

"Are you implying that this is somehow *my* fault?"

"I just think we need to keep Jonah's health in mind," my mother insisted.

"Why do you think I sent him to this *useless* therapy!" my father screamed, throwing his frozen dinner across the room.

"Dad, *stop*," I yelled, standing to confront him. He pushed me to the ground and stepped over my body. Seconds later, his study door slammed.

The following week, Doctor Jim was unusually solemn. He explained that we'd come to a critical point in my treatment. "I know how seriously you've taken our sessions and how hard you're trying here. But because you can't remember the specific moment that led to your same-sex attraction, I believe that you may be repressing this memory."

At last, an answer. A way out. A reason. An end to this torture. Tears welled in my eyes. I wanted to scream, I wanted to dance, I wanted to leap out of my seat and hug Doctor Jim. *Here will be the thing that heals my family*, I thought, *the thing that repairs all that is broken in my life*.

"Jonah, I believe that you were molested as a child," Doctor Jim said gravely.

My feelings of relief vanished. My rib cage tightened; my breathing grew shallow.

"But I . . . I don't remember . . . that never happened to me," I sputtered. "I would've told you, I promise."

"I know you would've told me if you *remembered*. But many of our most traumatic childhood memories evade our conscious recall, and childhood trauma frequently causes the same-sex attraction you struggle with."

"What do we do?"

"We'll recover these memories, Jonah. And with the Lord's help, we'll work through them. God will heal you if you let Him."

Doctor Jim instructed me to lie on the thin carpeting of his office floor. Tough red fibers dug into my shirt, making my back itch. Doctor Jim told me to relax, told me that we would pray for the Holy Spirit to "join us in this room today." I closed my eyes. As Doctor Jim prayed, his voice dipped lower, flattened, lulled me into a hypnotic state. Doctor Jim asked the Holy Spirit to guide me into my unconscious, and soon I felt my body melt into the floor. Doctor Jim's words floated at the edge of my thoughts. I was both in the room and not, both conscious and unconscious. My breath grew deeper, calmer, as Doctor Jim began to delve into my childhood. He mined it for past trauma, searched for the awful memory of a male relative or family friend or stranger from the park. Once I had discovered that memory, I was supposed to go beneath the surface and unearth the horrible truth. *You said you want to be a playwright, Jonah. What we're doing here is kind of like that—we're building a story. Building it with little blocks of truth, truth from deep inside you.*

This process continued for months. At first I came up empty, nothing but happy memories of my father at my tenth birthday party and the head deacon pushing me on the swing behind our church and the ice cream man handing me a dripping vanilla cone in a strong, hairy fist.

My father's rage deepened. He stopped speaking to my mother and me save for resigned grunts of acknowledgment in the hallway of our home. He spent an increasing amount of time in his study, eventually sleeping there, away from my mother, away from me, as if the knowledge and theology contained in his personal library could somehow shield him from his family's collapse. I, too, grew increasingly despondent, removed. I would hole up in my room and dream of ways to kill myself, listing them in the notebook I'd once devoted to ideas for plays. The only thing that stopped me was the literal fear of hell; the sinful double whammy of suicide and homosexuality would keep me toiling in the underworld for eternity. I resigned myself to life on earth while fantasizing of ways to leave it.

The more the men in her life pulled away, the more desperately my mother attempted to bring us together. Mirthless Parcheesi that ended in screaming. Dinners no one ate. Church functions where we drifted to opposite ends of the room immediately, repelled like magnets with warring poles. My mother begged my father to put an end to my treatment. My father refused. Instead, he called Doctor Jim nightly from his study, unleashing rage and blame and fire and brimstone. *Why isn't it working?* My father's shouts filled the house, echoing up the stairs and into my bedroom, where I would sit alone and clutch my pillow and cry.

Over the months, a story began to emerge. A story that Doctor Jim coaxed out of me, session by session. It started with the shameful memory of my Adventure Bible. The way Jesus made me stiff. Made me ashamed. Made me gay. We traced it back to that one memory: Dottie Tripplehorn frowning in my direction, knowing something was awry with one of her pupils. *Yes, that was the moment I knew. Looking at Jesus in that book.* The blasphemy of my suggestion terrified Doctor Jim at first. It was not possible that Jesus caused my same-sex attraction. But soon, Doctor Jim developed a theory to explain it all: *What if it was not, in fact, Jesus who turned you gay? What if it was someone from that period of your childhood, Jonah? An authority figure that your young mind confused with Jesus, the ultimate authority figure in our lives? What if your*

memory of abuse was so traumatic that you repressed it and con-
vinced yourself that it was Jesus who disordered your desires? Jesus
didn't molest you, but we will figure out who did.

Gradually, we "reconstructed" the memory of the trauma that
"turned me gay." But which authority figure in my life had preyed
on me? My Sunday-school teacher was ruled out: too female, too
shrewish, too sexless. The ice cream man was too distant, too unin-
volved, the church deacons too holy (and, I would later suspect, too
friendly with Doctor Jim).

One day during hypnosis, Doctor Jim asked me to see Jesus as He
had appeared to me in my earliest sexual fantasies. "And now, Jonah,
we're going to peel away that fantasy and unearth the reality behind
it. Look hard at this figure. It's not Jesus, is it, Jonah? It's someone
else. Someone who hurt you, someone who touched you, someone
who sent you down this sinful path. Someone with authority, someone you trusted with your entire heart and soul. *Who is there, Jonah?*
Who molested you?"

As he spoke, I pictured a pair of male hands as they touched me,
embraced me, aroused me. I imagined this man's scent, the sweetness of his breath, the smell of his robes. Yes, I knew that fragrance;
I smelled it every Sunday, starch and detergent and cloth. As I lay on
Doctor Jim's floor, the answer occurred to me. Finally, a way out of
this torture. Finally, a story that made sense, or at least the type of
sense that would satisfy my conversion therapist. Finally—through
the fog of confusion and coercion and suicidal ideation—I saw it:
an escape.

"My father." I gasped. "It was my father who molested me."

At the moment, I wasn't sure if it was a lie. But I knew it would
save my life.

Doctor Jim hugged me. I wept in his arms, willing my statement
to be true. Because if it was true, then there was a clear path to salvation. A way to fix this, even if it meant destroying my father.

Revenge, sanctioned by our Savior.

The devastation of my family was swift. That afternoon, Doctor Jim summoned my mother to his office and calmly told her that I had been molested by my father. My mother collapsed in panic, her knees hitting the thick red carpet on the very spot where I'd been lying for months, conjuring the image that would devastate us all. She cried and said it couldn't be true. Doctor Jim insisted it was.

After our session, my mother rented a hotel room outside of town, the same Best Western I had secretly visited with so many older male companions. "I love you, Jonah," she said through tears as she shoved the key card into our door. "And we'll get through this together."

She left me alone and went to confront my father. It all happened so quickly, too quickly. Had my father really molested me? It suddenly seemed impossible; absurd, even. Alone in the hotel room, I began to doubt my own recollection, the memory I'd constructed under Doctor Jim, lead architect. *No, my father never molested me.* But Doctor Jim seemed so sure of his methods, so confident in his discovery. What choice did I have but to believe him? Yes, I would believe *him.* That felt much easier than believing *myself.* If Doctor Jim, an expert on this issue, said it was true, then it must be.

I climbed into the hotel bed, turned on the TV to numb my nerves, and waited for my mother to return. I watched QVC on maximum volume, attempting to drown my thoughts with the deafening promises of an over-tanned jewelry saleswoman. *The whole set can be yours for the low, low price of $29.99.* I found myself longing for the uncomplicated moral universe of the home-shopping channel, where the only choice was the right choice, the easiest decision you'd ever made. *Just call now.*

Doctor Jim held an emergency meeting that afternoon attended by my mother, my father, and the entire elder committee of our church. My father denied everything, insisted he'd never molested me, wept before the baffled committee. Never had the church dealt with such an issue. The committee removed my father from his position as head pastor and forbade him to set foot on the church campus. Furthermore, they demanded he visit Doctor Jim for counseling. This would be kept a secret from the church congregation to avoid scandal, and a mysterious "medical issue" would be the explanation provided for my father's sudden disappearance. Divorce was a sin in the eyes of God, so my mother was instructed to remain by his side as he worked to "cure his brokenness" with Doctor Jim.

That night, she returned to the Best Western.

"Jonah, what on earth are you doing?" my mother yelled over the cacophony of QVC; she grabbed the remote and hit Mute. She sat on the bed and hugged me and told me about the surreal events of the day. We returned to our house the following morning. My father was gone. He'd drained our family's bank accounts. He'd left no note. He never returned.

Gossip spread. The "medical issue" excuse the church provided was flimsy. My mother got a job as a receptionist at the local dentist's office. The dentist was a major donor at the church who took pity on my mother. She was desperate for a way to support us now that her husband, the sole breadwinner, had vanished, so she endured the daily indignity of curious stares from patients who knew her history. The meager receptionist's salary was not sufficient to replace my father's considerable megachurch earnings (or pay the mortgage on our stately McMansion), so she took a second job at a local diner, heading there every day after clocking out at the dentist's.

My mother grew depressed and distant. She was rarely home, and when she was, it was only to down a bottle of wine before crashing. She was forced to sell our house, and we moved into a small, one-bedroom apartment, where I slept on the giant leather sectional that had fit perfectly in our former home but now crowded the tiny living room of our new place. Somehow, in the midst of everything, I managed to graduate from Wheaton. My mother wanted me to get a job, help her pay the bills. I never got one. Employment would only anchor me to my hometown, give my mother an excuse to keep me trapped in her apartment.

I was supposed to complete the remainder of my therapy with Doctor Jim, but my mother was far too exhausted to make me go. We had both been so traumatized by the results of my treatment it was impossible to summon the strength to return.

"Was this all *my* fault, Jonah?" she'd slur after polishing off a magnum of grocery-store chardonnay. "Did I fail you?"

"You didn't, Mom," I'd always reply, clenching my jaw. "You didn't."

My claustrophobia grew, followed me outside the confines of our tiny apartment. I needed to get away from my mother, from our tiny apartment, from church, from God. I needed to cut ties. To erase my past.

I weaponized my mother's guilt, used it as a tool to engineer my escape. I applied to graduate school in Ohio, desperate to put a state line between us. I'd study playwriting, focus on dreaming up other people's misery instead of fixating on my own. My mother cobbled together my tuition using a small chunk of money the church had given her out of pity (a sum that would've been my missing father's severance), her own meager earnings, and a considerable amount in cosigned student loans.

I thanked my mother by rarely calling her, desperate to pretend she didn't exist. But then I'd cry myself to sleep in my dorm room, longing for her. I missed the way she used to stroke my hair as we danced to Amy Grant in our big, beautiful living room, in the happy, innocent years of my childhood.

Most often, I would think of my father. Think of the way I'd ruined his life to save my own. I was racked with guilt, weighed down by the truth that haunts me to this day: my father never molested me.

12

I TOLD RICHARD the truth. Fear brewed in my gut as he listened.

"I'm so sorry, Jonah," Richard said once I'd finished. He stroked my hair.

"You don't think I'm a terrible person?" I asked, surprised by his tender reaction.

"A terrible person? Why on earth would I think that?"

"For what I did to my father . . ."

"I think the bigger issue here is what your father did to *you*." His anger on my behalf made me love him even more. Richard, my protector.

"But what I said about him wasn't true."

"Of course it wasn't. But you can hardly be blamed for your reaction to the wildly unethical and damaging treatment you received during conversion therapy. That therapist was *insane* for doing what he did. Forcing you to 'remember' something that never happened just to justify his own fucked perspective on homosexuality."

"But I just let my lie live on. Ruin my father's life."

"But don't you think he deserved it? For putting you through all that trauma? Think about it, Jonah."

And I did. I thought of my father, his face red with rage, gripping

my arm as he screamed at me in our family's living room, attempting
to shake Satan from my body, my mother crying on the couch, her
hands clasped in prayer.

"I . . . I guess."

"That's right."

"But shouldn't I . . . call him back?"

"And why would you do that, Jonah? So he can hurt you more?
Remind you that you're going to hell? Tell you that you're disgusting,
that you make him fucking sick?"

I started to weep softly. Richard put his arm around me, drew me
close.

"No, Jonah," he continued. "You're with *me* now. I love you. And
we don't need your father fucking that up. We don't need anyone
fucking that up."

"You're . . . you're right."

"Just you and me. Those are the only two people we need now."

"Yes."

"I love you, Jonah."

"I love you too."

———

And then my father arrived.

A figure in the distance, in the dawn. Stumbling through the mist,
dragging his left leg with both hands, his face crusted with blood.
Someone, something had harmed him. I sat up in bed, heart racing. I felt heavy, unable to move as he heaved himself closer. *Why is
he here?* I looked to my right—Richard was gone. I turned back to
the window. Scamp appeared, barking, nipping at my father's ankle. The Doberman sank his teeth into my father's left calf, tear-
ing through cloth and muscle and sinew, biting right down to the
bone. My father kept trudging forward, dragging the dog with him. I
wanted Scamp to make a meal of my father. But then, just as quickly,
the opposite desire swelled in my heart: I wanted to rush into the

wildflowers and haul my father to safety. Run a hot shower and strip
him down and lay him on the tiled floor and let a cloud of healing
steam consume him. But I didn't. I just watched as Scamp went back
for more. My father fell to the ground, landing by the hedges that
lined the gravel drive. Moaning. Was he speaking? Speaking to me?
But still, I couldn't move. A small red cardinal landed on the shrub
above my father. He fixed his gaze on the bird. The cardinal was
joined by another and then another and then another until the air
was filled with hundreds of them, the sky ablaze with a burst of red
wings. But then I squinted. Looked closer. No, they weren't cardi-
nals. This was fire. It spread quickly, lighting the row of hedges until
Richard's home was surrounded by a wall of flames. My father lay in
the grass, unconscious. The flames licked his flesh. He jolted awake.
By then it was too late—my father was burning; his clothes seared
to his flesh and his flesh seared to his bones and his bones crumbled
to ash. The fire only burned stronger. It became a ball of flame, a divine inferno hovering above the earth, a small sun.

It shot straight toward me.

I woke up screaming.

"Jonah! Are you okay?" Richard bounded into the bedroom,
holding a stainless-steel bowl filled with pancake batter and blueberries. He was making my mother's recipe, the same pancakes I'd
made for him on our first morning at the compound.

"Sorry, just a nightmare," I said, my heart still pounding.

"You scared the shit out of me." Richard sighed, sat on the bed.
"You okay?"

"Yeah, I'm fine."

"What was it about?"

"I . . . I can't remember," I lied.

"Well, lucky for you, I'm making your mom's famous blueberry
pancakes," he murmured sweetly, kissing my cheek. "Known nightmare antidote."

I realized how hungry I was and plucked a blueberry from the batter. "Delicious," I said. Richard danced out of the room, stirring batter as he left. I closed my eyes and saw a flash of my father in flames. "I . . . I think I'm gonna call my dad today," I yelled to Richard in the next room.

"Are you sure that's a good idea?" Richard called back.

"No. But I can't stop thinking about it. I need to see what he wanted. I mean, maybe it's even a good thing. Maybe he wants to make amends."

"Whatever you think is best, honey," Richard cooed from the kitchen. I heard his mixing spoon clanging against steel. I turned to the nightstand to retrieve my iPhone from its usual overnight charging spot.

It wasn't there.

"And I'm sorry, by the way," Richard continued. "I didn't mean to pressure you last night. I shouldn't get involved. It's your family."

"It's okay," I said, distracted. I ripped the duvet cover off the mattress, shook it. Still no phone. I dropped to the floor and searched under the bed. "Hey, have you seen my phone?" I called into the kitchen.

There was a brief pause. A pancake sizzled in the silence. "No. It's not on your nightstand?"

"No," I grunted. I ran into the closet, scanned every surface.

"I mean, you could use my cell."

"I don't have my estranged father's number *memorized*," I snapped as I reemerged. I searched increasingly unlikely locales— deep in dresser drawers, on the floor behind Richard's potted palm, under the dusty cushion of the bedroom's neglected Milo Baughman recliner. Nothing. I felt caged, claustrophobic. My phone was my sole connection to the world beyond the compound. A lifeline, should I need it.

But you won't, I scolded myself. *Stop being so paranoid and just eat some fucking breakfast with your boyfriend, who loves you.*

I came out of the bedroom, sweating from my search. There,

on the dining-room table, sat a tray of perfect pancakes, steaming below Richard's smiling face.

"Nothing." I sighed and sat.

"Don't worry, I'm sure it'll turn up."

It never did.

I needed air.

It was too overcast for a swim after breakfast, but I went to the pool anyway. You were already there when I arrived, Mace. Swaddled in a towel, reading *Variety*.

"You're too late," you said without looking up. "The sun's gone."

My pulse quickened—I always felt slightly starstruck in your presence. "Catching up on breaking news?"

"Just reading a charming little story about my mother's latest DUI."

"Oh, wow. Really?"

"Really!" you chirped sarcastically. "Bailing her out of jail is my favorite hobby."

I laughed politely. Your precocious, jaded wit made it easy to forget you were sixteen.

"Her timing couldn't be better. I'm heading to New York tomorrow for the press junket of my Sundance movie. Can't wait for literally every single reporter to ask me about my alcoholic mother."

"That sucks. But at least you have a great movie to promote."

"I hate doing press. It's a parade of bullshit."

"But people care about your work."

"I wish *I* cared about my work."

"You don't mean that."

"I've been working since I was six years old. Supporting my whole family. Sometimes I want a fucking break. Sometimes I wanna open up a magazine and *not* read about how my drunk mother crashed another car I bought for her."

"I'm so sorry."

You sighed, softening. "Thanks."

Silence descended, mixing with the unbearable humidity. The clouds were swollen black balloons. Distant thunder rumbled.

"Maybe when I'm back from this press junket, we could hang or something," you suggested warmly. "Go into town, just you and me. Without our lame daddies watching over us."

My heart surged. I looked up to you, Mace. Your approval, your attention meant everything to me. Meant that I was worthy of all our new "family" had to offer. You'd figured out how this world worked. I hoped I could scale the same mountain, that its peaks were meant for me. Your friendship confirmed that I belonged here, that my dreams and desires mattered. "I'd love that. I could also use a break from work. I'm having a miserable time with revisions to my play . . ."

"You're a . . . writer?"

"Yeah, trying to be."

"Just like Evan."

His name hit me like an insult. He'd been a servant, not a success. "Nothing like Evan," I blurted out defensively.

"Oh, okay. Sorry." Pity dimmed your expression.

Then the clouds burst. We hugged goodbye in the downpour and went our separate ways through the field. Rain turned the soil to quicksand. My feet sank deeper with every step.

Nothing like Evan, I assured myself. *Nothing at all.*

———

It rained for three days straight. "Let's get the hell out of here," Richard said on the fourth day once the sun made its comeback. "If I have to read one more word about Thomas Cromwell, I will fucking kill someone."

Earlier that week, Richard had received an advance copy of *Wolf Hall* from his agents, their attempt to prod him into writing the television adaptation of Hilary Mantel's novel. An executive from the company producing the miniseries had been at the opening of Richard's play and, according to Richard's agents, "fell in love" with his brain. Richard was in his self-described "fallow period" and didn't wish to even *think* about work, but after much harassment from his reps, agreed to at least skim *Wolf Hall*.

"I didn't realize it was ten thousand pages long," he'd complained as he removed the volume from its FedEx box three days prior. "But what else am I going to do in this shitty weather?" Richard disappeared into the novel, spending most of his time cocooned in a striped Pendleton blanket on the couch as the rain pelted the glass walls of his home, forming vertical rivers that striped the towering panes.

Meanwhile, I failed to work on my play. Each morning, when Richard assumed his position in the living room, I'd sit at the desk in the bedroom and stare hopelessly at my laptop. I was attempting to turn my play from drama to comedy, from a cautionary tale about the dangers of ambition to a Cinderella story about a young man rescued from poverty by an older, wealthy playwright. Much to my dismay, every scene I attempted to write fell completely flat. As soon as I wrote a line of dialogue, I'd erase it, already frustrated by its wooden rhythms.

It's so hard to write autobiographical fiction, I thought. *So difficult to accurately reflect one's personal experience.* It didn't help that I hadn't been sleeping, that every evening marked the arrival of the same nightmare about my father. I'd sit at my computer each morning, eyelids drooping, coffee doing little to cut the fog of exhaustion.

You were gone, Mace. Off to your press junket in the city. I missed you. You were the only person who could understand my life, my relationship with Richard, and this dysfunctional Southampton family. Without your reassuring presence, a low-grade anxiety hummed at the edge of my consciousness. There were few distractions that week—Charles was also away, producing a Broadway workshop

in New York. Sandro was in LA for meetings on his upcoming superhero film. Only Ira and Ethel remained, and they largely kept to
themselves. There would be a group dinner at their house on Saturday when everyone returned to the compound. Despite my restless-
ness, I tried to enjoy the intimacy of those quiet, rainy days with
Richard. I played house with Daddy like a good boy.

But now it was Thursday and the first sunshine we'd seen since
Monday sliced through the living room. Richard squinted as he
thumbed through the final pages of *Wolf Hall*.

"I do not give remotely enough fucks about Cromwell to waste
years of my life on this," he decreed, tossing the tome on the coffee
table. "I'd much rather go to the beach with *you*." Richard pulled me
to the couch and attacked my face with kisses.

"Let me change into my new suit." I laughed.

I wriggled out of his grasp and vanished into the walk-in closet.
I stripped down and slid into the tight red Speedo Richard had pur-
chased for me during our shopping spree. By the time I emerged,
Richard had disappeared.

One of the waiters—I still didn't know any of their names; Richard had never offered to introduce them and I'd never asked him to
—stood in the kitchen, putting bottles of rosé into a cooler for our
excursion.

"Richard's just packing the trunk outside," he said.

I saw a flash of this waiter in the basement, on his knees, his arms
bound behind his back, his eyes dull and dead.

"Okay, great," I murmured. I wanted him gone.

The waiter positioned a pile of artisanal cheeses next to the bottles of rosé. I watched his hands as he worked. There were matching
red burns circling both his wrists.

From the rope.

"I'll finish packing," I said, pushing him from the cooler. "You
can go."

"But I promised Richard—"

"*Go!*" I shouted, surprising myself. He shrank from me and left the room, ducking out the sliding glass doors. Relieved, I watched him vanish into the wildflower field.

It was time to go to the beach.

———

"Jonah?"

I wheeled around, sweating from my attempt to plant our beach umbrella.

It was Rashad, his presence an impossible mirage. Skintight beach trunks gripped his thighs. He approached with a tall, beefy redhead. They were holding hands. Unexpected jealousy constricted my gut.

"Rashad!" I rushed up to him and gave him a warm hug. His smell—that sweet, heavy scent of coconut oil and shea butter and sweat—filled me with longing. I was glad to see him.

"This is Chad," he said, motioning to his companion.

"What's up, dude?" Chad offered an affected, masculine fist bump. There was an 85 percent chance that Chad took steroids and an even greater likelihood that he pretended to enjoy football. Rashad and I used to spend hours at the restaurant ridiculing the Chads of the world. *Maybe he's born with it; maybe it's anabolic steroids,* we'd sing to the tune of the Maybelline jingle. Yet here Rashad was, sleeping with the enemy.

"Hi, I'm Jonah," I said, then returned my attention to Rashad. "What the hell are you doing here?"

"Um, don't pretend you don't know," Rashad huffed.

"But I don't . . ." I trailed off, confused.

"Bitch, come *on.* I texted you, like, fifty times."

"I lost my phone."

"You *really* expect me to believe that?"

"It's true!"

"Whatever. I'll forgive your sketchy ass if you come to our barbecue tomorrow."

"You're staying up here?"

"Yeah, a bunch of Chad's friends rented a share in Montauk. We're here for the weekend. Seriously, you should come. I wanna hear all about your fancy new life."

"Yes! I'll totally come."

"Great, we'll pick up some extra meat."

"Wait." I winced. "I mean, I have to ask Richard first." I motioned to my boyfriend. Richard lumbered our way wearing an awkward green bucket hat, carrying the cooler from the car. "Ask me what?" Richard said breathlessly as he set down the cooler.

"Rashad, Chad—this is Richard," I said.

"Nice to meet you finally," Rashad teased. "I work—sorry, worked—with Jonah before you stole him from us. Jonah told me all about you."

"Only terrible things, I hope," Richard joked dryly.

"The worst."

"Rashad and Chad are having a barbecue at their place in Montauk tomorrow night, and they invited us," I interjected.

"Oh, how lovely," Richard said politely. "But we have reservations at Nick and Toni's."

"We do?" I asked.

"Well, it was going to be a surprise. Until Rashad here ruined it," Richard replied with mock outrage.

"Sabotaging surprises is my favorite pastime," Rashad quipped.

"We should get back, babe," Chad grunted.

"Let me at least give you my number again, Jonah," Rashad offered. "Maybe we can hang some other time this weekend."

"I don't have a phone . . ." I trailed off. Richard claimed he'd ordered a new one for me online, though it still hadn't arrived. It will, I told myself. It will.

"Oh, duh. And I, unfortunately, forgot to stick a pen and notepad in my Speedo."

"Here, you can put your number in my phone," Richard said, offering his cell to Rashad. "We'll call if things free up."

Rashad put in the number, gave the phone back to Richard. "Take care of yourself, Jonah," Rashad said, sweeping me into a concerned hug. I was surprised by the sudden urgency of his embrace. "I hope to see you soon."

"What about *me?*" Richard shouted to Rashad as he and Chad made their way down the beach.

"Oh, honey, I think I got a full dose of you today!" Rashad called back, a salty gust swallowing the final syllables of his reply.

"Ugh, I can see why you hated working at that restaurant. Rashad is *so* annoying," Richard said once they were out of earshot. "And the other one—the redheaded lump—he seems barely sentient."

"I mean, Rashad isn't so bad," I said meekly.

"Sweetie, it's okay if you don't like him anymore. Sometimes we outgrow people."

"I guess . . ."

"We clearly won't be needing this," Richard continued as he deleted Rashad's number from his phone.

"Yeah," I said, distracted, watching as they ventured farther down the beach. Wishing I could take Chad's place. Longing to hold Rashad's hand in my own.

13

I WAS IN the basement again.

Tied to the leather sling. Naked. Gagged. But the dim red bulbs were gone, replaced by a searing floodlight. Its blinding white glow nearly erased the room. I squinted in the direction of the glare, unable to determine its source. A masculine figure stumbled in front of the harsh beam. I couldn't make out his face. In his hand, a blunt instrument. He stumbled closer.

And then he was on top of me, his body pressed against mine, his face still impossible to see. He raised his instrument to the sky and then brought it down with terrible force. But instead of thrusting it into my stomach, he gored his own, screamed, then collapsed onto me.

His face. So close. The figure gained definition—it was Richard. His dying breath brushed my lips.

But wait. No, it wasn't Richard. It was Ira. No, it was Sandro. No, it was Ethel. No, it was Charles. No, it was my father. No, it was Richard.

Yes, it was Richard. I felt him shudder. Grow heavy. He was dead and I was stuck here forever. Tethered, forgotten, alone.

I screamed.

Suddenly, I was back in Richard's bed. It was morning and I was fine. Just another nightmare.

Shaking, I turned to my right. Richard was gone. I stumbled into the living room searching for him and found a note on the dining table next to an open box of granola and a pot of lukewarm coffee.

At the farmers' market. Be back soon.
Love you,
R

————

RAYMOND: Why don't you spend the summer here, Jacob?
JACOB: But what about my job in the city?
RAYMOND: What about it? When you're here with me, everything is taken care of.
JACOB: Including me?
RAYMOND: *Especially* you, Jacob.

It sucked. Of that much I was certain. I slumped over my laptop, defeated. Nothing could fix this shit play. Raymond and Jacob felt as false as their pseudonyms, like two-dimensional cutouts with cardboard hearts.

Richard was still at the farmers' market. Three cups of cold coffee did nothing to erase my hangover from the previous day; beach rosé had turned into dinner rosé had turned into late-night rosé. I'd been trying to drink enough to black out, hoping that obliterating my consciousness would stop my recurring nightmares. It hadn't worked and now here I was, struggling to scrub another horrific dream from my memory. Every time I attempted to write a line of dialogue for Raymond, I saw Richard's agonized face, saw his mouth dripping with blood, saw the dream basement drowned in white.

Which reminded me of the real basement.

And then my thoughts abandoned fantasy for reality. I was back in the actual sling, in the actual basement, with actual bodies circling my own. It was worse than a nightmare because it was real. The stuff of snuff films.

I could have died that night.

I attempted to suppress my rising panic. But once the phrase lodged itself in my brain, it was impossible to remove. *I could have died that night.* The more I tried not to think about the basement, the more I thought about the basement. *I could have died that night.* That one thought put an end to the intricate narrative of denial I'd constructed, the delusion that allowed me to believe that I was safe, that Richard loved me. *Richard didn't love me, Richard raped me, watched as his friends raped me, heard my screams and did nothing.* I felt so stupid, so ashamed that I had somehow allowed him to seduce me in the aftermath, that I had believed him when he told me he loved me, that I was so desperate for love that I would forgive everything after a fucking shopping trip.

I could have died that night.

Wake the fuck up, Jonah.

Before I knew it, I had erased the scene on my laptop, erased the entire play, deleted Raymond and Jacob, and written the real story, the one I'd pushed to the back of my mind. This scene wasn't good either, there was no poetry here, no dramatic arc; it was nearly incoherent, but somehow it contained more truth than the bullshit I'd labored over that summer. I typed without thinking, typed the things I should've said when I was at that gate, when I faced freedom and flinched.

JONAH: Let me go, you fucking asshole. I deserve more than your abuse, you sick fuck, let me go let me go let me go
RICHARD: But Jonah, I love you—
JONAH: You don't fucking love me. This isn't love. This is abuse, this is a sickness that's infected my fucking mind and my heart and I will never forgive you for what happened in

that basement, you sick fucking joke, you twisted fucking
monster, you deserve to die die die DIE DIE DIE

I stopped typing. I was exhausted. My mania receded; my temples
pounded. I needed sleep. I slid from the desk chair onto the floor and
nestled into the thick shag at the foot of Richard's bed, too drained
to climb onto the mattress. I was gone in an instant, fading into un-
interrupted darkness. For the first time that week, the nightmares did
not arrive. I drifted somewhere deep, somewhere safe.

Peace at last.

————

I awoke disoriented. It was evening. Richard sat at the desk reading
something on my laptop. A small frown cracked the lower half of his
face. I watched him for a moment, panic rousing my body. He turned
and jumped when he saw me.

"You're awake! Couldn't make it to the bed?"

"Sorry . . . I just . . . fell asleep here."

Richard smiled strangely. "Well, you better shower quickly. We
don't have much time."

"Much time?"

"Before our reservation!" he said with forced cheer. "Nick and
Toni's. Remember?"

"Oh, that's right."

"You're going to *love* it."

————

"*So good* to see you again, Richard," the hostess gushed. She was a
handsome woman, late fifties, with a wispy brunette bob that contrasted with her tough demeanor. Her slight Boston accent was the
only echo of whatever working-class pit she'd clawed her way out of
to arrive here, queen of the most coveted tables on Long Island. She

beamed brightly at Richard's entrance, but I could tell she was not to be fucked with. She clocked my presence with a short, steely wince. Richard did not attempt to introduce me.

"Hello, darling. How has the season been so far?"

"I've missed you, Richard! Where have you been?"

"I've been a busy boy, but I'm here for the rest of the summer."

"I've heard marvelous things about the new play; I simply can't wait to see it," she said, pulling two menus from the hostess stand.

"Where are we sitting tonight?"

"I have a table in the front if you'll just follow me." She led us into the dining room. Dusk filtered in through the windows that lined the restaurant's perimeter, casting a purple pall over the bone-white interior. The cottage-like comfort of the room did little to ease my nerves. Richard had remained oddly upbeat throughout our car ride to the restaurant, keeping the conversation fixed on the weather, never once mentioning what he'd discovered on my laptop. I was too fearful to broach the subject myself, and I nursed the faint hope that he had somehow not read what I'd written earlier that day. Regret, stronger than the rage that had inspired my tirade, consumed my thoughts.

How can I have been so fucking stupid?

"Enjoy," the hostess said as she sat us. She beamed at Richard, frowned at me, then vanished.

Did I even mean the things I wrote? Or was I just exhausted, cranky, not thinking straight?

"*That* is the most powerful woman in the Hamptons." Richard shook his head in admiration. "Trust me—we wouldn't have gotten this table if my play had been a flop."

I perused the menu, feigning interest in food. Panic ballooned in my chest, making it difficult to breathe. *Maybe he didn't actually read it.*

"You want the chicken," Richard decreed. "It's everyone's favorite."

"Okay," I murmured.

Maybe I woke up before he had a chance to scroll through the document.

"Well, hello, Richard," our waiter said as he approached. "It's been a while."

"Yes, I'm finally home," Richard cooed.

He would have brought it up by now if he'd read it.

"Your usual?"

"Times two," he said, motioning toward me. "It's his first time."

I'm surely in the clear at this point.

"Well, lucky for you, you're dining with the expert," our waiter chirped in my direction. I felt a sudden urge to pulp his face with my fists.

"Lucky me," I managed.

"Jonah, we need to talk," Richard said once the waiter had left. My rib cage tightened.

Fuck—he did read it. "About what?"

"About us." Richard sighed. I gripped my napkin, forced myself to breathe.

"Okay . . ."

"I love you, Jonah, I really do. But sometimes love isn't enough."

"What . . . what do you mean?"

"We're in such different places in our lives. And sometimes it's hard to bridge that gap of experience. I mean, I'm old enough to be your *father.* I just feel like there's a bit of a disconnect because of our age difference."

"So this isn't about . . . my play?" I ventured tentatively.

"You mean that thing I read on your laptop today?"

"Yeah."

"Of course not. Though I don't know that the revisions you made were quite"—he paused, teasing me with a patronizing grimace—"*successful.*"

"So you're breaking up with me?" I took a giant breath, exhaled. At last it was over. My body relaxed.

"I'm so sorry, Jonah."

But then a realization obliterated my calm: I had no money, no home, no family, no friends, no phone, nowhere to go other than back to Richard's compound. "I totally understand . . . it's just . . . I was planning on spending the summer with you . . ." Tears slid down my face.

"I know . . ."

"I could maybe stay with Rashad in Montauk for the weekend, at least . . . do you still have his number in your phone?"

"I'm so sorry. I deleted it back at the beach, remember?"

"That's . . . okay." I sobbed in short, hushed bursts, trying not to attract attention. "Maybe I could . . . go down to Montauk. Walk around and try to find Rashad or—"

"That's the other thing we need to discuss, Jonah."

I wiped my cheeks and waited for Richard to continue.

"I think you should stay at the compound for a while longer."

"That . . . that would be amazing," I stammered. "Just for a couple weeks while I get back on my feet, figure out what I'm gonna do—"

"I think you should stay longer than a few weeks."

"Oh . . . really?"

"I hate to do this." Richard sighed. "But there is the issue of the money you owe me."

I stared at him, baffled. "The money I owe you?"

"Ugh. I'm sorry, this is so awkward."

"But I don't owe you any money."

"Excuse me, but you owe me a great deal of money," Richard insisted, his tone sharpening.

"But—"

"Two months rent—twenty-two hundred dollars. The clothes I bought you—three thousand, four hundred, and sixty-seven dollars. You owe me a total of five thousand, six hundred, and sixty-seven dollars. Were you really planning on just *never* paying me back? Are you truly *that* selfish? I thought you were better than that, Jonah."

"No . . . no . . . I . . ." Vertigo seized my skull. The room tipped.

"Sorry, I didn't mean to snap." Richard sighed. "But there is a way you can pay me back."

"How?" I gripped our table for balance, bunching the white table-cloth in my fists.

"You could join our waitstaff. You'd stay on the property with the rest of the boys. There's an extra bunk now that Evan's gone. We pay two hundred dollars a week."

I wanted to hurl my bread plate to the floor. Watch it shatter. Run into the night.

"We'll put your initial salary toward the money you owe me, of course. At two hundred a week, you'll have paid off your debt in, what, about seven months? Then, once that's taken care of, you can start saving to make a move back to the city. It's a pretty good deal, all things considered. Not everyone in my position would be so generous."

"*Generous?*" I snapped. "This is *totally fucked.*"

"Jonah, I'd appreciate it if you didn't take that tone with me. I'm offering—"

"You aren't offering *shit.*"

"I'm offering you a *job,* Jonah. Jesus."

"What you just described is indentured fucking servitude."

"Perhaps you'd prefer to live in the Southampton homeless shelter?"

"*It's fucking medieval, Richard.*"

"Though I'm not sure the gruel they serve would satisfy your rather expensive tastes."

"*Fuck off.*" I slammed my fists on our table. My fork flew to the ground.

"Is there a problem here?" the hostess barked from behind me.

The restaurant fell silent. Diners stared at me. Richard stared at me. The hostess stared at me. Her pursed lips a warning: *I will fuck you up, little boy.*

"No," I mumbled, shame flushing my cheeks.

She picked up my fork. "I think you dropped this," she hissed in my ear.

"Thank . . . thank you," I stammered, my indignation curdling into embarrassment. I realized why Richard had brought me to Nick and Toni's: so I wouldn't make a scene.

"I think we both got a bit overheated," Richard cooed after a brief silence. "I'm sorry if I was overly harsh. I know this is a lot to take in . . ."

I said nothing. Sudden fatigue turned my limbs to lead.

"But I'm only trying to help. I think this job would be good for you."

"Sure," I managed.

"It's your decision, of course."

"Of course," I echoed numbly.

"Though I'm not quite sure what other options you have at the moment."

"I'll do it."

"Wonderful! I promise it's a great gig, especially off-season. The winter months are much less busy for the staff. We come out only about every other week or so."

"Right."

"*So* glad this all worked out. It's a win-win for everyone, really."

"Your chicken, sir." A food runner placed my meal in front of me. "Excellent choice."

The sight of the steaming carcass turned my stomach.

"And don't worry." Richard winked. "Dinner's on me."

14

SERVANTS' QUARTERS. That's what Richard called the windowless shack.

"The servants' quarters always feel a little snug at first. But all the boys get used to it eventually."

"Thanks," I mumbled.

"And that's your bed." He pointed toward the immaculately made bottom bunk in the corner of the shack shadowed by its unkempt twin above. A white sheet dangled in front of my bed like a curtain. I snapped it aside and sat on the tough, thin mattress, wondering how I'd ever sleep here. "It used to be Evan's before we . . ." Richard paused. "Let him go."

"And so all the servants . . ." I drifted off, staring at the impossibly small space.

"Sleep here, yes. Michael, Seb, and Chase. Lovely boys, you'll get along famously."

I looked to the floor. Directly next to my feet was the hatch. Its dull, rusted ring was a reminder. Pull it, and the portal opened.

A flash of you, Mace, on that night: *It's a little strange at first.*

Then your face against the concrete, bloodshot eyes watering.

I threw my duffel bag on top of the hatch, as if hiding it would help.

"I'll let you get settled. The rest of the boys are shucking oysters

for tonight. You should join them when you're ready—they're at Ira
and Ethel's."

"What do I wear?"

"The boys all wear black."

"So . . ."

"Wear the Alexander Wang T-shirt. The one you bought?"

You bought it, I countered in my mind. *For me. For this moment.*
I unzipped my duffel and confronted my new clothes, freshly ripped
from Richard's walk-in and now crammed into my battered bag.
How stupid I've been.

"Oh, and this is your light," Richard said, motioning to a small
red bulb protruding from the wall above my pillow. Below it, a label
that read EVAN. "It'll flash red if I need you. There's also a buzzer
that goes off, in case you're asleep."

This is only temporary. A way to get back on my feet.

"Okay," I said, surveying the room, no more than two hundred
square feet total, determined not to cry. It felt like a garden shed, a
place to store tools, that had been hastily converted into living quarters. My bunk stood in the right-hand corner, mirrored on the opposite side by an identical stack of beds, only a few feet between them.
Claustrophobia seized my chest. It would've been cramped for one
person, let alone four. Fluorescent rods on the ceiling cast a grim, industrial glow over the interior. The only light. Day or night, it didn't
matter—inside the small shack, it could be any hour. The only teth-
ers to time were the small digital clocks embedded in the walls beneath our lights. All the boys had one: the same red bulb hovered
over each pillow. To summon us.

"I know it's a bit of an adjustment, but I'm honestly *so* thrilled
you'll be joining our staff. Ever since we let Evan go, I've been absolutely *lost* without a butler."

"Yeah, this will be great." I wanted to scream.

"I'll leave you to it, then," Richard chirped as he opened the door, letting a rare blade of sun slice through the airless concrete box. "See you at dinner!"

And then he was gone, taking the daylight with him.

———

He was twenty-three. He hunched over the sink, scrubbing an oyster shell with a little brush. His swollen triceps twitched with every jab, his muscular arms comically large for such a small task. He wore a tight black shirt, one that looked suspiciously similar to my own Alexander Wang tee. His olive complexion contrasted with his white-blond hair, a disparity heightened, no doubt, by the summer sun. His face was a lesson in symmetry, his cheekbones two perfectly matched cliffs that plummeted to a devastating pink pout. His eyes were dead and blue and beautiful, like an over-chlorinated pool too poisonous for a swim. His stare made me itch.

"I'm Sebastian," he said. A slight Southern drawl tinged his vowels. "You can call me Seb."

"I'm Jonah."

"I know." He frowned.

"Oh, right," I mumbled. "I'm sorry I didn't know your name."

"It's okay." He shrugged. "I don't really care."

And he clearly didn't. Care about anything. His apathy terrified me. Or, rather, I was terrified by how much I understood it.

"I was wondering how long it would take," he continued.

"What?"

"Until you joined us. On this side of things."

A series of questions, each more paralyzing than the last, roiled my thoughts and left me speechless. Or perhaps *questions* is the wrong word for the nebulous turmoil that rippled through my brain, triggering a bout of vertigo. I leaned against Ethel's immaculate marble counter, bewildered by my new circumstances. Seb seemed completely unconcerned. My presence was expected.

"Have you shucked an oyster before?" He picked up an oyster knife, clutched its white handle in his sunburned fist. Dead skin dusted his knuckles, his fingers like five peeling snakes.

"No . . ."

"You stab it," he said, plunging his knife into the oyster. "Right here in the hinge. Then slide the knife between the shell. But make sure you don't mangle the meat inside." He cracked it open, revealing a little puddle of muscle ready to be eaten alive. *"Et voilà."* He gestured with grotesque flair. "Oysters for assholes."

"Where's everyone else?"

"Michael and Chase are pulling wine from the cellar."

My eyebrows twitched upward. Seb laughed. "No, not *that* cellar. Ira and Ethel's wine cellar."

"Oh," I managed. My thoughts flashed to that night — a shock of Seb's white hair in the dark basement.

"Your turn." He handed me a knife. So naturally, like he was living in a universe where this all made sense, operating under a dream logic from which I was excluded. I wanted to wake up screaming.

"Thanks." I grabbed an oyster and stabbed as instructed, but the shell slipped and the knife sliced my finger. Blood bloomed from the cut. *"Shit."*

"Here, I got you." Seb grabbed a paper towel and wrapped my finger. "Are you okay?"

"Fuck you, Ira!" Ethel's scream emanated from the bedroom before I could answer. Seb and I froze, listened as Ira issued apologetic murmurs, too faint to make out. A door slammed. Silence.

"The happy couple at it again." Seb sighed.

I looked down at my finger, mummified in Bounty, a crimson stain stretching across the white paper. "Do you know if there are bandages somewhere or . . ."

"Yeah, check the bathroom."

I made off in the direction of the nearest bathroom. Seb yelled after me, "Actually, Chase just cleaned that one for tonight. Maybe use the one in the guest cottage instead."

"Got it," I said. I slipped out of the kitchen through the sliding glass doors and crossed the white gravel drive. The guest cottage was cut from the same architectural cloth as the other buildings on the compound, though it was much smaller in size, a less lofty replica of its modernist sisters. I stepped inside, marveling. Two of the walls were entirely covered by bookshelves that mirrored each other across the minimal interior, only a small orange love seat, a clear glass coffee table, and a gray rug between them. The other two walls were massive rectangular windows. The room was all sun and books. Beautiful.

I wanted to cry.

I had, just days prior, believed all this beauty belonged to me. The buildings, the books, the art, the wildflowers. I'd felt like I was entitled to the abundance of Richard's compound, that I owned it by proxy. Not realizing that it owned me. Or, rather, Richard did.

I marched up the stairway that floated at the back of the space and led to a lofted bedroom. I passed the plush queen bed, straitjacketed in beige linens, and opened the bathroom door.

Ethel stood inside, weeping over the sink.

I jumped in surprise. She wheeled from the mirror, wiping tears from her bloodshot eyes.

"Ethel, I'm sorry. What are you doing here—"

"It's *my* guest cottage, isn't it?" She silenced me with a withering frown.

We froze in an uncertain tableau. I'd caught Ethel in a rare moment of vulnerability; neither of us knew how to proceed. I'd never seen her without makeup. Her face didn't make sense without paint to cover the seams of her many surgeries. It looked like something assembled in a lab, a mad scientist's mistake, like hocks of meat Frankensteined to a skull.

"What are *you* doing here?" she spat. "That's the question we should be asking."

"I—I cut myself. I was looking for a bandage."

"Well, I suggest you look elsewhere."

"Yes, I'll go." I retreated from the bathroom and ran down the stairs. I was almost to the door when I heard Ethel murmur something from above. "I'm sorry, did you say something?"

Ethel appeared at the top of the stairs. "I said stay away from my husband."

"Excuse me?"

"Don't think I don't know what goes on in that basement." Ethel's voice shook with quiet rage. "And I think you're disgusting."

A sick feeling hit my gut. Not because I resented Ethel for her judgment, but because I agreed with it.

———

"Another Campari soda," Ethel intoned from her position at the head of the table.

"Yes, of course," Seb said, jumping into action. She gripped his arm, stopping him.

"No. I want Jonah to make it for me," she trilled meanly. This was a different Ethel than the one I'd encountered in the guest cottage earlier that afternoon. Her countenance was now complete, painted and contoured and smeared into a human face. Her stiff bob helmeted her head, bleached to straw-like perfection, hairsprayed to within an inch of its ebbing life. Order restored. She pulled her pink pashmina tight around her shoulders and squinted at me. "Jonah?"

Everyone at the table looked in my direction. I hated them all: Richard, Charles, Ira, Ethel, Sandro. And you, Mace. I hated you in that moment. Your words echoed in my mind: *Wanna be my big brother?* You were supposed to be my friend, my ally. But you just sat there, silent. I would soon learn my resentment was shared by my fellow waiters; the boys despised your ability to come and go as you pleased, jetting off for press junkets and film shoots. Of course, when the sexual roles were drawn, you joined the rest of us in being gagged and bound. But in the harsh light of day, you were free to leave the compound. So why did you keep coming back? I imagine the answer had something to do with a fear that all your success would vanish if you betrayed the systems of abuse that bolstered it. Your contract with evil.

"Campari soda. *Now.*" Ethel grimaced.

You stared at me, oyster shell in hand. You sent me a look of pity. I could've slapped the oyster from your fist. I didn't want you to look down on me; I wanted you to look me in the eye, be my equal. But I'd been banished to the realm of the waitstaff, a role I occupied easily, thanks to my experience in Perdition. Still, I should've accepted your acknowledgment, Mace. At least you saw me. Everyone else acted as if I were just another server, had *always* been a server, had never occupied a seat at the very table I now stood above, tending to the demands of people I'd mistakenly assumed were my new family.

"Yes, I'll make it."

It felt like the previous two weeks had been erased. The promises never made. The love never shared. As if Richard had never been my boyfriend.

He did love me at one point, I reminded myself. *Maybe he still does.*

"Get me another one too," Richard said, punctuating his demand with a sick oyster slurp.

Or maybe he never did.

I marched to the kitchen, anxiously pinching my bandaged finger, each squeeze sending a pulse of pain through my hand. The pain felt good. It kept me alert, kept me from drifting too deep into darkness. I had a job to do. A job I needed to keep. A job keeping me alive. A job that was killing me.

"They *all* want them now," Michael said, appearing next to me at the sink, rolling his eyes. Of my three fellow waiters, Michael was the kindest. He was only nineteen, tall with lanky arms that usually dangled at his sides. His every gesture seemed to apologize for the length of his limbs; he never extended them fully, opting instead to fold them at awkward angles in front of his torso. His lopsided grin and flitting fingers resulted in a goofy demeanor that almost overpowered his beauty. Almost. But in rare moments, Michael's features settled and his beauty emerged, as shocking as a slap.

"We're going to run out of Campari," I said.

"Never!" Chase cried, rushing into the kitchen. He opened a Campari-stocked cabinet with dramatic flair. "They have enough of this stuff to stay wasted through the zombie apocalypse."

Chase was warming up to me. He'd been the most aloof of the three on my first day of employment, his Chiclet-toothed smile vanishing the minute I appeared. He was a compact square of muscle. I could tell by the way he sashayed through the kitchen—feet turned out, perfect posture—that he was a dancer. He had a tendency to hum to himself during repetitive tasks, songs that stopped whenever I looked his way.

None of the waiters trusted me that first day. It was clear that they'd all predicted my menial fate, though *how* they'd been so confident I would end up among their ranks was still a mystery. We'd not had time for candid conversation—the afternoon was spent under Ethel's disapproving stare. She monitored us as we shucked oysters and salted steaks and made brownie batter and set the table. Everyone proceeded with an air of forced normalcy, though my presence added an underlying tension.

"Can you grab some ice from the freezer?" Michael asked me.

"*Someone help!*" Ira's terrified call emanated from the dining room.

We rushed from the kitchen. Ethel, the color of eggplant, gurgled in her seat. She stood sharply, knocking over her tumbler. It flew off the table and onto the floor, exploded in a mess of glass and ice and red liquid.

"She's choking," Richard cried, recoiling from Ethel in horror.

"Fucking do something!" Charles shouted at the waitstaff, as if lifesaving were a duty we'd neglected.

"Does anyone know the Heimlich?" Ira exclaimed.

I did. It had been part of my training at Perdition—we'd learned to save the lives of customers we wanted to kill. I said nothing.

"I do!" Michael yelled. From behind, he wrapped his arms around Ethel, thrust his fists into her stomach. How small she seemed, crumpled in his urgent embrace. A sack of bones, jostled with each jab.

One, two, three, four, five, six thrusts.

I wanted her to die. It was a strange feeling to realize I wanted another human to stop breathing. Wanted to watch her eyes empty. Watch her crumple to the floor, clutching her pearls one last time, her neck bulging beneath them, face red until it went white and her body went limp and the ambulance arrived, far too late.

One, two, three, four, five, six thrusts.

And why stop there? I looked around the room in disgust, at you and Richard and Charles and Sandro and Ira, imagining your heads exploding spontaneously, detonated by my psychic stare. Brains landing with a wet smack, followed by the bodies above.

One, two, three, four, five, six thrusts.

I watched the color drain from Ethel's face.

I wondered who I had become.

———

To my dismay, Ethel survived. Michael successfully dislodged the oyster from her throat, and Ethel and Ira retired for the evening, exhausted by her brush with mortality. The rest of the party retreated to Richard's home. The night, Charles insisted, was not over yet.

I was alone in the kitchen, uncorking a pinot noir, when I felt your hand on my shoulder.

"Jonah, I'm . . . I'm sorry," you whispered urgently.

"So you knew," I hissed.

"Knew what?"

"How this whole thing works. The boys, the shed—"

"I didn't know it would happen to you—"

"Oh, I think you could have fucking guessed."

Sandro swooped in and massaged your shoulders. "Guessed what?"

"The vintage of this pinot," I said, suppressing my rage. "More for you, Mace?"

I poured red wine in your glass, intentionally splashing your shirt. A crimson blotch spread across the fabric. Like blood from a stab wound.

"Jonah, what the fuck?" you cried, jumping out of Sandro's embrace.

"I'm so sorry. It was an accident."

"Too bad you're so poor that you'll never be able to buy another white T-shirt again," Sandro quipped, pushing us both into the living room. Michael, Seb, and Chase were already shirtless, sitting on the shag, looking like bored statues. Charles cut cocaine with his Amex.

"Why don't you just take it off?" Charles said to you before snorting a massive line from Richard's coffee table.

"That's a great idea," Sandro said, ripping the shirt off your body.

"*Stop,*" you snapped at him.

"Someone's sensitive tonight." Richard laughed, emerging from his bedroom. "By the way, we have treats."

Richard approached, carrying a metal tray dotted with eight tabs of ecstasy. He passed the drugs around the room. One by one, each person took a pill, but when the tray got to me, I said, "Sorry, guys, think I'm actually going to call it a night."

I bent down to place the wine bottle on the coffee table. Charles grabbed my arm, arresting me at a ninety-degree angle.

"I think you should reconsider." The room fell quiet.

"No, I'm good. It's been a long day." I wriggled out of Charles's grip, stifling the urge to kick him in the gut.

"Jonah, we're not done yet," Richard said. "Your services are still needed."

"I *said* it's been a long day." I moved toward the door, but Richard blocked my exit.

"And *I* said we're not done yet." He grabbed my hand and forced a pill inside it. I turned back toward the living room, hoping for a sympathetic look from one of the waiters, or even you, Mace. No luck. All eyes were cast down, as if the entire room were in prayer.

But God had clearly abandoned us all.

I sighed and closed my eyes. A flash of my father in the darkness. I had brought this on myself, after all. This is what I deserved. God's punishment. My hell on earth.

I opened my eyes and accepted the pill.

Later, in the basement—leather restraints, abuse, violent fantasies made real in the dark. Only this time, I didn't fight, didn't scream, didn't run.

There was nowhere to go.

15

"THIS IS A BAD IDEA," Michael hissed.

"Why are we whispering?" I sipped from our handle of stolen vodka.

"Because we're breaking into Sandro's fucking house?" Seb deadpanned.

"Guys, relaaaax." Chase stumbled drunkenly through the field. "No one's here."

The compound was empty for the night, a first since I'd become a servant. Richard and Charles were in New York, Ira and Ethel were speaking at a costume-design conference in Toronto, and Sandro was back to Los Angeles for a second round of meetings about his superhero movie. You had taken Scamp and driven to the city earlier that evening, telling Chase you thought it was "spooky when everyone is gone." But everyone wasn't gone. Seb, Chase, Michael, and I were still on the compound. Clearly, you felt uncomfortable around us. Outnumbered.

"*Ladies and gentlemen,*" Chase slurred as he opened Sandro's sliding door. "The servants take over the castle." He sashayed into the living room, flipped on the lights, and scream-sang Lady Gaga's "Just Dance."

"You can take the gay boy out of musical theater," Seb observed, grabbing the vodka from me, "but you can't take musical theater out of the gay boy."

"I once got *two* callbacks for *Mamma Mia,* you bitch," Chase said, flipping both middle fingers and then blasting the actual Lady Gaga over Sandro's sound system.

"Never booked it, though," Seb fired back.

"Not so loud!" Michael shouted over the music. "You guys are making me nervous."

Michael grabbed the handle of vodka from Seb but fumbled it in his lanky arms. I dived for the plummeting bottle, caught it before it smashed to the ground.

"Jonah for the win!" Chase yelled. "Jonah! Jonah! Jonah!" The rest of the boys joined in Chase's chant, drunkenly shouting my name over the thumping bass.

"Y'all are a mess," Seb drawled, his slight Southern accent amplified by the alcohol. "Feels like I'm on spring break at Fort Lauderdale."

"Boys gone wiiiiiiiiiiiiild," Chase shouted. He grabbed the bottle again and chugged it empty. "I just killed the vodka!"

"Well, good thing I stole a Beaujolais from Richard's cellar." I held the wine aloft, triggering more cheers. Chase danced his way over and swigged from the bottle.

"Careful, honey," Michael murmured, concerned. "You might wanna slow down."

"Noooo, I wanna go *fast*." Chase did a pirouette and spun rapidly before jumping to the ground and landing in a split. Everyone screamed and laughed in amazement. I felt, for the first time in weeks, a flicker of joy.

At that moment, the front door slammed.

There you stood, Mace. Face twisted in shock. Scamp whined at your feet.

I rushed to the speakers, shut off the music. We all froze.

"What the hell . . ." You seemed afraid to finish your sentence.

"Thought you were going back to the city." Seb gritted his teeth.

"I . . . I forgot Scamp's squeaky frog," you said delicately. "He can't sleep without it."

"Well, why don't you *go ahead and . . . and get it,*" Chase slurred aggressively.

You moved toward Scamp's dog bed in the corner of the living room as the rest of us watched, hostile. We held a collective power — maybe it was the booze, or the bonding, or the fact that there were more of us. But whatever it was, we refused to surrender our one night of fucking fun. Refused to scatter like roaches.

"You know, I . . . I don't think Sandro would like this," you murmured as you picked up the dog toy. It let out a shrill squeak that echoed in the silence following your statement.

"Well, we don't have to tell him, do we?" I snapped.

"I just think—"

"Actually, none of us give a fuck what you think."

"Jonah, come on. I'm on your side—"

"Are you? 'Cause it doesn't feel that way."

"Of course I am—"

"In fact, feels like you pulled a bait and switch. Made me feel *right at home* before I became trapped in this fucking prison—"

"That's *not* fair."

"Wanna be my big brother, Jonah?" I mimicked you. "Come join the family."

"I wanted to be your friend. I . . . I really did," you stammered.

"And what about now? Now that I've joined the fucking help, you don't seem quite as interested, for some reason."

"I—I'm sorry." You started crying. "Sometimes I just feel so . . . alone here."

"Well, then, why don't you become a *servant* like the *fucking rest of us?* Oh, that's right—because you're too good for this shit."

I waited for your response, but your gaze shifted to something behind me. I turned to find Chase, bent at the waist, vomiting.

You helped us clean it up.

I rubbed Chase's back as he sat on a dining chair, head hung low. Seb grabbed paper towels; Michael got the bleach. You dropped to your knees and scrubbed the floor.

Then you left.

"Stay as long as you want," you said at the door. "I won't tell anyone."

But it didn't feel like a party anymore.

———

By mid-August, I'd occupied my role as Richard's butler for a little over a month. Grim math dominated my thoughts: each day I was twenty-eight dollars closer to freedom. I never saw an actual paycheck, though Richard assured me he was deducting my earnings from my overall debt of five thousand, six hundred, and sixty-seven dollars. I didn't trust him to accurately record my income, so I kept my own ledger. Thus far, my earnings totaled nine hundred and eighty dollars, a sum I worked out on stolen stationery due to the fact that my laptop had "vanished" just like my phone had. Without my devices, I found it increasingly difficult to imagine life beyond the walls of the compound. Richard insisted he had no idea where my laptop had gone. I was infuriated by his second attempt to gaslight me; I wasn't stupid, and besides, there was nothing I could do. He had all the power. *Just admit you took it, you fucking coward.* But sometimes I felt like his lies were more for himself than for me. A way to deny the reality of what he was doing. To pretend it was all perfectly ordinary.

This is not normal. It was my mantra, my only remaining tether to reality. Each morning, we'd sit inside our windowless shack waiting for our red lights to blink. *This is not normal.* Once they did, we'd run to our respective households and attend to the daily needs of the men who assaulted us nightly. *This is not normal.* I became increasingly grateful for our boring chores; laundry and cleaning and meal prep kept the dread at bay. *This is not normal.*

Despite my mantra, the constant abuse weakened my resolve: *This* feels *normal.*

Late afternoons were the worst; we knew what horrors awaited us as dusk descended. *This feels normal.* If there was a group dinner on the compound, we could expect the evening to end in the basement. *This feels normal.* There was no way out; none of us had the code to the gate, and none of us had anywhere to go. Life was a horror movie on repeat, less shocking because we knew the twists by heart: the drugs, the bondage, the rape. *This feels normal.* My body had stopped producing adrenaline, or maybe it was constantly producing adrenaline. Panic deadened into helplessness. *This feels normal.*

In my darkest moments, nihilism poisoned my thoughts: *This* is *normal.*

When there was no group bondage session, each of us was often required to have a solo encounter with his designated employer in the middle of the night. *This is normal.* Every time a red light above one of our beds illuminated, it was accompanied by a loud buzz, so if we were sleeping when the men summoned us, we'd be roused to meet their needs. *This is normal.* Often, we were called under the pretense of fixing a midnight snack or changing a light bulb, an excuse that quickly collapsed as we were forced into a rough and rapid fuck. Other times, there was no pretense, and when one of the boys entered his employer's home, he'd be greeted by a stiff cock and expected to do something about it. *This is normal.* Our windowless confines were so small that when a buzzer went off, it woke everyone up. Nights were sleepless after that. We lay in silence, waiting for whomever had been summoned to return. We never articulated our fears—we didn't need to. The quiet that swelled around us was enough. The dull refrain echoed: *This is normal. This is normal. This is normal.*

I needed to act before it was too late. Before I lost my mind completely.

———

"Are you finished with the fifties, hon?" Chase called.

"Yeah," I replied, hefting two fifty-pound weights into his grip.

"Spot me, will you?" he asked, leaning back on his bench, a dumbbell in each hand.

The gym was a welcome distraction for all of us. Something else to occupy our minds—our bodies. For a brief period every morning, they were ours again, free from the men who owned them. Each day at 6:00 a.m., we went to Sandro's gym, a small annex hidden behind his home. Inside, it was spare. A white room with one mirrored wall, concrete floors, and an array of weights and workout equipment.

We were only to use Sandro's gym when he wasn't there. Sandro didn't like sharing but felt it was a necessary concession. How, after all, were we supposed to stay sexy for our basement rendezvous? What our employers didn't realize was the relief these moments brought. We watched in Sandro's mirrors as our muscles strengthened, sinew fortified for an uncertain future. Even if our minds had given up hope, our bodies had not. They grew stronger, faster, leaner, larger. Bodies that could run if required to.

"Have you ever noticed the wall behind Richard's kitchen?" I asked Chase.

"What"—he panted between reps—"do you mean?"

"There's a section that's sinking. Into the ground."

"Really?" He grunted, completing his final chest press. Behind us, Seb ran for his life on the treadmill, a strange stare fixed on his face. Only Michael was absent from our workout this morning, detained by one of his "moods." There was a dark side to his sweet demeanor, a depression that could keep him bedridden. He rose only for his professional duties, the very tasks that were the source of his misery.

"Yeah," I continued. "I heard him screaming to his architect on the phone yesterday."

"Always such a sweetheart to his employees." Chase wiped his brow with a rag.

"Something about a shoddy foundation. The rainy summer. The weight of the wall."

"That architect is a con man." Seb panted. "This place is held together by Silly String."

"Anyway, I took a look myself. There's an extended section that slopes downward, right behind his kitchen. It's about three feet lower than the rest of the wall."

"So?" Seb shrugged as he hit the Stop button on the treadmill.

My breath quickened. "If we work together, I think we can get the fuck out of here."

"You're insane." Chase laughed warily.

"I'll get the ladder from the pool house." I talked faster, attempting to mask my anxiety. "We'll take it out in the early morning. To the wall. The ladder won't be tall enough but if we can somehow boost each other once we reach the top, we could scale the sunken section. Sure, it'll be a drop to the other side, but even if someone sprains an ankle, it's not that far to the Jitney stop, only about a mile, and the first bus leaves around five a.m., and maybe if we stole cash from Sandro's or Richard's wallet, stole enough for Jitney fare, we could get back to Manhattan."

I stared down at the sweat-splattered concrete, afraid to meet their eyes.

"And then what?" Chase sighed.

I looked up. Chase pierced me with a pitying stare. Seb's gaze was dead, distant.

"What do you mean?"

"Even if nothing goes wrong—we miraculously fail to trip the wall's alarm system, we manage not to break our legs on the twenty-foot drop to the ground, we steal money and no one notices, we take the bus back to Manhattan—then what, Jonah?"

"We . . . we start our lives over."

Seb fired off a bitter laugh. "Where? A park bench? Or maybe you're sitting on a classic six off Gramercy Park that you never told us about?"

Each boy had been selected by Richard's cohort for the same reason: his vulnerability. Seb was estranged from his mother and father. As a child, he'd slept in the kitchen closet because his alcoholic parents cared more for Jose Cuervo than they did for their own son; every night it was margaritas and screaming matches while Seb cried in a sleeping bag beneath an empty spice rack. College was Seb's only hope of escape, and so he poured his soul into studying, something his parents resented: *You think you're fucking better than us, well, news flash, we're not paying for some hippie scum college, you're staying in fucking Florida.* It got worse when his dad discovered Seb was gay; the margarita rants became salted with *faggots* and *fudge-packers*. All the while, Seb kept the bulb in his closet burning. He studied and studied until the impossible happened: a full scholarship to Yale. A final fuck-you to Mom and Dad.

But Seb's elation was short-lived. At college, no one wanted to be friends with the poor Floridian loner who wore the same shitty clothes all the time and worked at the local pizza parlor. *White trash,* his classmates whispered. He hoped to save enough to move to New York City after graduating, but minimum wage failed to make money accumulate in his bank account. Seb had nearly surrendered hope when his queer-theory professor—a man of forty who had become Seb's surrogate father and sometime lover—mentioned that his friend Charles Moore was looking for someone to work at his Hamptons estate. Charles would provide Seb with lodging on the compound and a modest paycheck for his services. It was a solution to Seb's dilemma, a loophole through which he could shimmy into the lower ranks of New York City's creative class. Charles wasted little time in forcing himself on his new employee. Then Charles started to share Seb with his friends. Seb endured these unwanted sexual encounters as best he could; he had nowhere else to go. Still, the servants' quarters were better than a kitchen closet. Weren't they?

That was spring of 2008. Soon thereafter, Michael arrived on the compound. Michael never went to college; the near-daily beatings from his mother proved too strong a distraction from studying. The only subject he excelled at was theater; applause provided the love he lacked in his New Paltz home. After high school, at the unripe age of eighteen, he fled to New York City. He'd planned to be a great actor but became a mediocre cater waiter instead. One of Michael's first gigs was passing appetizers at the intimate penthouse soiree of a gay financier who frequently funded Sandro's films. Sandro cornered Michael at the party and laced his flirtation with promises of movie roles. But when Michael's boss walked in on Sandro and Michael fucking in the bathroom, Michael was promptly fired. Sandro apologized and insisted that Michael come to the compound the following weekend. Michael agreed, secretly thrilled to sacrifice his lame job for a trip to Sandro Rüegg's summer estate. Perhaps Sandro would cast Michael in a small role in one of his films. Or a supporting role. Or a lead.

A few weekend trips later, Sandro offered him a job as a waiter alongside Seb—not quite the Oscar-winning role he imagined. Still, Michael jumped at the chance. Their affair was quickly cooling, Michael needed money, and the job was an opportunity to stay in Sandro's exclusive circle. By the time Michael realized his mistake, it was too late. His first attempt at escape resulted in a black eye; the next, a bruised rib. Then he stopped trying. In a way, the abuse felt like home.

"Do you know Sandro still hits Michael?" Chase snapped.

"I . . . I didn't," I muttered, surprised.

"On his rib cage, on his lower back, spots guests won't see."
Chase's tone was accusatory, as if I were somehow responsible.

"Sandro still hasn't forgiven him for trying to escape," Seb murmured.

"And you know who else wanted to get the fuck out of here?"
Chase asked. "Evan."

Evan was, of course, the only waiter to successfully leave the compound. Though no one knew where he'd gone. Or when he'd left.

Or if he was alive.

Evan had, as I'd guessed on first seeing him, briefly dated Richard. The two had met at a gallery opening for George Condo that
Evan had attended as the intrepid, unpaid intern of *Artforum.* Evan
was angling for a position as a staff writer, so he had taken to re-
viewing art shows for free. Evan didn't want to be an art critic, he
wanted to be a novelist, but novel-writing wasn't paying the bills,
and Evan was getting tired of squatting in a condemned Bushwick
warehouse with a group of gutter punks he'd met at a Throbbing
Gristle show. Plan B was to write for *Artforum,* but at the time he
met Richard, plans A and B were both failing. Richard became plan
C. Richard was surprisingly amenable to funding his younger lover's
life. Clothing, dinners, phone bills—all taken care of. A couple of
months after Michael's and Seb's hiring, Evan accepted Richard's invitation to live on the compound and work on his novel.

According to the rest of the boys, Evan's path to servitude was
chillingly similar to my own: the breakup, the surprise bill, the indentured servitude. But Evan worked on the compound long enough
to settle his tab and even save a small sum for a move back to Brooklyn. When he told Richard and Charles he wanted to leave, they refused to pay him; they claimed his math was off, that he still had
months to go.

Evan snapped. He grew increasingly rebellious, punched Charles
during a routine rape. The afternoon of that pool party—the last
day anyone had seen Evan—Charles barged into the servants'

quarters and demanded they pack Evan's things. Charles offered no information about where Evan was going, simply grabbed the suitcase and stormed across the wildflower field.

"I swear to God, he's . . ." Seb trailed off, terror swallowing his sentence.

"I'm sure he's fine," I murmured unconvincingly. "He has to be."

"He *has* to be?" Chase snarled. "Says who? Your guardian fucking angel?"

"Maybe he just decided—"

"He's dead, Jonah."

"But you don't *know* that—"

"Why do you think Richard brought you here?" Chase snapped, his voice rising. "Because he loved you?"

"No . . . I . . . obviously not," I stuttered.

"He brought you here because you're *worthless.*"

"Excuse me?"

"Because you're a fucking *loser,* because your family *hates* you, because you're *poor,* because you have *nowhere else to fucking go*—"

"Chase—"

"Because you're just like the rest of us," he screamed.

"Stop."

"Because no one would give a shit if some rich fuck slit your throat after a fucking pool party."

"Chase, stop!"

And he did. It was as if the outburst had drained all the strength from his body. He leaned against the concrete wall and sank to the ground. Exhaustion burdened his features; his frown looked like it might slide off his face.

"Are you okay?" I asked, concerned. "I'm sorry if I—"

"Don't you get it?" His voice was a lifeless monotone. "We're all the fucking same."

"But don't you want to leave?"

Self-hatred burned in his eyes. "And go back to what?"

Chase was the last hire before me. He'd met Sandro at a sex party in the Manhattan apartment of Trent Rogers, a wealthy pornographer. The sex party was not to be used as content for his porn site—it was simply a private gathering of Trent's favorite people to fuck. Chase made the list, barely. Trent had briefly considered hiring Chase for his roster of "exclusive" talent; he'd even filmed a few "audition" videos that had been featured on Trentrogers.com. But auditioning had never been Chase's strong suit—a fact underscored by his two-year string of failed attempts to join the choruses of various Broadway musicals—and after Chase's initial lackluster performances, Trent made the executive decision to bar Chase from future videos. Still, Trent had a soft spot for poor, lost Chase, who'd grown up in foster homes and struggled with meth addiction for years. Trent looked out for him, keeping Chase in his orbit if not in his employ. Trent told Sandro this entire story on the phone when describing the guest list for the sex party. Later, after Sandro had finished fucking Chase that evening, he invited Chase to the compound for the week. Shortly thereafter, in the fall of 2008, Chase was hired.

That's when things started to change. Sandro, inspired by Trent's parties and encouraged by Richard's proclivity for bondage, began to outfit the basement with a variety of torture instruments: a rack, a sling, ball gags, whips, cuffs, ropes, chains. Once the basement was fully equipped, the orgies began. Drugs became increasingly common as well, a rote prerequisite.

"You'll get used to it, Jonah," Seb mumbled apologetically. He looked to Chase for backup, but Chase's mind was somewhere else. He sat on the floor, head between his knees, his back heaving with slow sighs.

"I don't *want* to get used to this," I told him.

"But there's nothing you can do," he insisted. "And if you keep fighting this, it's only gonna drive you crazy."

In the corner, Chase began to shake. An animal moan escaped

his lips and devolved into guttural sobs. Seb joined him on the floor, rubbing his back tenderly.

"It'll drive us *all* crazy," Seb warned as Chase shuddered in his arms.

"*Wake up,*" I snapped. "What's *crazy* is the fact we are *rotting* in this *awful fucking place* just because we're too scared or beaten down *to do something.*"

Suddenly, Sandro burst into the gym. "What the fuck is going on down here?"

Seb and Chase scrambled to their feet. I stared at the ground. Sandro circled. His face was red; the tendons on his neck bulged.

"Jonah, is there a reason you were yelling like a fucking maniac at six forty-five a.m. in *my* gym?"

"I . . . I . . . no."

He punched my rib cage and I dropped to the floor. "No what?"

"No, sir," I murmured. He slapped my face, just light enough to not leave a mark.

"Now get the fuck out."

This isn't normal, I thought, clinging to my rage like a life raft. *This isn't fucking normal.*

———

Richard's mother was coming.

"What happened to the 2003 Beaujolais?"

Richard frowned as he surveyed the assortment of wines lined up on his dining-room table. I'd been responsible for pulling tonight's selection, a task that involved multiple trips to the wine cellar as Richard anxiously changed his mind about the pairings for each course of this evening's meal. There was only one wine cellar on the compound, shared by all residents, and each household possessed its own panel of oak shelving that stored the best bottles. I'd shuttled back and forth all day, attempting to keep up with Richard's agitated whims. I'd not seen him this strung out since the opening of his play. His mother clearly fucked with his sanity.

"I . . . I'm not sure." Of course, I knew precisely what happened to the 2003 Beaujolais; Chase had puked half of it onto Sandro's floor the night of our secret party. I'd stolen just that one bottle—I never thought Richard would notice.

"Well, either we were visited by a thief with exquisite taste in French wine, or someone fucked up."

"I—"

"Who fucked up, Jonah?"

"I don't know."

"Well, we need to find out."

"Richard, come on. We have so much to do before your mother comes and—"

"And one of those things is finding out who fucked up."

"Richard—"

"*Who fucked up, Jonah?*"

"I . . . I dropped it," I blurted. This lie was less incriminating than the truth. "It shattered."

"You *dropped* it?" Richard shut his eyes and clamped his left hand to his temple.

"I'm sorry. I can just pull a similar bottle from the cellar . . ."

"There is no substitute for a 2003 Beaujolais."

"Oh, come on, Richard."

"That year was a near *perfect* grape harvest."

"Well, what do you want me to do?"

"How about booking a ticket on a fucking time machine and going back to the summer when my mother and I bought that bottle directly from a French vineyard and promised to share it together over a special occasion. Because that is the *only* thing that will satisfy my bitch of a mother on her fucking birthday."

"Richard—"

"Do you know how much that bottle cost?"

I refused to play whatever new game this was.

"I *said,* do you know how much that bottle cost?"

"No," I said, relenting.

"Two hundred dollars."

I stayed silent, afraid to respond.

"Two hundred dollars that will be added to your overall debt."

"That's not fair!"

"It's absolutely fair, Jonah," Richard said, plucking a 2007 Sancerre from the table and extending it to examine the label. "And do you know how much this cost?" Richard lifted his gaze to meet mine. I said nothing, gnawing my inner cheek, fighting back fury.

Richard threw the bottle to the ground. The Sancerre detonated, sending a network of red stains across the gray concrete — a spider-web spun with blood. "Ninety-five dollars."

"Richard, don't."

Crack. Another bottle hit the floor. "And that's seventy." *Crack.* Another bottle. *"Fifty-five."*

"*Richard* —"

Crack. Another. *"One hundred,"* he roared.

"Stop it," I screamed.

Richard stepped toward me, shoes crunching in the puddle of wine and glass that pooled between us, his face red, eyes wild. He raised another bottle in the air, clutching the neck like a baseball bat. I flinched, fearing it was headed for my face.

"Clean this up," he spat, shoving the last bottle into my arms.

The room tilted around me. Vertigo again. "But I didn't break those —"

"But you did upset me, Jonah. And because you're my butler, my happiness is your responsibility. So the way I see it, this little" — he suppressed a wave of fury — "*episode* is a failing of your overall purpose here."

"I didn't break those bottles," I repeated, conviction draining from my tone.

"It's not about *who* broke the bottles, it's about *why* they were broken. And they were broken because *you* fucked up and made me frustrated."

"I'm sorry," I murmured, clutching a chair for balance.

"Apology accepted," Richard snapped, a petulant look puckering his face. "And you don't have to look so sad. It's not a big deal."

I could feel my anger fading, eroding into apathy. Seb's hopeless face burned in my mind. *You'll get used to it, Jonah.* But I couldn't give up. I'd make another plan. Dangerous, desperate, it didn't matter. I needed hope, whatever the cost.

"I'm gonna get some air," Richard said, making his way to the door, leaving a trail of crimson footsteps.

"Okay . . ."

"And don't forget—you just added five hundred dollars to your tab."

This was the moment I began plotting Richard Shriver's murder.

16

"'HAPPY BIRTHDAY TO YOU . . .'"

Poisoning Richard was a possibility. Unfortunately, my education in chemistry had ended with a C plus in high school science, and while I could slip bleach into Richard's pinot noir, I had no clue how to create a formula that was subtle in taste and lethal in effect.

"'Happy birthday to you . . .'"

Slitting his throat was also an option. Though this would require a great deal of courage, a sense of determination I feared would vanish the minute I climbed into Richard's bed clutching one of his Williams-Sonoma butcher knives. Plus, there was the mess to consider. I hate blood.

"'Happy birthday, dear Patricia . . .'"

And then there was the problem of escape. None of the waiters knew the code to the gate; even if I did manage to successfully poison or stab or strangle Richard, I would be unable to flee.

"'Happy birthday to you.'" The diners wrapped up their flat serenade. Richard's mother frowned slightly before she blew out her candles, as if it were her birthday wish to discover us all dead when the lights came up.

Michael switched on the pendant lamp that hovered over Richard's dining table as Seb stepped forward to slice the cake. Patricia recoiled.

"Is this *coconut?*" she spat.

"Yes," Richard murmured. He was a completely different person in the presence of his mother, a mere shadow of the monster I knew. A fearful, petulant child.

"I'm *allergic* to coconut."

"Mother, you've had coconut cake every year for the past ten years."

"Yes, ten *awful* years when I was unaware of my coconut allergy, and now, when Dr. Rosenblatt has *finally* found the source of my debilitating gastrointestinal issues, you serve me coconut cake on my *birthday.*"

"I'm sorry. I didn't know," Richard whined.

"You *did* know. I told you a month ago. I called you immediately after Dr. Rosenblatt diagnosed me, so relieved was I to have solved the terrible mystery of my chronic indigestion."

"I don't think you did . . ."

"Oh, I most certainly did. Which means you forgot. Your own mother experiences a *major* medical victory and you just *forget.*"

"I'm sorry."

"No, *I'm* sorry that everyone else has to sit through this."

Patricia motioned to the stricken faces of her fellow diners. Everyone had been summoned for Richard's mother's birthday — "She's turning seventy-five, I need serious backup," he'd told each compound-mate he called that afternoon as I knelt on the floor below him, scrubbing red wine out of the concrete with a steel brush and a bucket of Clorox — and Patricia's disappointment had been the recurring theme of the meal. First it was the table settings ("Oh, Richard, you know I *abhor* this china"), then the Caesar salad ("*Far* too much lemon in this dressing, dear, I can't take another bite"), then her cocktail ("I'm impressed—there are a mere two ingredients in a gin and tonic, and your sensationally inept waitstaff still managed to ruin mine"), then her steak ("Like sawing into a leather wallet"), and now the mountain of coconut frosting that towered before her. Ironically, of all the insulting aspects of her dinner, the lack of the 2003 Beaujolais was the least important to Patricia. When Richard preemptively apologized for its absence, throwing me under the bus for breaking a bottle that was of such great sentimental value, she merely sniffed and said to Richard's crestfallen face, "Oh, that's quite all right. Truth be told, I'd completely forgotten about it."

As dinner stretched on, it became clear that Patricia was the type of woman who derived great joy from being disappointed; each of Richard's failures gave her greater power. Even though some of her comments were directed at the private chef Richard had hired or the waitstaff, it was clear that all of the barbs were meant for her son.

"Should I still serve the cake to everyone else?" Seb ventured warily.

"No," Richard snapped.

A tense silence descended as Seb swiftly removed the cake from the table. I stood in the corner of the room holding an open bottle of dessert wine, unsure if I should pour it now that dessert had been banished from the room.

It was at this juncture that you stepped in, Mace, attempting to save the evening in its final hour. "So, Richard. Sandro tells me that Meryl Streep is interested in starring in a film adaptation of *Flesh and Blood*," you said, steering the conversation into cheerier territory. "You must be very proud, Patricia."

Patricia ignored you and instead turned to Richard with a furious grimace, the same contorted expression that I'd seen on Richard's face so many times before. *So that's where he got it from,* I thought.

"Is this true?"

"Well, nothing's been solidified yet, but—"

"Answer my question, Richard. *Is this true?*"

"Yes."

"I suppose she's interested in playing the *mother.*" Patricia spat the final word like it was one of the pieces of too-tough steak she'd coughed onto her plate earlier this evening. Richard said nothing.

"Well, *is* she?"

"Yes," he admitted.

"I don't see why anyone would want to produce such a vulgar work, let alone play that dreadful role."

"Surely you don't mean that," you said, attempting to play peacekeeper but only digging yourself deeper. Patricia swiveled toward you.

"Oh, I most definitely mean it. That play is disgusting and"—she turned back to Richard—"I have made you more than aware of my opinions on the matter." Her eyes burned with rage although her tone remained staid and condescending. "I am shocked that even after hearing my perspective, you would pursue a *film adaptation* of such vile trash."

"Mother, I . . . I'm sorry. I don't have to do it—"

"Oh, but you *will*, won't you? You'll do exactly as you please, as always. With little consideration of how it might affect your mother—"

"But how *does* it affect you, Mother?" Richard fired back, finally trading meekness for anger.

"Don't press me on this subject."

"No, really. I'd like to know how it affects the great Mrs. Shriver."

"Richard, stop."

"Please, tell me, *Mumsy*. How has my little vulgar piece-of-shit play affected someone so superior?"

"*Richard, you know very well*—"

"*How does it affect you, Mother?*"

"*Because it's* about *me!*"

Her final outburst echoed through the room. No one moved. Even Charles, an expert at filling awful silences with dreadful jokes, remained tight-lipped. No one wished to fuck with Patricia.

"Well, I think we'd better retire for the evening," Ethel said finally, practically pulling Ira from his seat. "A pleasure as always, Patricia."

"Same here," Charles said, uncharacteristically sober.

"I would like to go home as well," Patricia announced, her voice wavering for the first time this evening. Ethel, Ira, and Charles all stopped in surprise.

"But Mother, it's too late to go back to the city. Just stay in the guesthouse like we planned and—"

"I *said,* I'm going home."

"Fine. I'll call Carlo and have him bring your car around."

There was something about Richard's devastated expression as he called Patricia's driver that brought vengeful joy to my heart. A taste of his ruin. I wanted more.

"Carlo will be here in ten minutes," Richard said after a hushed and tense phone conversation in the far corner of the room.

"Good," Patricia said.

"And it isn't about you," Richard whimpered. "My play."

"Good," Patricia repeated flatly.

"On the contrary, Mrs. Shriver," I interrupted, a giddy, vindictive thrill burning my spine. I wasn't sure what I was doing—my words gained a momentum that outpaced my thoughts. But the fog of fear and helplessness had finally lifted. Rage, my long-lost friend, emerged. "Richard once told me that his play was *all* about you."

A violent glare lit Richard's face. He looked like he wanted to kill me.

That's it, I thought, solving the problem of Richard's murder. *I'll say it was self-defense.*

———

"Mace, let's play my favorite game," Richard slurred.

"I don't know if I'm in the mood," you mumbled nervously.

"Oh, *come on.* You're an actor. You're *always* in the mood for more attention." Richard's drunkenness converted his attempt at flirtation into something that sounded like an accusation. He sidled up to you on the couch and licked your ear. Sandro, four martinis deep and completely passed out, snored with his head in your lap. Charles, Ira, and Ethel were long gone, all back at their respective homes, safe from the blotto aftermath of Patricia's birthday.

"C'mon, it's Daddy's favorite game," Richard cooed.

In the kitchen, tense looks passed between the waitstaff. Each waiter focused on his individual task with exaggerated attention to avoid being drawn into the scene. Michael wiped down the already sparkling table for a second time, Chase scraped the remains of leftover fillets into the trash with the slowness of a sloth, and Seb scrubbed a saucepan like his life depended on it. Perhaps it did. Clearly, my fellow servants were aware of what this game entailed and did not wish to play. I, however, was completely in the dark. It must have been a game developed before my tenure. The fear in their expressions filled me with hope. I needed a trigger, something to set Richard off. Then, with a roomful of sympathetic witnesses, I would defend myself until Richard's face was merely a stain on the concrete, something to be scoured from the floor in the morning after the coroner came to his conclusion. *Self-defense. Jonah killed Richard, but who could blame him?*

"No," you said, forceful this time.

"My *least* favorite word in the English language," Richard growled.

"I want to play," I said. You shot me a warning look. I ignored it.

"But you don't know *how*," Richard whined, his eyelids drooping, the irises underneath drifting upward.

"*Well, wake the fuck up and teach me,*" I shouted and slapped him across the face. That brought his fire back. *Challenge accepted.* You looked at me in horror. The boys in the kitchen stopped their busywork, jolted by my outburst.

"Okay, let's play, then," Richard slurred once his shock subsided. He waddled into his bedroom like a giddy, drunken child.

"Are you *crazy*," you hissed once Richard was gone.

But before I could answer, Richard was back, carrying a white-blond wig, a short, tangled bob. It looked strangely familiar, and I struggled to remember where I'd seen it before.

"Put it on," Richard barked as he threw the mess of hair at me.

I caught the wig in my fist. That's when I remembered: Richard's play. This was the wig that Richard's fictional matriarch wore in *Flesh and Blood,* the wig that bore a striking resemblance to his actual mother's hairstyle.

"Now play Mommy," Richard demanded.

"What do I—"

"He wants you to do an impression of his mother," you snapped. Your tone implied that you thought I should do the opposite—put the wig down and end this portion of the evening. But you didn't know my plan.

"Oh, I see." My body tensed. Richard stepped closer.

"Play Mommy." His sour whisper stung my nostrils.

I put the wig on. The coarse lining made my scalp itch. Beads of sweat bloomed on my forehead.

"Oh, Richard. There's *far* too much lemon in this dressing, dear, I can't take another bite," I cooed, imitating Patricia.

"You're very good at the game!" Richard laughed and clapped his hands. You and the boys looked on in terror. "Another, another!"

"I said *medium rare,* darling. Cutting this steak is like sawing into a leather wallet."

"That is perfect." Richard was laughing violently now, tears dripping from his chin.

"And you know I simply abhor this china."

"Yes, yes, good!" Richard clapped again. "Now tell me that you love me, Mommy."

"Oh, darling, but I *don't* love you."

His face darkened. "I *said,* tell me you love me."

"But then I'd be *lying.*"

Richard barreled at me, grabbed my face.

"Richard, stop," Chase shouted from the kitchen.

"Tell me . . ." Richard growled, forcing a kiss on me mid-phrase. He pushed his tongue into my mouth, white strands from the wig mixing with spit. *That you love me.*

"I'm afraid you just made a common mistake, son."

"Tell me you love me."

"I just *fucked* you, dear. Not the same thing."

And that's when Richard punched me.

I dropped to the ground, hitting my head on the coffee table.

Black.

17

WHEN I REGAINED CONSCIOUSNESS, I was looking at myself. For a brief, disorienting moment, I thought you were me, Mace. I winced from my position on Richard's rug as a wave of pain shot through my skull. There I was, or, rather, there *you* were, looking like me, looking at me, tears staining your cheeks as Richard pressed your face against the floor and forced himself inside you.

It was the wig that threw me. The wig I'd been wearing moments before was now on your head, its tendrils obscuring your face, allowing me to imagine myself in your position. All animosity I'd felt toward you vanished. We were the same. It could've been either of us wearing that wig, pinned to the floor.

It was difficult to say how much time had passed since I'd lost consciousness. The waitstaff had vanished, likely ordered out of the room by Richard. Sandro was still passed out, deadweight sinking into the couch above me.

You would be the only witness.

I rose from the carpet, careful not to make a sound. Silence filled the room, unbroken save for an occasional grunt from Richard or sob from you. I stepped slowly toward the wall covered in a collage of artworks. I selected Richard's favorite—the George Condo painting depicting a grotesque orgy, with distorted bodies locked in naked chaos, their faces staring straight at the viewer—and removed it from the wall. Richard once boasted that the painting had cost him three hundred thousand dollars, a sum that came to mind as I held my makeshift weapon. Richard's demise would be appropriately expensive.

The frame was heavy and gold, with sharp corners. My biceps strained under its weight as I carried the canvas silently across the room. Richard knelt on the ground, completely naked, hunched above your motionless body. His fleshy back jiggled with each thrust. You were still largely clothed, your pants bunched around your knees. I trod lightly, approaching Richard from behind. I raised the canvas far above my head, fixing my stare on the back of his skull, imagining the moment I would split it open with the gilded edge of the Condo. I wanted to batter him senseless. Erase him from this earth.

But God had other plans for me.

I brought the painting down, aiming for Richard's skull, directing the edge of the frame like a dagger. Richard detected my presence and jerked to the side, so I merely clipped him in the shoulder, failing to deliver a fatal blow. He screamed and swiped at the painting, sending it clattering to the ground.

"*What the fuck,*" he yelled, scrambling to his feet. He clutched his bleeding shoulder. You curled into a ball on the rug, shaking in terror.

We all froze for a brief, terrible moment—you on the floor, Richard above you, me across from Richard. It was clear that this moment represented a threshold; our lives would be forever changed once we passed through.

And then Richard screamed, an animalistic howl that echoed through the room as he charged in my direction, blood streaming down his chest, dick bouncing between his legs, his gut swinging with every drunken stagger. I ran out of his house, across the gravel drive, into the wildflower field. Scamp appeared in the brush. He barked and nipped and circled. I looked back and there was Richard, bounding through the grass behind me, quickly gaining speed as I kicked the dog out of my way. I was headed for the pool house, uncertain of what I'd do when I got there, but it was at least a destination, one that would hopefully supply new options for ending this nasty game. Mr. Keller in the Pool House with the Gardening Shears. I looked back again and there you were, trailing behind Richard, the last float in our grim parade.

Finally, the pool. My feet slapped against concrete as I rushed around the perimeter of the water, surprised to find it glowing. Seb must've neglected his nightly duties and forgotten to turn off the pool lights. I turned to discover you and Richard struggling on the deck, lit from below by the teal glimmer of the water. Odd shadows rippled across your face as you attempted to hold him back. I reached the pool house, rushed inside, and flipped on the fluorescents. I squinted under the harsh glare and scanned the room, searching for a weapon.

"Jonah, watch out!"

But your scream came too late. Richard was already tackling me to the ground. I struggled under his naked body as he strangled me. Scamp rushed into the shed, barking and barking. But Richard was never one to let something stand between him and the thing he wanted.

Suddenly, you appeared above Richard. Seb was there too — perhaps he had heard shouting; perhaps he had remembered the pool lights. The two of you grabbed Richard's shoulders and pulled him off me. Richard reared upward. You and Seb retreated from the shed and backed onto the pool deck. Richard stormed toward you, and Scamp circled, unrelenting in his furious yapping.

"Shut up," you screamed at the dog, diverting your focus from Richard to Scamp for no more than two seconds. Just enough time for Richard to backhand your face.

Richard's slap sent you sailing into Seb, who then staggered back and tripped over Scamp. Seb flailed his arms as he fell, hitting his head on a corner of the pool. Seb's skull emitted a sick, wet crack when it struck the concrete. He slid into the glowing water, unconscious. We stood there in shock, considering his silhouette as it drifted, a stream of blood coursing around it.

You jumped in, Mace, and I followed. We dragged his body from the water. Richard looked on in horror.

"He's still breathing," you shouted. We knelt by his side, fully clothed and dripping wet. Chlorine stung my eyes and mixed with my tears.

"He can't die here." Richard's rage morphed into fear.

"We need to call an ambulance!" I shouted.

"He can't die *here*," Richard repeated. Implying Seb *could* die, just not on his property.

"It'll take forever for an ambulance to get out here," you said. "We need to take him ourselves."

"He can't die here."

"Grab his shoulders!" you yelled to me. "I got his legs."

We hefted Seb's unconscious body into the air and carried him across the wildflower field. Richard trailed behind.

"You were *never* here, understand?" Richard panted, his hysteria rising. "I don't want this coming back to me."

"It won't," you said, attempting to placate Richard.

"This never happened, you were never here, you found him in a ditch on the side of the road, anywhere but on *my compound*."

"Here—lay him down in the back seat," you said as we arrived at Richard's BMW.

"This can't be happening, this can't be happening." Richard spiraled into panic. "Do you know what something like this could do to me?"

"The keys," you barked at Richard, who stared back blankly. *"Give me your fucking keys."*

Moments later, we were speeding down the gravel drive—you at the wheel, me in the passenger seat, Seb's crumpled body in the back. We reached the gate and a terrifying realization crossed my mind.

"I don't know the code," I said as we pulled up to the call box. "Do you?"

Pity darkened your face. "Yes." You sighed. "Zero, eight, sixteen."

Today's date?

I punched the numbers into the box. Fresh indignation coursed through my body. There it was—Richard's code finally cracked, the answer so obvious, so simple: his mother's birthday.

The gate buzzed. We were free.

———

Later, after we'd hauled Seb's unconscious body onto the concrete outside the emergency room, after we'd flagged down a nurse, after she'd checked his vital signs and asked for information about what happened, after we'd endured her unconvinced response to our foggy answer, after she'd said she'd be right back with help, you turned to me and changed the course of my life.

"Here," you said, handing me a fistful of twenties. "Take it."

I dumbly accepted the bills. "What do you want me to do?"

"Run," you replied.

18

"YOU CAN'T SLEEP HERE."

A gentle kick to my thigh roused me. I looked up to discover a frowning Long Island Rail Road attendant, a gaunt, redheaded giant who looked about as tired as I felt after having trekked the two miles from the Southampton Hospital with no idea where I was going, certain only that I needed to go somewhere. I'd ultimately selected the train station and attempted to sleep on the platform. I drifted in and out of consciousness, my mind replaying terrifying flashbacks. *I'll choose a destination in the morning,* I told myself, shivering from my position between the tracks, unsure if my shudders were spurred by the unseasonably cold night or by the shock of freedom.

"C'mon, let's go," the attendant barked.

"Sorry, I—I just fell asleep."

"There's a shelter in East Hampton. Sleep there."

"I'm not homeless," I said. It seemed absurd that I needed to articulate that, and yet as I spoke, I realized that I *was,* in fact, homeless. I had nowhere to go. No apartment, no possessions, no clothing except for the bloodstained jeans and T-shirt I'd slept in, no money except for the two hundred dollars that you'd pressed into my fist outside the emergency room—a wad of bills I'd gripped anxiously in my pocket all night long, fearing someone would steal my only hope of survival.

"I'm just waiting for the train," I insisted as I rose to my feet, brushing dirt from my body.

"Nothing's coming for another hour," the attendant said, softening. He was clearly too exhausted to invest any more energy on this encounter now that he'd deemed me nonthreatening. "Just stop sleeping on the ground, okay?"

"Okay," I mumbled, sitting on a bench as the attendant limped away.

I faced the tracks, waiting—for what, I didn't know. An hour later, a train arrived. I boarded it with no destination in mind, no luggage, nothing but the fear in my heart. I found a seat as the train pulled away. The scenery outside my window started to blur. I fantasized that the ride would last forever, that I'd remain in this limbo, speeding nowhere fast, hurtling through time and space eternally, never facing the consequences of a destination.

———

When she saw me, my mother shrieked as if she'd seen a ghost. Her son, the prodigal phantom, home at last to rattle some chains in the attic. To remind her of the past.

"Jonah!" she cried, that one word containing millions of questions. But I had no intention of answering them. All I wanted was a shower, a meal, and a bed. I'd dreamed of Richard on the train ride; each time I managed to drift to sleep in my seat, his face would appear and his hands would wrap around my neck and I'd jolt awake, gasping for air, eliciting concerned stares from my fellow passengers.

I was betting big on this trip home, spending the majority of my limited resources on the Amtrak ticket from New York to Chicago, then the Greyhound ticket from Chicago to Lake Bluff. I hadn't called my mother ahead of time—whenever I imagined punching her number into a pay phone, my chest tightened in panic. There was a strong possibility she would've told me not to come home. I had no choice but to show up on her doorstep unannounced.

"Come in," she said after a beat. A familiar claustrophobia overwhelmed my senses. I was greeted by the too-large leather sectional, an artifact from my childhood, back when we were a family, and my father was still my father, back when we still lived in the gated community in our massive McMansion. The leather sofa was the one piece of furniture my mother refused to relinquish in the move, and it now dominated her tiny apartment. It was where I'd slept while my family collapsed around me, before I escaped to grad school.

My mother was twenty pounds thinner, her ruddy cheeks replaced by sallow swaths of skin that hung from protruding cheekbones. Her hair—previously light brown and shoulder-length—now stretched to the middle of her back in a cascade of blinding white curls. Her shoulders were hunched, like they were apologizing for her presence. But it was her wild eyes that shocked me the most—I didn't recognize the woman behind them. Her gaze had grown feral.

"What are you doing here?" she asked once we were sitting at her small kitchen table.

"I . . . I need to lie down for a bit," I said, avoiding her question, beyond exhausted.

"You can nap in my bed if you like," she offered. "I know how much you hated that couch."

Moments later, I drifted to sleep tucked into my mother's sheets. Her smell hadn't changed; that comforting rosewater scent was still on her linens. I slept soundly at last. That evening, I was roused by another comforting aroma from my childhood: my mother's macaroni and cheese.

When I emerged from the bedroom, the skittish stranger who'd greeted me at the door was gone, replaced by the mother I remembered—a familiar light had returned to her eyes. This was the woman who'd raised me, who'd loved me so hard it hurt.

"I made your favorite," she said, placing a steaming casserole dish on the counter.

"Thank you," I replied, sitting at the table.

We ate in silence, neither of us wanting to rupture this Rockwellian portrait of domestic normality: a mother serving her son his favorite dish. A pleasant trip home.

We maintained that silence for a week. My mother went to work, still answering calls at the dentist's office, still booking root canals for the gossiping townsfolk scandalized by the scorned preacher's wife, the Fallen Woman of Lake Bluff. I had no desire to confront people from my past so I spent most days inside, watching television. My favorite show was *Snapped,* the trashy, true-crime documentaries they marathoned on the Oxygen network. Each episode featured the story of a different female felon—typically a woman who'd been abused or cheated on or both, a woman who wanted revenge, a woman whose rage had driven her to madness. These women's lives were incredibly tragic, but the trauma was diluted by camp—B-movie horror soundtracks, low-budget reenactments, and melodramatic interviews with dumbfounded locals who "never imagined that such a sweet girl could do something like this." I'd binge episode after episode, imagining my own story rendered with such crudeness, transformed into trash, something for people to eat ice cream to while frozen on the couch, something that meant nothing.

I always rooted for the murderers.

Every day when my mother returned from work, I'd switch off the television and we'd reenact our performance of domesticity. Dinner was always the same, always macaroni and cheese. We never questioned the repetition; I never asked for a different meal, nor did my mother offer one. We were scared to alter one detail, as if a single false move could cause the entire act to collapse. I thought we could maybe continue this way forever, locked in a living lie. But one day, over yet another macaroni dinner, I burst into tears.

"Jonah . . ." she whispered, placing her hand on mine. Her touch was delicate, like she was caressing something fragile. "Jonah, what's wrong?"

I told her everything, finally shattering as she'd feared I would. Her broken boy, in pieces again.

It was then I knew my visit had come to an end. I needed to leave before reality came rushing back.

Before someone got hurt.

———————

She wanted me to go back to therapy. She wanted me to see Doctor Jim again. She was afraid for my soul. She felt that there was still hope—even after everything that had happened—because God had delivered me to her doorstep. God had brought me back for a reason. We could maybe try a sleepaway program, one of those conversion-therapy camps she'd heard about. A kid in town, the Mullen boy, had gone to one for a year, a whole painful year, but it had worked and he'd come back changed and he was now married to a woman and they had a child and if God had shown such grace to the Mullen boy then surely there was hope for me. Yes, conversion-therapy camp was the ticket, my mother told me just minutes after I'd related the awful events of my summer. I'd sobbed in her arms and told her how Richard had raped me. She told me that everything was going to be okay, that we'd rescue me from Satan's grip, we'd save me from myself. And the camp was only about thirty miles away, so she'd visit me every weekend. We wouldn't let my sin pull us apart again, we were stronger than that, we had God's love, and God's love would guide us through.

"I named you Jonah for a reason. Yes, Jonah was my idea. Not your father's. He can—and will—rot in hell," she said as I wept in her embrace. "I named you Jonah after my favorite person from the Bible. All that time in the belly of the whale. But he survived and washed up on the shores of Nineveh. God gave Jonah a second chance. Just like you're getting one now. We'll get through this, my sweet baby boy. I love you."

Later that night, as my mother slept, I left for good.

———

It took me three days and six Greyhounds to get back to New York. I'd stolen four hundred dollars from my mother's Rapture box, a small shoebox containing cash she'd squirreled away in case of apocalyptic emergency, grocery money for when the battle of Armageddon was finally unleashed by the Antichrist. My bus ticket cost me one hundred and fifty dollars, which left me only two hundred and fifty dollars to reestablish myself in the city. The sum was terrifyingly small. But I knew of a cheap hostel in Bushwick. It was a shithole with shared rooms, but it cost forty bucks a night. If I spent ten dollars a day on bodega food, if I jumped turnstiles to avoid buying a MetroCard, I could limit my spending to fifty dollars a day. That gave me five days of food and shelter before my cash ran out.

Five days to find a job.

I spent those five days looking for a gig waiting tables, stopping at every restaurant I saw, dropping off my hostel-printed résumé (a favor I'd flirted out of Gordy, the front-desk clerk, a sad, defeated gay man who allowed me to use their printer for free). Hosts and hostesses invariably looked at me with pity and disgust as I explained to each of them that the phone number listed on my résumé was actually the pay phone at the youth hostel where I resided, and if they wished to reach me, they'd need to call between the hours of six p.m. and eight p.m., when I'd be back at the hostel, waiting. They all promised they'd call if something opened up.

No one called.

As each day passed, my desperation grew. I managed to squeeze one extra night out of Gordy at the hostel, a thank-you for sucking him off in the employee restroom. But after that, I was on my own. On my seventh day back in New York, I emerged from the hostel carrying the small backpack I'd poached from my mother's closet and marched bravely into the early-September afternoon.

I knew what I needed to do.

"I had a feeling you'd be back," Mommy said, a triumphant smirk lighting his face as I walked through the doors of Perdition. "Things didn't work out with your daddy, I take it?"

"Not quite," I muttered.

"Let me guess—you want your job back?"

"I was wondering if you had any open positions."

"Well, that depends. Do you have any apologies to offer me?"

I paused for a moment, hate festering in my stomach. "I'm sorry, Brett."

"Aww, apology accepted." He sneered, slapped my butt. "You're lucky your ass is still tight."

I slept on a park bench that night, using my backpack as a pillow. I started work the next day.

————

YOUR TIME IS ALMOST UP.

PAY FOR ANOTHER SESSION?

I never have more cash to give, so this is when I always stop—when my money runs out. I don't have a computer, so I work at the ratty internet café down the street from the restaurant. I write my pages, e-mail them to myself, then leave when my minutes are up. I find the time limit comforting; I'm allowed to think about this past summer for only one hour a day.

But in this document, I've recorded it all.

I need to tell the story of what happened to us. Even if the only person listening is me. So here it is, a journal, like the one I kept as a teen. A private space to store my pain. Or maybe this is really a letter to you, Mace, my unlikely savior. A message of gratitude. Regardless, I can tell the truth in these pages. The other aspects of my life have become a well-rehearsed lie. The restaurant is unchanged, as if time stopped when I vanished into my summer fantasy and resumed when I returned. My old life, waiting for me.

If only I could just pick up where I left off. Forget about the compound. Reading this over, tracking the pitiful arc from beginning to end, I'm filled with self-loathing. How did I allow myself to be so degraded? So manipulated? So used? *What the fuck is wrong with me?* I want to take these pages and delete them. Drag them to the trash.

I want my history to die in this document.

But I know it can't. My story is entangled with so many others'. What will happen to the rest of those boys? What will happen to you, Mace? I was so cruel to you that night you discovered our party at Sandro's. But what happened this summer wasn't your fault. So why did I act like it was?

The guilt weighs on my chest. Robs me of sleep.

You saved my life. I would do anything to repay you. Anything you ask.

But where have you gone?

2017

19

I SAW IT on TMZ, the video of you emerging from a Denny's. Your left eye pink with blood, skin vacuum-sealed to your skull, face a starved outline of its former, fatter shape. Cheeks mottled with strange sores. Knuckles bursting from your fight with the cashier over his refusal to give you one hundred individual packets of honey. What you needed them for, you never said. You probably didn't need them at all, just wanted someone to pull the trigger on all that rage. Maybe you were looking for a fight, determined to act out a luke-warm spaghetti Western at a fast-food joint in Burbank, praying that someone, anyone, would pay attention—something that hadn't happened in years. And the world did start paying attention, Mace —it still is. People are watching you on their iPhones and laptops. They're watching you march out onto the pavement and stumble into the sunlight, your bones straining against skin. Your skeleton is an open secret—death right under the surface.

"He was, after all, a *former child star*," reporters reminded us hourly, the phrase implying a generally applicable horror, as if child stardom were a disease that produced the same symptoms every time. Late-night hosts got in on the action too, mining your story for com-peting punch lines. "It's Mace's Last Supper," one host joked, Pho-toshopping your deranged visage onto the body of Jesus at a burger joint. Even the battered Denny's cashier came forward to comment on his violent brush with stardom and his heroic denial of your out-size sweetener request. "We have a *five-packet limit,*" the employee intoned with valiance on the evening news, a sound bite that was im-mediately auto-tuned and mixed into a viral hip-hop anthem that then inspired the "Five-Packet Limit" dance challenge in which kids around the country filmed themselves pouring honey packets onto their asses while twerking to the song. I spent hours watching those videos on YouTube, my nausea growing, disgusted by the distance between your experience and that of the sorority girl in Racine, for example, who bravely accepted the dance challenge from "Kate and Jess," her "two BFFs," who "knew she was gonna go viral with this one." I doubt she even knew who you were.

Much was made of the dress. That thin white baby-doll gown, tattered and dirtied and hanging loosely from your emaciated frame. Your chest partially exposed, the outline of your ribs heaving with every breath. An op-ed in the *Daily Beast* said it was more grunge than drag, defending your sartorial choice by citing history—Kurt Cobain did it; you were just referencing him—and claimed that your *rock-star style* was a chic throwback to simpler times. We should cel-ebrate your *unfiltered attitude* in an era of *hypersensitivity online,* the author argued, which triggered a hypersensitive online backlash, complete with hot takes and multipart Twitter rants about the ar-ticle's lack of sensitivity surrounding drug abuse and depression and the dangers of glamorizing addiction while ignoring mental illness.

The debate raged on for a week, but I ignored it, knowing bet-ter than to expect answers from the internet. I was more concerned with your wig—that white-blond bob. The sight of it made me sick, a sickness I'd worked so long to suppress.

I'd worn that wig once myself, of course. On the night you saved me.

I can't believe you kept it.

———

Things intensified this morning.

"Have you seen that video of, uh, what's his name? Mike? Mace? That child star. The one who broke down at a Denny's."

Time stopped. My body tensed. "No . . . I . . . what video?"

"It's everywhere. You really haven't seen it?" Jeff asked, sitting on the edge of my desk. "He's, like, in methed-out drag screaming in a Denny's parking lot. It's *hilarious*."

"Nope, haven't seen it," I lied. The room started to spin.

"It's, like, if *I* was going to have my child-star-meltdown moment, I would at least pick a *good* fast-food chain. Has he not heard of In-N-Out?"

Someone somewhere once lied to Jeff and told him that he was funny. One of my responsibilities as his employee is to uphold this delusion. Jeff is my editor at the *Profile,* the popular entertainment-news site—or "a thinking man's *Us Weekly*," as I prefer to call it. After three years of Jeff's "jokes," I have perfected my fake laugh. But I couldn't muster it today.

"Anyway, I thought it might be a good news peg for a long-form piece tracking the history-slash-psychology of child-star meltdowns. Would you be down to write something?"

"I don't think so."

"Um, may I ask *why?*"

"Aren't child-star breakdowns well-trod territory? I'm sure there are about eleven thousand think pieces on this very topic already."

"But none have been written by Jonah Keller. Come on, dude. People look to you for this type of stuff and—"

"*I'm not fucking doing it, Jeff,*" I snapped. Jeff jumped off my desk like I might hit him.

"Jesus, bud. You on your gay period again?"

My "gay period" was typically invoked in times of conflict. Jeff mistakenly assumed that his "edgy humor" had the power to defuse any tension. In reality, it whittled my patience down to an impercep-tible nub.

"I've got enough on my plate as it is." I sighed. "Please find someone else?"

I was hired at the *Profile* in 2014, three years after your trial. I was
eager to start anew, desperate for a fresh identity divorced from my
horrific past. I began as a staff writer but was quickly promoted because I churned out celebrity profiles and movie reviews and cultural
commentary with impressive speed, numbing residual trauma by
working late into the evening and straight through weekends. I developed two identities: the public Jonah—a Twitter-verified "name"
in entertainment journalism—and the private Jonah, the man with
the awful secret who needed whiskey and Xanax to sleep, the man
who woke up screaming nightly, the man ravaged by so much misery
that there were days he couldn't go into the office, days when panic
attacked his nervous system and made his limbs ache and his mind
spin and rendered his body immobile.

"Eh, maybe I'll just toss it out," Jeff said, sulking. His delicate
ego had once again been bruised. "It's a lame idea."

"Whatever you think is best."

"Besides, isn't this Mace kid, like, evil anyway? I think he was the
one that lied about getting raped. For career revenge or something."

My chest seized. A flash of you in the sling. In the basement.

"He probably deserves all this shit."

"Probably," I echoed, my voice dry and small and distant.

———

I bolted from work early. Took the stairs instead of the elevator,
dreading even a moment of stillness, and pushed myself out into the
busy Manhattan streets. I walked the three miles home. It was a way
to occupy my time, expend the adrenaline flowing through my body.
As I raced down Third Avenue, I saw flashes of Richard, felt his hands
on my neck, heard his laughter, smelled the scent of sex and blood on
his body. I stopped in Union Square and collapsed on a park bench.

My phone vibrated.

It was you.

Or, rather, a notification about you. I've set a Google alert for your name.

Panic coursed through me as I clicked the article link.

You were safe. Checked into a rehab facility in Albuquerque, New Mexico. I stretched out on the park bench, closed my eyes. Tried to calm down, slow my breath, steady my pulse. I gave up on God ages ago, yet something like a prayer drifted through my thoughts. A desire to connect with an entity that could make sense of our history, our hell. Or maybe I simply wanted to talk to you.

You have a choice to make.

It's one I've had to make countless times since that summer.

I pray you choose life.

———

Back at my apartment, where I'm writing this now, I find myself fixated on our past.

I swear, I only wanted to help. When you reached out to me in the fall of 2011 and asked me to be a witness in your civil trial, I thought, *Yes, this is where we get our revenge.*

"The defense will try anything to discredit you," your lawyer warned me during one of our prep sessions. "They'll call you a liar, a criminal, a gold digger, a whore. They'll challenge your every memory, pounce on the slightest inconsistency."

But he didn't warn me about the things they'd do outside the courtroom.

At the time, I lived in an illegally converted warehouse on a deserted block that bordered the Brooklyn Navy Yard. Occasionally, massive trucks parked outside the neighboring factory. Other than that, the street was always empty.

Until the car started showing up.

A black Mercedes. With tinted windows.

It parked on my block for three weeks straight during the days leading up to the trial. When I went to meet with your lawyer, it was there. When I went to work at the restaurant, it was there. When I came home from my shifts at midnight, it was there. Shining its high beams in my face. Every time I left or returned to my apartment, it was there.

It's nothing, I tried to convince myself. *No one.*

Meanwhile, prep sessions with your lawyer intensified. I would break down sobbing as we rehearsed for cross-examination. He'd pretend to be the defense, launching rapid-fire attacks, picking apart every detail of my trauma. Though he'd comfort me afterward, I could detect his trepidation. It was essential that my testimony seemed credible. So I manned up, put on a brave face, cried *before* our meetings. I didn't tell him about the car parked outside my house, because I didn't want to upset him. This case felt so fragile, my own sanity so tenuous, that I worried the additional stress would cause everything to collapse.

Ultimately, your lawyer decided I was strong enough to take the stand, and I—well, I didn't decide anything, preferring to let others dictate my fate. I was paralyzed by mounting anxiety and the realization that soon my secret past would be public knowledge, that the entire world would be judging me. The truth didn't matter—my performance did.

The day of the trial arrived. I left my building and discovered a dead cat by my doorstep. Its body was a pulp of blood and bones and fur. Denial kicked in—my neighborhood was industrial, untended, feral-cat fights weren't uncommon, and it wasn't directly on my doorstep but two feet to the left. I took a deep breath and looked up.

There was a man standing in front of me.

He was white, late fifties, with a bulbous gut and bearded jowls. A cigarette burned between his lips. He leaned against the Mercedes that had been parked outside my apartment for the past three weeks. Fear shot through me. I nodded at him—he didn't nod back. Didn't even shift his expression or ash his cigarette.

"Meow," he whispered. I ran all the way to the train.

For the rest of the day, all I could see was that rotting carcass. Flashes hit me as I entered the courthouse, as I dodged reporters, as I spent hours waiting to testify, as I opened the door to the courtroom. As I ruined your life with my lies.

I rode the train home after the trial, convulsing with sobs. Strangers turned away, moved their seats. I stumbled out at my stop, pulse pounding as I approached my building.

The car was still there.

I almost collapsed on the pavement. Would Richard really keep torturing me? Even after I'd betrayed you? Would I be followed forever?

Inside my apartment, I sat down at my computer. I opened the document I'd started in that internet café back in 2009, after that awful summer. I hoped it would provide some answers, but all it did was raise more questions. How could I have ruined your one chance for justice? After all we'd been through? How could I have been so weak?

I started adding to that document. I realized I was writing to you — searching for clarity, searching for forgiveness. I wrote down what happened at the trial, how I'd lied on the stand. All the things I wished I'd said to you in that courtroom. When I was finished, I looked out the window.

The Mercedes was gone.

I shut my computer. No more writing. No more processing. This chapter was closed, and I would never open it again. I would lock these memories away in a file on my computer. Let them fade like a nightmare.

Let them vanish like the car.

————

But after I saw you on TMZ, I reopened this file.

One trigger is all it took.

I'm still not sure what to call this document. At times, it feels like a diary, a secret record of a truth I'm too terrified to share with anyone. Other times, it feels like a memoir, a cautionary tale to sell to the masses. And sometimes it's my therapy substitute, a way to purge the suicidal thoughts, the dark images that haunt my sleep. Even if I'm unsure what to call this work, I know the reason I always return to it: my guilt.

In 2010, about a year prior to the trial and about six months after my escape, you were fired from Sandro's superhero movie and replaced with another actor. Rumors appeared in the trades about how you were "difficult" on set, how you would scream at Sandro in front of the entire cast and crew. You gained a reputation as a diva, though I knew the true reason for your outbursts. The same rage burned in my brain.

Your failed trial fit perfectly into the narrative the press had already created with your firing from Sandro's movie. You wanted someone to blame, and so you blamed Richard and Sandro and Ira and Charles, the men you'd formerly praised as your "mentors." You made up awful stories about them to ruin them, to rob them of their money now that you were no longer capable of making your own.

Richard was acquitted on all counts of rape, aggravated sexual assault, and human trafficking. My false testimony was the seed of doubt that allowed him to continue working completely unscathed. The trial was the first in what was supposed to have been a series of four, with cases brought against Charles, Ira, and Sandro as well. But as your credibility crumbled in the media, your lawyer withdrew the remaining cases.

It was all my fault.

Run, you said, and I did. *Run,* you said and handed me cash for my escape. *Run,* you said and stayed to endure whatever torture awaited you back at the compound.

Run, you said, and I repaid you by ruining your life.

Can you ever forgive me?

20

"THANK YOU for speaking with me, Cameron."

"You promise you won't use my name?"

"We're gonna use an alias. Like I told you in my e-mail."

"I just feel weird about everybody knowing this happened. I mean, I've told my parents and stuff. And my therapist. But not—"

Cameron's reedy tenor came to a nervous halt. I waited on the line, not wanting to push him. His breathing became heavier, gave way to muffled sobs.

"—not anyone else," Cameron gasped out.

"I wanna be really sensitive here. If you don't feel comfortable telling your story—"

"No. I want to talk to you."

"Okay. Just let me know if you ever need to stop, if it's too much."

"I fucking hate him," Cameron spat. "Let's start there."

In many ways, Cameron reminds me of you, Mace. He was also a child actor, though he has since abandoned that career path to pursue a nursing degree at UCLA. *I want to help people,* he told me via e-mail when I inquired about his reasons for abandoning show business. *I want to ease their pain.*

But nursing was not the focus of our phone call this afternoon. Cameron had additional reasons for leaving the entertainment industry, reasons I hoped would serve as the foundation for an article I was writing about Doug Sheffield, famed agent to a roster of A-list child stars. Doug had, over the years, raped and assaulted many of his underage male clients.

"It was four years ago," Cameron continued. "So I was, like, fifteen? And Doug wanted to represent me. He took me out to dinner. I told my mom I wanted to go by myself 'cause I was a teenager and I didn't want my mom tagging along."

"And what happened at dinner?"

"He ordered a glass of wine for himself but let me drink it. And then he ordered another one for me. And another one. And then he said we could keep hanging out back at his place, that his clients were also his best friends and they all liked hanging out at his place. He said he had the new Grand Theft Auto. We could go play video games and have a few more drinks . . ."

Cameron's story was just one in a series of similar accounts I'd heard this week. I'd been tasked with covering stories of sexual predators for our website and rushing them to publication. The reason for the sudden deluge of assignments at the *Profile:* Harvey Weinstein. I'd grown so sick of typing his name. The accounts of these women stoked a wild rage within me.

But underneath that fury was another, less assured feeling, one that dovetailed with a newfound paranoia. I guess you could call it dread, though that seems too trivial. Waves of vertigo attacked my body; I rushed to the office bathroom for jags of muffled, snotglazed sobbing. I avoided even the slightest of workplace *hello*s out of fear that bloodshot eyes would betray my secret.

Our stories will resurface, Mace, regardless of whether we want them to or not. There were too many witnesses, too many rumors, too many boys that summer. It will all come out—and what happens when it does?

"I went back to his place. He poured me some red wine in a regular drinking glass. Filled it all the way to the top. I drank some

more and the room started to go black and that's where things get
blurry . . ."

"Just tell me to the best of your memory what happened."

Of course, you'd already attempted to shine a public light on the
events of that summer. Your 2011 lawsuit against Richard was ahead
of its time. I can't shake the image of you sitting in that courtroom
as I delivered the testimony that sealed your fate.

"I can trust you, right?" Cameron asked.

"You can trust me."

———

"We have to be the first to break the Doug Sheffield story," Jeff
barked after I briefed him on my call with Cameron. "We've been
eating shit on sexual-misconduct stories this week, picking up scraps
from every other site on the internet. We are supposed to be a *leader*
in the entertainment news space, but as far as I can tell, we're just
following everyone else."

"I've got the entire story lined up, but none of my sources are
willing to reveal their identities. We can still publish with aliases —"

"A piece that doesn't name at least one source is worthless. I've
heard that Lindsay Gardin at *New York* has at least three sources on
the record for *her* Doug Sheffield article."

"Well, I don't know what to tell you."

"Have you heard the term *pivot to video*?"

I rolled my eyes. "Of course I have."

"Well, in about one month the *Profile* is making that pivot, and
about a quarter of the editorial staff is gonna be laid off to make
room for a new video team. Now — you're one of my favorite writers here, and I would hate to see you go. But moving forward, I'm
gonna need people who can prove their worth."

I stared at Jeff, astonished. He looked drained from the stress of
the impending layoffs. He sighed, softening. "Just get me *one* name.
Please."

And so I placed a second call to the nineteen-year-old nursing student and appealed to his previously stated desire to help people. I assured him that coming forward in the article and letting me use his name would be a way for him to touch the hearts and souls of a great many more than he could ever hope to reach in the entirety of his nursing career.

"But what about me? Am I gonna be okay?"

"What do you mean?" I winced.

"Like, after the piece comes out. Are people gonna . . . mess with me online?"

"That's always a risk, of course. But you're doing an incredibly brave thing—a lot of people are going to be very proud of you. You'll have so much support."

"Okay. Use my name."

"You sure?"

"I'm sure. And thanks for everything, Jonah. I can't tell you how much our conversations mean to me."

I hung up the phone and burst into tears.

Despite my assurances, I knew this kid had a lot to worry about. I could catalog a comprehensive list of what might haunt him for the rest of his life, how his feelings would likely intensify once his story was released into the unpredictable waters of the Twitterverse as chum for verified sharks. Catharsis was possible, but so was further trauma, and when Cameron saw his name in print—when the public eye twitched in his direction—I would not be around to find out which of these feelings surged in his heart.

I placed Cameron's name in my article and sent it to my editor.

I prayed this boy was stronger than me.

———

Sleep is impossible despite the fact that I've finished the wine bottle on my nightstand. I spend hours in bed with my phone, scrolling endlessly in the dark, my face illuminated by the screen.

Searching for you.

I don't know what I'm hoping to find. News of your improve-ment, I suppose. Though if I'm being honest, I'm also hoping for news of my own absolution. A public statement from you forgiv-ing our history and the lies I told at the trial. It's an absurd fantasy, of course—that my words have reached you via some sort of tele-pathic channel.

But all I find is evidence of my guilt. Like the 2011 op-ed from the *Wall Street Journal* I discovered at four in the morning, buried in the eleventh page of Google search results for your name, under piles of headlines about your recent meltdown. It was published dur-ing your lawsuit against Richard, and its main thesis was that your accusations of rape were absurd because it was clear that the young men who maneuvered themselves into Richard's orbit all possessed the same duplicitous motives: to exploit his wealth and fame. The author argued that the trial was nothing more than the final chap-ter in a yearslong "shakedown." My own testimony was used as the primary evidence of the columnist's theory: *If Jonah Keller—a young man with nothing to gain—says that the claims are baseless, then how much credence can we really give to Mace Miller, a bitter, washed-up star looking for a final payday? Mr. Miller claims there was a ring of abuse, multiple victims. Why, then, did none of these men testify?*

Because they were boys with ugly pasts. Questionable characters with histories of substance abuse, broken families, sex work, and desperate ambitions to be in show business. It was a cruel irony— the vulnerabilities that made these boys perfect targets for Richard and company were the same vulnerabilities that destroyed their cred-ibility as witnesses in a court of law. *As much as I am sympathetic to Chase's plight,* your lawyer said to you during one of our meetings, *I cannot, if you wish to have any chance of winning this thing, call a porn star who has a meth addiction to the witness stand.* Michael wasn't an option either; he was homeless, living in a queer-youth

shelter in Brooklyn. Seb was in rehab. And Evan was still missing—
he had no social media profiles, no family, no evidence of his presence on earth.

No one will believe them, your lawyer said. *But thank God we
have Jonah.*

I was cast as the wholesome Midwestern boy with a preacher father and a bright future. It was bullshit, but it was what your lawyer
needed and so I agreed to play the part.

It backfired. From the same *Wall Street Journal* piece: *Jonah
Keller, the preacher's son who could not ignore his strong moral
compass, bravely spoke his truth and brought Richard Shriver's un-
warranted nightmare to an end.*

Dig deep enough and you'll find more articles just like this one.

How long until someone else finds them?

———

A week has passed since I published my exposé of Doug Sheffield.

I was wrong to worry about Cameron. As it turns out, the un-
assuming nineteen-year-old nursing student was serious about his
previously stated desire to help others, and he went on a media tour
following the publication of my article. Cameron—beautiful, baby-
faced, hazel-eyed Cameron—retold his story to Anderson Cooper on CNN, and I found myself in awe of the boy I had underesti-
mated just one week prior. I'd awakened something in Cameron and
launched, for lack of a better word, a star.

"He raped me," Cameron said with a steely glint in his eye. "I
stayed silent because I was afraid of my abuser, because I gave him
power over my life. Even after I dropped him as an agent and left the
business, he held that power over me. But by speaking out, I'm taking it back."

Watching the interview this morning, I finally understood the incongruous nature of his appeal: Cameron's vulnerability was also
the source of his power. It was this paradox, no doubt, that had first

attracted Doug Sheffield, a man who understood the allure of this boy's open heart—and knew precisely how to exploit it. Knew the way Cameron's doe eyes would fill a movie screen. He appreciated the cash value of Cameron's innocence but also recognized how it could be abused. It would lead the boy to either incredible fortune or absolute ruin. Ever the businessman, Doug hedged his bets and played the game from both sides—he pushed for public adoration and private devastation. It was a win-win for Doug.

This is why Cameron's performance on *60 Minutes* was so remarkable. We were watching someone reverse the trajectory of his fate. Cameron took his rightful place on our TV screens—not as the star of a scripted cable soap but as the leading player in a real-life drama, a role far more powerful than Doug Sheffield could've booked for the young actor on HBO. There was something otherworldly about Cameron's suffering. It seemed bigger than everyone else's, more beautiful, more devastating. His face was the perfect canvas for projection, warm and open and intelligent. His rawness was a force, one that spoke to the darkness in everyone's heart. Or at least, it stirred the pain fixed in mine.

I'm sitting at home now, late for work, consumed by the need to process the emotions triggered by Cameron's interview. I have to admit, I'm jealous. Not of the publicity—I've turned down every interview request I received in the wake of my article, instead referring reporters to a more-than-willing Cameron, terrified of the parallels between his narrative and my own history. I know that someone will eventually make the connection and comb through Google search results to arrive at the thing he'd suspected: Jonah Keller was *that* boy, the one from Richard Shriver's trial, the one who took a stand against the exact brand of justice for which he had recently become an advocate. No, there's not one bit of me that envies Cameron's fame.

I'm jealous of his strength. His courage to confront what I never could. His ability to not only process his trauma but offer it up to the masses in digestible sound bites in an attempt to make the world a safer place. The bittersweet truth: I've turned someone else into the survivor I always longed to be. The perfect victim.

Meanwhile, I'm a liar, a drunk, a loser unworthy of redemption.

I've failed myself, but more important, I've failed you. I lied to the world, but I lack the courage to fix what I've done. The public sphere is a dangerous arena for healing. And yet, Cameron inspires me. What would happen if I, in the words of Anderson Cooper, "bravely come forward"?

Come forward. I hate that term. When you tell your story, you don't *come forward*—you *let people in.* Into the dark place you've occupied for years. And what happens when the public enters? Maybe they rush to you with open arms, tell you the things you've longed to hear.

Or maybe these people stomp inside with their muddy boots, accusing you of crimes, confirming your worst fears about yourself.

But how to know which future awaits? Maybe it's time to tell my story, our story. Pray we both survive.

I guzzled coffee at work, fighting my daily hangover as I drafted my public apology.

In October 2011, I was asked by Mace Miller to testify against Richard Shriver . . .

I worried you might interpret a private apology to you as disingenuous if I sent it before I'd corrected our shared story in the press. However, there was also the risk that you'd view my public statement as an attempt to get ahead of the story, to respond to accusations I knew would inevitably arise in our current climate. I suppose, in some respects, this *was* what I wanted: to control the narrative. But isn't that what all writers do? I needed to tell the truth before it became impossible, before the internet's collective opinion was already tweeted in stone, informed by old headlines, false information, and the distorted echoes of the think-piece industrial complex. I feared that if I didn't, we'd never heal.

I revised and revised my statement, burning through the morning hours at my desk, trying to get it right, knowing I never would. Unable to summon the courage to post it.

And then I saw that article on Twitter.

There on my feed, quickly racking up retweets, was a picture of my face accompanied by the headline "Why Is Jonah Keller Allowed to Cover Sexual Assault for the *Profile*?" My phone started vibrating —a waterfall of notifications from my social media accounts cascaded down the screen. The vibrations pushed my cell across the desk. I watched, numb, unable to move even as the office stirred and my coworkers shot suspicious glances in my direction. I sat there, arrested, entertaining the panicked delusion that if I didn't move, then neither would time.

An e-mail hit my in-box. From my boss. The entire message contained in the subject line: *Come See Me in My Office*.

Instead, I ran. Back to my apartment, back to this document, back to the one place where the truth lives, even as the rest of the world writes its own story.

21

HE CAME AT ME from across the street, running despite the
DON'T WALK sign. He dodged a speeding taxi and leaped onto the
curb in front of me.

"*Jonah!*"

My pulse quickened.

"You're Jonah Keller, right?"

He wore acid-washed jeans and a ratty black T-shirt. A gold sep-
tum piercing glinted beneath his nostrils. Matted blond hair ob-
scured his youthful, acne-pocked face.

"Leave me alone."

"Dude, you know your address is online? Some troll posted it on
Twitter."

I stopped on the sidewalk, stunned. I'd just emerged from my
apartment building.

"But don't worry," he insisted nervously. "I'm not a troll. I'm a reporter from *Vice*."

"Isn't that the same thing?"

"Come on, bro. That's not fair. We, like, won a Peabody Award—"

"Fuck off."

"I just wanna give you a chance to tell your side of the story."

"I said *fuck off.*"

I stepped forward. He blocked my path.

"Can you—"

"This . . . this is stalking." I tried to step around him. Again, he blocked my path. I reversed course, headed back toward my apartment.

"What are your thoughts on the recent article about your history with Mace Miller?" He ran past me and stood in front of the building's entrance.

"Get out of my way."

"Did you—"

"*Out of my way.*" I shoved him aside. He stumbled, fell into a bush.

"You just . . . just *assaulted* me, dude."

"*Well, you fucking deserved it.*"

It was then I noticed the voice recorder in his hand.

———

For the past forty-eight hours, I have been unable to sleep, unable to eat, unable to do anything but drink the cheap red wine from my corner bodega. I have declined or ignored the inquiries of all reporters. Their voice mails and e-mails aggregate on my phone, each message some version of *We want to give you a chance to tell your side of the story.* But it's far too late for that; public opinion has already cemented, and I've been cast as an accomplice to Richard—the very man who has robbed me of sleep for the past eight years, who has made me terrified of sex, terrified of love, terrified of even the most basic human connection.

Still, I can't tear myself away from the headlines. I drink straight from the bottle—wincing as the sour red floods my mouth—and Google Richard's name. So many victims have come forward in the press with stories of the abuse they've suffered at his hands. A sick thrill courses down my spine as I comb through news of his destruction in the wake of these unearthed allegations: rumors of a state investigation into his crimes, the Broadway transfer of his most recent play canceled, a major studio film shelved, honorary degrees rescinded, his friends distancing themselves from him in the press. Even Kristen Sloan, so devoted that summer, has denounced him. Sandro, Charles, and Ira face allegations of their own as victims come forward, men I've never met yet feel I understand. Strangers who have seen the basement.

I read, with considerably less enthusiasm, about my own downfall. I never bothered to return to work, assuming I'd been fired. Yesterday, my editor issued a statement claiming he hadn't known of my relationship with Richard Shriver or my testimony at the 2011 trial, that if he had, I would not have been hired at the *Profile*. Whether or not this is true, I'll never know. It's possible that he simply failed to conduct a deep enough Google search before hiring me in 2014. It's also possible that he *did* know my history and simply didn't care. Perhaps he believed my testimony and sided with Richard in the case —2014 was a different time.

The reporter who first broke my story—or re-broke it, rather, deconstructed it in light of #MeToo—has made quite a name for herself as the expert on Jonah Keller. Prior to publishing "Why Is Jonah Keller Allowed to Cover Sexual Assault for the *Profile*?," twenty-three-year-old Jessica Ronson was a celebrity gossip editor with 467 Twitter followers, employed by a fledgling website with the dubious name of PopCandy.net. She now appears hourly on cable news to discuss my story, has amassed over twenty thousand Twitter followers, and has spawned her own controversy over the legitimacy of her reporting, which—as more seasoned reporters at the *New York Times* have pointed out—is rife with defamatory conjectures. Jessica favors sensation over accuracy, as demonstrated by her widely spread theory that I "procured young men for Richard Shriver" and "brought them back to his lair" despite her having zero evidence to back this up. This has served her, and PopCandy.net, rather well in our current climate. She herself has become a headline, which has boosted the site's traffic and raised her own profile. Jessica Ronson is the face of my waking nightmare, the avatar for the cultural hatred aimed in my direction.

And yet, there is a part of me that wonders if I deserve all this, if Jessica's story, however incorrect, contains a kernel of truth. I didn't procure young men for Richard, but I did prevent those men from receiving the justice they deserved. This is all I can think about as the e-mails and calls and texts and tweets continue to flood my phone. Each alert triggers a flash of that basement. It's like I'm back there again. Like I never left.

"This sinful lifestyle will lead to your ruination," Doctor Jim, my ex-gay counselor, assured me all those years ago. Now—sweating in my apartment, sick on cheap merlot, panic racing through my body —I can't help but wonder if he was right. What if homosexuality *was* the first step on my path toward damnation? What if it *was* Satan's grip that dragged me into Richard's basement?

Hell on earth, just like Daddy promised.

"YOU F***ING DESERVED IT"—*JONAH KELLER ASSAULTS REPORTER*

The *Vice* article was savage, but one line in particular set the internet on fire: "Though I was physically unharmed by Keller, the emotional trauma inflicted by this encounter has been brutal."

In other words, my septum-pierced nemesis sustained zero injuries from my push. This renders his claim of assault legally inaccurate in the State of New York, a fact neither he nor his editors seem interested in. He couldn't press charges if he wanted to. Though why should he press charges when the public has already convicted me?

It was the perfect headline. The quote so awful; the word *assault* so triggering. The headline did not claim *sexual* assault, but that didn't stop the Twitter trolls:

@JONAHKELLER *is now raping reporters??!? How is he not in jail yet?*

@THEPROFILE you should be ashamed of yourselves. Letting convicted abuser @JONAHKELLER report on sexual assault is an insult to victims everywhere

Fun fact of the day: jonah keller's e-mail address is jonah. keller.84@gmail.com. Direct your hate mail to this predator accordingly

Die die die die die @JONAHKELLER. Roy in hell, you fat fuck

All these tweets contain a terrifying amount of misinformation, but I find myself particularly offended by the last. I *am* in hell, but I can't confirm or deny the presence of a Roy here. Also, I am not remotely fat. I've maintained a svelte figure throughout my adulthood, not for the purposes of luring potential mates (sex fills me with fear and shame), but because my body often feels like the only thing I can control.

Exercise keeps me grounded. I perform set after set of crunches and lunges and push-ups and pull-ups on the bar mounted on my bathroom door frame. I don't stop until my entire body throbs with pain. Then I strip for a shower and evaluate my body in the mirror. I'm dismayed at the ring of flab that has accumulated around my waist, eroding the valleys of muscle that once defined my stomach. Too much cheap wine and frozen pizza from my corner bodega. It's the only place I dare to go outside my apartment. The owner's daily greetings torment me: "Jonah! Ah, DiGiorno again. Your favorite! I have a new wine that I think you'd *love!*" Lorenzo has no idea what I did, and his efforts to befriend his new regular depress me. Then again, maybe I can use his ignorance to my advantage. Maybe I can run away with Lorenzo—the one person in the world who doesn't loathe me—and retire to a tropical island where we'll gorge on defrosted pepperoni and five-dollar magnums of merlot until we die.

I need to escape Manhattan. I live in constant fear of running into someone I know or someone I don't know who knows and hates me. But every time I consider a getaway, I am faced with the terror of my potential freedom. I no longer have a life here, but I also don't have a life anywhere else. I could move, probably *should* move—my savings account is dwindling. If I go, I'd need to act fast, while I still have the cash for a plane ticket to my new home, first month's rent, last month's rent, and a security deposit. I'd need enough money to keep me afloat while I find a new job—doing *what,* I have no idea, as the only items on my résumé are writer and waiter. The former is no longer possible, and the idea of reverting to the latter makes me want to choke down a bottle of barbiturates. Still, I suppose diner-employee-in-Kabumfuck is probably my best option, but which Kabumfuck to choose? I hear Kabumfuck, Kansas, is particularly bleak this time of year, though others prefer the ripe garbage smell of Kabumfuck, Delaware, and then there are the passionate proponents for Kabumfuck, Utah, who say there is no better place to fade into oblivion, that its hopelessness is unmatched, that the suicide rates are soaring.

"And now Jonah Keller is *assaulting* reporters? Just more proof that he is a dangerous, violent person," Jessica Ronson, my sweet angel of destruction, asserted on *Anderson Cooper 360.* I watched the clip on Facebook this morning, contributing to the 3.6 million views. "But let's not let this recent headline distract us from the most important issue here: Jonah Keller is an accomplice to a vicious sexual predator."

"*Accomplice* is a strong word, Jessica," Stephanie Hagger, a *Times* reporter, interjected. "We don't know that he was an accomplice, we simply know he testified in defense of Richard Shriver and—"

"Oh, *please,* you're splitting hairs, Stephanie," Jessica interrupted.

"I'm not. I'm trying to distinguish between theory and fact here—"

"Fact: Jonah Keller is a fucking crony for Richard—"

"Jessica, Jessica, let's keep this—" Anderson said, trying to referee.

"We don't *know* that, Jessica," Stephanie cut in. "It's possible that at the time of his testimony, he wasn't aware of Richard's history of assault—"

"Then why has Jonah said *nothing* in the press? Nothing to confirm or deny—"

"I'm just saying, you shouldn't present your opinion as fact because a lot of people pick that up and run with it—"

"I'm allowed to have my opinion, Stephanie, it was an op-ed—"

"Oh, I'm sorry, I forgot about PopCandy's lauded Opinion section."

"Guys, hold on. I want to give Cameron Davis a minute to weigh in," Anderson said. My chest tightened. "What's your take on this, Cameron? You got to know Jonah fairly well while he reported on your own sexual assault."

"My contact with Jonah was limited to a journalistic context, where he operated with the utmost care and respect," Cameron said. "But I had no idea of his history at the time. And this news is, well, it's just sad. To challenge or discount victims of sexual assault is reprehensible for anyone, but especially for someone who now reports on this important issue."

And that's where the clip ended. Frozen on Cameron's frown. It pulverized my heart.

What do you make of all this, Mace? News outlets have also reported on your own surprising silence, your refusal to comment on these unearthed allegations. Do you agree with Jessica? Do I deserve all this hatred? Am I the true monster in this story?

These are questions only you can answer, which is why I've yet to contact you. I want to know I'm more than the sum of my demons, but I'm too afraid to ask.

22

I TRACKED HIM DOWN. Showed up outside his dance studio this morning.

The building was a glass-walled space on a busy Bushwick street corner. Mirrors lined the far wall of the room so that passersby could see their own reflections behind those of the dancers. I stood there, watching myself watch Rashad. He darted back and forth at the front of the room, yelling to the people who leaped and spun in front of him. I caught his gaze and he jumped in surprise. Like he'd seen a ghost.

He squinted in my direction, then waved his arms at the dancers. They stopped and retreated to various corners of the room to grab their water bottles and stretch. Rashad clenched his jaw, exited the building, and marched toward me.

"What the hell are you doing here, Jonah?"

"I . . . I wanted to see you."

"I know." He sighed.

I've spent over a week in isolation. I'm losing my fucking mind. I have no job, no friends, no life, nothing to fill my days. All I have is time—infinite and empty and terrifying time. I needed someone, something, outside of my apartment. So I texted the one person who could, perhaps, restore my faith in humanity, my faith in anything other than a vengeful God. "You never returned my texts," I murmured.

"I know," he repeated, more firmly.

There were a few times Rashad contacted me over the years, attempting to reconnect. I deflected or ignored his every communication, hiding behind the emotional walls I'd erected after that summer. I preferred to watch his life unfold from a safe distance via various social media feeds. Rashad left Perdition shortly after I did. Petra—his indie-rapper roommate and artistic collaborator—parlayed her MySpace fame into a lucrative record deal and hired Rashad as her exclusive choreographer/creative director. Petra soared to international stardom, and Rashad became a minor celebrity in his own right, creating pieces for other pop stars and eventually opening his own dance studio. A pang of regret clamped my heart with each sighting of his smiling face on my phone or laptop, his social media posts celebrating yet another professional success or life milestone. A series of what-ifs always run through my mind: *What if I'd never gone to the Hamptons that summer? What if I'd dated Rashad instead?*

Who would I be without Richard?

Who could I have been with Rashad?

"I wanted to talk . . ." I continued, drifting off nervously.

"About what, Jonah?"

"I'm going through a hard time."

"I've seen the headlines," Rashad said, softening slightly.

"It's not what you think. People have the story wrong. I—"

"What did he do to you, Jonah?"

"Who?" I asked. An unconvincing performance.

"Richard."

"He . . . he . . ." *What am I doing here? This is insane. I show up like some fucking stalker, show up after years of ignoring Rashad, begging for . . . well, what exactly? What do I want?*

"Did he . . . hurt you?"

The question lit my heart on fire. Sobs bubbled in my throat, escaped in short wet bursts.

"Hey, hey . . . come here," he said, pulling me into his embrace. I wanted to stay there forever. We'd be two figures locked together permanently, a statue on a Bushwick street corner. Safe, stable, cemented. I sighed, settling in his arms. Rashad stepped back.

"Maybe we could go somewhere and talk?" I asked.

"Jonah, I'm in the middle of class," Rashad said, frustration returning.

"Oh . . ."

"You can't just show up here out of the blue and expect me to drop everything."

"I'm sorry, I—"

"Are you sorry? Because you've ignored me for *years*, Jonah. I've tried again and again to reach out, to be your friend. And you always blow me off. That's why I didn't return your texts. Because I'm done trying."

"I just need . . . help . . ."

"You *do* need help, Jonah. But I'm sorry, you're not gonna get it from me." Rashad pulled out his iPhone and scrolled through his contacts. "Here, I'm texting you the number of a friend of mine. Jeremy's a great therapist. He's a trauma specialist with a lot of queer clients."

I knew I wouldn't call Jeremy. Therapy was not the answer here. If I'd learned anything, it was that therapists weren't to be trusted. People weren't to be trusted. Rashad, the one person I wanted to trust, was not to be trusted.

"I'm sorry. About everything," I said, flushed with shame, embarrassed by this whole pathetic episode. "I'm not really good at . . . dealing with people."

Rashad gave my shoulder a squeeze and shot me a pitying look. "Just see Jeremy, okay?"

"I will," I lied and watched him retreat back to his studio, back to his life.

———

I arrived home to discover an e-mail from my father.

I got only as far as the subject line: *I'm Praying for You.*

He's back from the dead, I thought as I slammed my laptop shut. *Back to exact his revenge.*

Four simple words—*My father molested me*—and he was gone forever. Redacted from our family. Banished from his church. His perfect Christian existence destroyed, decimated, dead, dead, dead. I felt profound relief in my father's absence. Some divine force had bestowed mercy on me, removed the violence of my father's disappointment, rescued me from conversion therapy, and delivered me from the brink of suicide. Whether it was God or Satan, I wasn't sure. I almost didn't care.

Almost.

If it was God who'd granted this mercy, what did that say about my father? That he'd been wrong all along? That God loved me as I was? Then there was the terrifying possibility that Satan had saved me. That I'd succumbed to homosexuality, to sin, and this earthly respite was only temporary, a prelude to the hell my father had promised. My unholy agreement with Evil.

I reopened my computer, shaking as the screen illuminated.

Jonah —

I've missed you.

I saw the headlines. Hope you're holding up, though I imagine you're struggling. If you ever want to talk, I'm here. Praying for you.

Blessings,

Dad

It was the first I'd heard from him in nine years. I read the letter over and over, attempting to find meaning in the space between sentences. His reemergence felt like a rip in time, one that revealed a parallel universe where my father was living and breathing and existing without me. It felt impossible that our two worlds should meet, something out of a scrapped episode of *Star Trek,* and yet there he was, fresh from another galaxy, praying for me.

Now, as I sit at my desk and write this, I wonder — have my father's prayers protected me this whole time? All these years, was he begging God to keep me safe even as I sinned? Maybe I have my father to thank for my survival. Maybe God can save me from this nightmare. Maybe it's time to return to His loving embrace.

Another painful question: What would've happened if conversion therapy had worked? Would we still be a family? Perhaps this is the only way to heal: To finally renounce what I am. To apologize to the man whose life I ruined. To ask my father for forgiveness. Ask the Father for forgiveness.

I feel sick. Dizzy. Vertigo again. I need to lie down. A terrible weight presses on my chest. Another panic attack?

Or maybe it's Satan reminding me of our pact.

———

It's three a.m. I can't sleep. The trauma feels as fresh as it did that summer. Time collapses. I can't endure this any longer, I can't wallow in pain and self-pity and cheap wine, I can't take another day trapped alone in my apartment.

I want out.

23

I WAS GOING to do it. I abandoned my bodega merlot for the harder stuff. A bottle of whiskey to bolster my courage. I sat with it all night and into the morning, forcing the alcohol down my throat, steeling myself for the end. Seeing the lackluster sunrise gave me new resolve, confirmed I'd be happy never to witness another. Around seven thirty, I wiped the tears and snot from my face, slammed back a final shot of whiskey, and set out in search of a Duane Reade.

Even the weathered, seen-it-all salesclerk—a grim Eastern European matron who looked about three whiskey shots from suicide herself—raised her eyebrows upon seeing my fifteen jumbo bottles of aspirin. I stared back, daring her to deny me. She paused for a brief moment, allowing her face to resettle into its stoic countenance, before ringing up the bottles, one by one. New Yorkers are reliable in this way—there is not a single person who'd miss the L train to save someone else's life. It's a selfish city, to be sure.

The perfect setting for suicide.

I stumbled out of the drugstore. My determination waned; my drunkenness became a headache. I needed more alcohol. Something to restore my resolve. I needed a liquor store.

I ventured farther down Eighth Avenue, regretting my decision as the Penn Station crowds swarmed around me. I turned off Eighth, walked west on Thirty-Fourth, trying to escape the throngs of slack-jawed tourists drifting from Marshall's to Macy's to Kmart. My path was barred by a group of high school boys wearing matching red T-shirts that read KIRKWOOD HIGH SOCCER TRIP 2017. I elbowed my way through their ranks much to the alarm of their Midwestern mama-bear chaperone, who grabbed my arm and said, "Watch where you're *going*." I shook her off, stumbling and falling to the ground in the process. She looked down at me like I was the type of urban degenerate she'd heard about, the type who would rob or rape or kill these innocent boys. She quickly ushered her flock into the steaming maw of the Thirty-Fourth Street subway station.

I sat on the sidewalk as the river of pedestrians parted unceremoniously around me, citizens sidestepping yet another drunk on the concrete, averting their eyes. Business as usual. It was surprisingly comforting to be erased in this way. A true ghost, at last.

Gone.

That's when I heard it. The gentle lull of a rock band. I turned to face the building behind me. Hammerstein Ballroom. The music crescendoed, pouring out of the open doors. A tenor voice cut through the hum of city traffic like it was calling me.

Oh, the overwhelming, never-ending, reckless love of God . . .

A woman in her early twenties approached me. A mane of blond, expertly tousled hair framed her beaming face. She wore a hip wide-brimmed hat and a simple white T-shirt tucked into faded jeans. The lanyard hanging from her neck read: MOUNTAINTOP WORSHIP TEAM. I'M COURTNEY. "Welcome," she said.

Oh, it chases me down, fights 'til I'm found . . .

Minutes later, I was inside the packed auditorium, bathed in a dark purple glow. All around me, people thrust their hands in the air, dropped to their knees, wept in the aisles. The scene felt not unlike a rock concert; the musicians' bodies thrashed under strobing spot-lights as fog machines filled the stage with white mist. Behind them, a Jumbotron projected a rapid succession of images: star-filled night skies, sweeping mountain ranges, vast oceans, and a diverse array of youthful faces that mirrored the ones in the crowd. Thousands of voices chanted in unison as the band built to a soaring refrain.

Oh, the overwhelming, never-ending, reckless love of God . . .

The music softened as the pastor took the stage. A reverent ex-pression radiated from his handsome, rugged face. He wore a black T-shirt that emphasized his muscular frame, dark jeans, and white high-tops. Gold necklaces bounced against his swollen chest. "God, we are gathered here today in awe of Your overwhelming love. And God, we pray that those here who are lost, who are in pain, we pray that they open their hearts to Your amazing grace. Amen.

"And I just want to say to anyone out there who feels hopeless: there's a reason you're in this room today. And that reason is God. He has brought you here to hear the Gospel, the Good News. It's a message meant for you no matter who you are or what you've been through.

"Because when God sees you, He doesn't see your failures. He doesn't define you by your past or your problems. And when you ac-cept God into your heart, His love becomes your new identity. And *that's* when everything changes. You become a child of God. You'll be flooded by the Holy Spirit, who brings immediate peace, hope, and joy. You'll be born again."

I wept. Nothing had ever sounded so true.

"During the next few songs, we're going to invite you to reflect on God's love in a variety of ways. You can raise your hands in a pos-ture of surrender, or you can come to the front of the stage and get on your knees before our King. Or, if you want to accept Jesus Christ into your heart for the first time today, there are prayer ministers positioned around the auditorium. They are ready to pray with you as you start your new life."

As he spoke, I drifted into the aisle, pushing through the crowd. Courtney, the blond woman who'd greeted me earlier, stood at the edge of the auditorium. I ran to her, quickening my pace as the band's music swelled. She greeted me with a hug. I didn't need to tell her why I was there—she knew. I dropped to my knees. She placed her hands on me and prayed. I felt God's love flow through my body, purging all the pain and trauma and abuse, promising me eternal life. I could hear His voice, I swear, hear the voice of God say: *You are no longer in darkness, you are in light.*

I stayed there all day. Stayed for the ten a.m. service and the noon service and the two p.m. service and the five p.m. service. I surrendered to the rhythms of the music and the Gospel.

I reveled in God's love, in my new life.

————

So much has happened over the past month.

After that first Sunday, Courtney invited me to join her at what Mountaintop calls a "small group." When you have a church with thousands of congregants, people need a way to connect with one another on a more intimate level. Small groups are the solution, weekly Bible studies with five to ten people held at the homes of various church members. This is how I found myself outside the Upper West Side apartment belonging to Matt, the music minister at Mountaintop, the beautiful man with the beautiful voice who led the band onstage every Sunday. Looking back now, I hardly recognize the person who knocked on his door that day.

A familiar panic stiffened my body as I waited in the hall. I had a choice. I could stay and fight the terrifying suspicions that constricted my heart—that every new relationship ended in betrayal and abuse, that I was unworthy of love. Or I could run, fly down the three flights of stairs, burst out of this stranger's building into the bracing November evening, and be safe from the horrific work of connecting with other people.

As I debated, the door cracked open.

"Rufus, no! You're not getting out," Matt shouted over his shoulder. He scooped up an ancient wheezing pug and turned to greet me. "Sorry—Rufus is attempting to escape. But we already took you out, didn't we, Rufus?"

"He's so cute." I laughed nervously.

"Don't tell *him* that." Matt smiled. "He's enough of a diva as it is."

"Nice to meet you, Rufus," I said, mussing the folds of fur between his ears. "I'm Jonah, by the way."

"And I'm Matt. Come on in." He swung the door open. "We're just about to get started."

Mere adjectives fail to convey Matt's appearance. I'm tempted to describe him in terms of how his beauty *felt:* like a gut punch, a slap, a stunning assault that awakened impulses I'd long thought dead. The possibility of love personified.

Compounding my attraction was the fact that Matt seemed totally unaware of it. Matt possessed the oblivious demeanor of someone who drifted through life with ease due to the sharp line of his jaw, the deep blue of his eyes, his perfectly tousled hair, the olive tint of his skin, and his lean, muscular frame. Matt could have, if he'd wished, gotten away with being a total asshole. And yet he was so relentlessly kind—his compassion almost felt like an apology for his appearance, a way to diminish the effect of an intimidating exterior. I could imagine the trail of broken hearts that had followed Matt from puberty to present, the many who had mistaken his kindness for romantic interest, who had fooled themselves into thinking they had a chance.

He led me into the living room of his sizable Upper West Side apartment, tasteful if unimaginative in its decor. It looked like a West Elm catalog, with a light gray couch, a green, midcentury accent chair, and a low-burning pendant lamp. The only marks of character were the vintage Dolly Parton record covers framed and hung above a bar cart. A group of five attractive, well-dressed people completed the catalog photo, drinking red wine out of elegant, stemless glasses. They turned to greet me with genuine enthusiasm. *You are welcome here,* their warm hugs suggested, *you are loved by us and you are loved by God.* I bristled a bit at first, skeptical of their kindness. But as each person embraced me, I realized it was easier to surrender to their compassion than reject it.

Truth be told, I was exhausted. Exhausted by the endless chore of maintaining the wall between me and the rest of the world. And in the buzzy warmth of Matt's apartment, I finally let go. Allowed myself to trust. The near constant pulse of adrenaline in my system quieted and I felt — for the first time in years — a sense of hope.

We settled in Matt's living room and began our discussion. The question for the meeting: How has Christ's love brought renewal and hope to your life? Courtney detailed her mother's death from breast cancer and how Matt had rescued her from deep depression, revived her sense of wonder, and reminded her of who she was in Christ. And Chris — a white twenty-eight-year-old meth addict who hadn't used in over a year — told us how he still struggled every day to resist the pull of the drug, how he felt that all that stood between himself and death was this church, this small group, the love of God, and that each time he felt called to use, he also felt a stronger call, the call of God's love, and it was His love that gave him the will to go on living. And Keke — a thirty-two-year-old Black woman who worked at a nonprofit called Seeds of Hope teaching ex-convicts the skills they needed to get green jobs — told us that though she loved her career at times, she was overworked and her program underfunded, and there were days she was so physically exhausted that she simply wanted to quit and take a cushy corporate job and never think about social justice again. And she told us that when she had these dark thoughts, she would think of this small group, remember all Christ endured and how her suffering would never match His death on the cross, and she was humbled and renewed and found the strength to go on. And a couple named Craig and Julia—he white and American-born and she a Mexican immigrant—told us how they had endured prejudice from both their families at the start of their relationship, prejudices that, with the help of God's grace, gradually disappeared. Their two families formed a beautiful bond, and life became a miracle, and they decided to have a child together, a child that—as they discovered early into the pregnancy—had Down syndrome, a fact that led the young couple to consider abortion until this group brought them back to the foundations of their faith and reminded them of God's perfect plan for all our lives.

And then there was me.

I told them the story of my upbringing, how my soul had been twisted by conversion therapy, how my sexuality broke my family, broke my spirit. The empathy on their faces inspired me to open up in ways I never had. We had all endured terrible events that tested our will to live.

And we had all survived.

In that initial meeting, I didn't have the courage to tell them about you and Richard and that awful summer. The root of the terror that plagues us both, Mace, that tempts us to self-destruct. But over the next three weeks, I told them my entire story, the plot to my private horror film that started with my childhood, climaxed with Richard, and ended with the miracle where I was saved by Christ, saved by the people with kind faces who sat across from me week after week and loved me and said I'd be okay, that the Lord had shown me grace.

God has given me a second chance, a fresh identity founded in Christ.

He's given me a new family.

———

"You know, I went through conversion therapy too," Matt said to me after our fourth group meeting. I'd stayed behind to help him with the dishes, though I really just wanted to flirt.

"You did?" I shouldn't have been surprised, given that most people in our group came from similar evangelical backgrounds. But something about Matt's assured gayness had led me to assume that he'd never been through the degradation of conversion therapy.

"It was the worst experience of my life," he said. "Only now, like, seven years later, am I starting to rebuild a relationship with my parents. We're still pretty much estranged, but they'll at least answer an occasional e-mail."

"What's making them come around?"

"This church. The fact that I've made such a commitment to Christ again."

"What about all the gay stuff, though?"

"Don't get me wrong, it's still a huge issue for them. But they're starting to understand how celibacy can be an equally faithful option for people who suffer from same-sex attraction."

Hearing those words — *same-sex attraction* — sent panic through my system. Those were the words that had been used to describe my sexual orientation during conversion therapy. I set my wineglass on the counter. The room began to spin. Matt clocked my surprise and placed a hand on my shoulder.

"Hey   are you okay?"

"I . . . I think I need to just sit for a second." I made my way to the couch.

Matt sat down next to me, put a hand on my knee. "I'm sorry, I thought you knew I was celibate."

"I didn't."

"I know it can be a lot to take in. It was tough for me too when I first started going back to church."

"I don't understand."

"The first thing you need to know is that God loves you exactly the way you are. Okay?"

"Okay," I muttered.

"We're all created equal in God's eyes, and He loves each and every one of us. But we're all sinners too. And *everyone* has strayed from God's design for sexuality, whether they watch porn, or cheat on their spouse, or have premarital sex. So it doesn't matter if you're straight or gay. The more important question is: Are you embracing a holy sexuality?"

"Right . . ."

"And so same-sex attraction is treated like any other temptation to sin. In order to remain holy, all we have to do is deny our same-sex attraction."

"And so you're celibate."

"Exactly. And I'm welcomed into our church with open arms. Lots of gay people attend Mountaintop. And they're all living life according to God's plan."

"And no one undergoes conversion therapy," I ventured, uncertain.

"Of course not. No one here will ever put you through that. Because God loves you exactly as you are. All you need to do is resist those sinful impulses."

"Is it ever hard? No pun intended," I said dryly.

Matt let out a giant laugh, a laugh filled with a self-awareness that set me at ease. He could joke about this; *we* could joke about this. As my shock subsided, I began to see a certain logic in his perspective. Here at last was the solution to the conflict between God and my gayness: I didn't have to deny my sexuality, just refuse to act on it. As he spoke, it started to seem like an understandable compromise, a way to find healing through Christ.

"Of course it's hard. But the sacrifice I've made is nothing compared to the sacrifice of Christ on the cross. Knowing the love of God overpowers any sinful impulses I experience."

"I'd have to delete Grindr from my phone, I assume."

Matt laughed again. "That's a definite yes."

"I'll need to think about this," I said, seriousness returning to my tone. But even as I said it, I knew my mind had been made up, that the riddle had been solved, that here, finally, was the way to align my spirituality with my sexuality. Deny the sin but stay the same.

Salvation through celibacy.

After all, what good had sex ever accomplished? Sex had only gotten me into trouble. Sex led me into Richard's clutches, into his basement. Sex robbed me of life, of joy, of meaning. Sex almost killed me.

Almost killed us both, Mace.

24

"NOW, *THAT* WAS A FEAST," Matt said as we finished our two-man Thanksgiving dinner, a holiday plan we'd hatched upon discovering that both of us were estranged from our families. We were on our second helping of turkey and third bottle of wine. I felt blessed that God had brought Matt into my life. He was the closest thing I had to family, a brother not in blood but in spirit.

"Not to be *too* Thanksgiving-cheesy, but I'm so thankful for your friendship."

"And I'm thankful for you," Matt replied sweetly. "You know, I've been thinking a lot about you recently. Have you ever considered sharing your story with Pastor Dane?"

"Why?"

"I think he'd be deeply moved by your journey. And he might even be interested in having you share your testimony onstage at church."

"Can . . . can I think about it?"

"Yes, of course," Matt said, though I detected a slight disappointment in his tone. "I don't want you to feel any pressure."

A sense of failure crushed my spirit. I knew that sharing one's testimony in front of the church was an incredible honor and that I should feel grateful that Matt, a member of the church's leadership, thought my story was worthy of such a platform. Matt once joked that he was "jealous" of my testimony—there was an unspoken sense in my new, born-again community that the greater your suffering, the closer you were to Christ, who'd suffered for all of our sins. I wanted to be Matt's perfect disciple, wanted to demonstrate my love for him, wanted to offer my suffering as proof.

But reliving the horrors of the compound with my small group had been difficult enough. I wasn't sure I had the strength to do it in front of thousands of strangers.

"It's . . . it's just hard for me to talk about this stuff," I stammered, eyes watering.

"I totally get it," he said, moving in for a hug. We embraced for perhaps a moment longer than our mandated celibacy allowed, a moment in which I felt the ripple of muscles on his back and his breath on my neck and smelled the scent of butter on his skin. Blood rushed through my veins and stiffened my cock. I pulled him closer, the wine dulling my judgment, flushing my cheeks.

And that's when I did it. Something awful. Unforgivable.

I kissed him.

He jerked back. Suddenly, I saw my new life collapse. Shame and terror stirred within me. "Should we clean up?" I leaped to my feet like there was a demon below the dining table.

"I think we should pray first," Matt murmured, a dark expression contorting his features.

"Okay . . ." I sat back down and clasped my hands together. A horrible silence filled the room. I prayed I hadn't ruined everything. I prayed I hadn't destroyed my relationship with Matt.

We lifted our heads. I didn't want to talk about the kiss. Talking about it made it real. Matt opened his mouth, but before he could speak, I said, "You know, after praying on it, I think we should share my story with Pastor Dane."

An olive branch. Or was it a bribe?

"I'm happy to hear it, Jonah."

———

"Lord, we pray that You offer Jonah guidance in this moment as he considers whether to share his testimony with our church. We look to You, Lord, in Your eternal wisdom, grace, and love. Amen." Pastor Dane lifted his head and stared straight into my eyes. "How are you feeling, Jonah?"

Things had moved at a rapid pace. I couldn't help but feel that this momentum was driven by a divine force, that Christ was compelling me to share my story with the world. Well, Christ and Matt. Matt had pushed my story on our pastor with surprising passion, offering my saved soul like a holy prize. Or a professional achievement. But I tried not to let cynical thoughts like that enter my mind. They were the work of Satan, who was trying to lure me from the righteous path that Matt had paved for me. I chose to view Matt's enthusiasm as evidence of his love for me, despite the tension that had grown between us. Matt brought me to Pastor Dane, a man with a direct line to God, because he believed there was still hope for me. Even after Thanksgiving.

"I . . . I guess I'm a little nervous."

"You don't have to be nervous," Matt said impatiently.

"Hold on, Matt." Pastor Dane held up his hand. Matt's face wilted at the rebuke. "I want to hear why, Jonah. You can talk to me."

"I . . . I can't believe you wanted to meet with me," I stuttered.

"Jonah—I canceled a meeting with Justin Bieber for you." Pastor Dane shot me an irresistible smirk. In another life, he could've starred in a Marvel movie, released a number-one album, or campaigned for president. "Trust me, I wanna be here."

We all laughed. The energy in the room became more relaxed. I glanced around Pastor Dane's NoHo office, with its lofted ceilings, white walls, and massive windows that overlooked the traffic jammed on Lafayette. There was something comforting about staring down at the bottlenecked cars but not hearing the commotion. We were safe from the city and its madness, secure in this idyllic office in the sky. We were closer to God.

"Because let me tell you something. I don't care if you're Justin

Bieber or Justin Nobody. We're all equal in the eyes of God. We all
have a story to tell. And our stories matter. *You* matter, Jonah. You
are loved by God . . . and by everyone in this room." Pastor Dane
looked to Matt, who nodded in agreement.

"Jonah has become an essential member of our small-group family," Matt said. "I've seen him completely transform, seen him accept God's pure design for our sexuality. I've witnessed his rebirth
in Christ."

"That's an incredible thing, Jonah."

"Your story would be an inspiration to so many," Matt continued. I was honored to think that my testimony might have special
significance, that it was not something to be ashamed of but rather
a model for salvation.

"I . . . I feel like Christ has healed me," I said, holding back tears.
"I have never, in my life, known this kind of peace. It's like everything weighing on my heart, all the trauma and pain, it's like all that
has been lifted. And all that's left is Christ's love. A love that gives me
strength. A love that fills my life with purpose."

"That's beautiful," Pastor Dane whispered.

I began to weep.

"And so the final question to ask yourself, to ask Christ, is this:
Do you want to share your testimony with our church?"

———

I told my story again and again onstage at the Hammerstein Ballroom—at the ten a.m. service, the noon service, the two p.m. service, and the five p.m. service. Pastor Dane asked me if I truly had
the strength to tell my story that many times, said he'd understand
if it was too much, but I was buoyed by a manic sense of divine purpose. I delivered my testimony four times in one day as Matt led
the rock band behind me. His music gave me strength; it swelled
as my story reached its climax. And each time—as I delivered the
Good News of how God saved me from suicidal despair—the crowd

erupted into Super Bowl cheers. They stomped and howled and ap-
plauded, and the volume of their adulation echoed in my body, overwhelmed my senses, left me weeping and shuddering onstage, my
palms turned up to heaven in gratitude.

I felt loved at last.

And you were right there in the audience, Mace.

For a moment, at least. Until your face vanished, replaced by an
anonymous worshipper. As I wiped the tears from my eyes, as my
vision cleared, I realized why I was there, on that stage, reliving the
most horrific chapters of my life.

Even if I have God's forgiveness, I still want yours.

———

"Congratulations, Jonah."

A flash of you, crumpled on the basement floor.

"Your testimony was so powerful today."

Richard on top of me, his hands constricting my throat.

"You must feel incredible."

The witness stand. Your sobs. Your lawyer's furious stare.

"We're so blessed to have you in our lives."

My friends' voices became a distant chorus, background noise to
the flashbacks flooding my mind. I closed my eyes, downed my wine.
My fifth glass of the night.

"You okay, Jonah?"

I opened my eyes. Keke stood above me, concerned. The rest of
my small group froze in place, waiting for my answer.

"I . . . I think I'm just tired."

"It's been a long day for you," Chris whispered.

"Yeah, we should let you get some rest," Julia suggested.

One by one, they drifted out of Matt's apartment, hugging me as
they departed. I kept drinking, desperate to dull my panic. A sixth
glass, a seventh. With each goodbye I said, my terror grew—another
person was abandoning me. They'd seen me for who I truly was, how

defiled, how rotten, how broken. And they'd left. Matt was the only person who remained. He sat on the couch next to me, rubbed my back. My breath came in short hiccups. I felt dizzy, drunk.

"I'm a little worried about you. You're looking—"

"I . . . can't . . . be alone right now." I gasped for breath.

"You're not alone. I'm right here. I'm not going anywhere."

I broke down sobbing in his embrace, searching for comfort that the cheers of thousands of strangers could never supply. I felt the warmth of his hand on my back, felt the strength of his body as he pulled me close. Animal whimpers bubbled in my throat.

"Hey, hey, it's okay. I'm right here," he repeated, his voice a soothing whisper.

I felt sick. Too much wine. I dipped in and out of consciousness. I don't know how long I stayed in his lap like that, but eventually I found myself in Matt's bedroom, in his bed, with no memory of how I'd gotten there.

"I think you should sleep here tonight." Matt crouched by the bed, whispering in my ear.

I let out a low moan of agreement.

"I'm just gonna be in the next room. Sleeping on the couch."

"Okay . . ." My mouth was parched. The room spun. My gut churned.

"We're gonna get through this. God will get us through this."

I shuddered and sighed, drifting.

"I'm praying for you. For us."

"Thank you," I slurred.

"I'm here for you, Jonah. I love you."

"I . . . I love you."

Black.

I didn't wake up until I felt an immense pressure on my wrists. I roused in confusion, drifting from my slumber to discover Matt on top of me, my underwear tangled around my ankles, my arms pinned to the mattress with painful force. My body understood what was happening before my mind did—adrenaline shot through me and my limbs tensed. By the time my brain caught up, Matt was inside me and there was nothing to do but let him finish. As he raped me, I imagined myself in heaven—as far as possible from my own reality, where it seems like every path leads to the same abuse, the same predetermined destruction. And there—on Matt's bed but also far above it—I imagined myself in the paradise I know I don't deserve and felt guilty for even dreaming about.

Back at my apartment now, I write to you for the last time, Mace.

I am cursed in life, damned in death. There is no way out. I want to give up, give in to the inevitable, feel the relief of the lost battle.

Let go of life.

There's just one final thing I need to do.

25

December 6, 2017

I want to address the stories that have recently circulated in the press regarding my testimony in the 2011 trial of Richard Shriver. I never once, under any circumstances—as some pundits have theorized—secured young men for Richard to abuse. I would also like to make it very clear that I have never sexually assaulted anyone, ever. I have nothing but the utmost respect and empathy for all the victims of sexual violence who have bravely come forward in recent months.

I did, of course, come to Richard's defense during his trial, something I deeply regret. I discounted true stories with my false testimony. I apologize for lying. I know for a fact that Richard Shriver assaulted multiple young men on his Hamptons compound.

I know this because I was one of them.

Richard Shriver raped and sexually assaulted me repeatedly during the summer of 2009. I know many will be confused as to why I decided to defend the very man who violently attacked *me. I can only say that trauma has warped my mind in strange ways, ways I'm only beginning to understand.*

I apologize to Mace and all the other men I've betrayed with my lies. Know that my mistakes haunt my every waking moment. I pray for your forgiveness but don't expect it.

— Jonah Keller

26

FROM: jonah.keller.84@gmail.com
TO: yesthatmace@gmail.com
DATE: Dec. 7, 2017
TIME: 2:17 p.m.
SUBJECT:

Dear Mace,

I did something stupid yesterday. I did it at three in the morning after finishing an entire bottle of Macallan 12. I did it because I thought maybe it would fix things and because I didn't know what else to do. I did it because it wasn't suicide.

I issued a public statement.

You have, by now, probably seen it. My grand mea culpa, typed in the Notes app of my iPhone, screen-grabbed, and tweeted. I passed out shortly after posting and did not wake up until eleven a.m. Already, the internet was hours deep into a referendum on my apology. My pounding hangover was quickly erased by sheer panic as I watched my Twitter feed fill with content dissecting the sincerity, timing, and phrasing of my statement.

The initial response was positive. A chorus of prominent voices came to my defense, with headlines like "Why We Should Forgive Jonah Keller" and "Jonah Keller's Brave Statement Is a Test of Our #MeToo Moment." I read each article, expecting catharsis, but felt nothing except rising panic. I had done it all backward. Exonerations given by anonymous internet pundits meant nothing to me. The only forgiveness I wanted was yours, Mace.

Yet you remained silent. Repeated requests for comment were declined.

By noon, the expected backlash started: "Why We Shouldn't Be So Quick to Forgive Jonah Keller" and "Factions of LGBTQ Twitter Question Jonah Keller's Apology." The mob was led by Jessica Ronson, who was eager to protect the crown jewel of her outrage empire. Her argument killed me: "Sure, we can empathize with Jonah Keller's agonizing position on the day of that trial. But does someone's past abuse excuse bad behavior for the rest of their lives? Does someone's personal trauma give them the right to inflict trauma on another human being? These are the vital questions that face the #MeToo movement at this juncture. Let us not forget the ways in which Mace Miller's life and reputation were destroyed in the wake of this trial. And here's another telling fact: Miller has refused to comment on this apology. If the victim has yet to forgive Jonah Keller, why should we?" The article currently has over 1.2 million shares and is the second-most-popular piece on PopCandy.net, just below a quiz about how your favorite flavor of ramen reveals your personality type.

By 12:30 p.m., there was backlash to the backlash: "How Can Anyone Attack Jonah Keller?" By 1:00 p.m., America had moved on to the Skirball fire—the inferno currently consuming Bel Air—and my story was abandoned in favor of pieces concerning the impacts of climate change.

By 1:30 p.m., I had no idea what my own apology meant anymore.

I'm lost, Mace. Which is why I'm writing to you now. I want to reconnect with reality. I want to remember my truth. I want to confess things the public could never understand.

I've attached a document to this e-mail. For years, I've been writing in it, unsure of what, exactly, it is. It tells the story of our past, our pain. And not just us—all the boys. Seb, Michael, and Chase too. It describes the things we lost that summer, the parts of ourselves we'll never get back. I needed to record it all somewhere, to create an artifact, something to leave behind that said: *This really happened. This matters. We matter.*

Finally, today, I realized what this document is, what it has always been.

A letter to you.

I was always writing to you. At first, because you saved my life, because I needed some way, somewhere, to thank you. Then I wrote out of guilt. About the trial, my betrayal. And now I write to you with the hope that this letter can somehow lead to our reconciliation.

Not a day goes by that I don't wonder what would've happened if I'd told the truth at Richard's trial. Words can't express my regret, can't express the level of shame and sorrow and self-hatred I feel when I think of how I failed you. Given the length of the attached document, it's ironic that language is ultimately insufficient. Still, I hope you can find some healing —or at least an explanation—in these pages.

Yours,

Jonah

27

FROM: yesthatmace@gmail.com
TO: jonah.keller.84@gmail.com
DATE: Dec. 15, 2017
TIME: 7:58 p.m.
SUBJECT: hi, jonah

I don't know what to say.

This is a common theme when dealing with this part of my life. Words like *horror* and *rape* and *abuse* have lost all meaning at this point. They can't express how I felt then or how I feel now.

A part of me was jealous when I read the document you sent. You're a writer. Language is your thing. Maybe if I could write, some of this would be easier to process. But child actors get a pretty shitty education. My on-set tutors sucked; my schooling was a joke. What really mattered was my career. And if I already had a career, who needed an education? From an early age I learned that career and money mattered most of all. Mattered more than education but mattered more than other stuff too — like family, friends, my own well-being. Maybe that's why I got into trouble with Richard and Sandro and everybody. Because I was willing to do anything for my career. I often blame myself for what happened. But I know I shouldn't. And I told my therapist that I forgive myself, even though some days I don't. Some days I still feel so fucking stupid about what happened. Like it all happened because of me.

But I'm getting off track. I guess I have learned a little about how to talk about this stuff. And talking does help. I think it's crazy you aren't in therapy. Like, *really* fucking crazy. You need to go to therapy, like, yesterday. Run, don't walk.

Anyway.

You don't have to forgive him.

That's what my therapist said when I told her about your letters: *You don't have to forgive him.* I felt so relieved when she said that. I thought that part of therapy meant forgiving your enemies, like all that shit we learn from movies and the Bible and the stories that we tell ourselves and each other about what it means to "move on." But my therapist said: *You don't have to forgive him.* I could choose how to deal with this. It wasn't, like, a preordained kind of thing.

And I was angry with you, Jonah. You fucked me over at the trial. Like, *really* fucked me. It hurt me so bad. To go through all that only to get fucked in the end, fucked by the one person who was supposed to help, who was supposed to *understand*. That hurt more than the verdict. Fuck the verdict. It killed me that you took the stand and said what happened didn't happen. It fucking killed me. I hated you.

But, really, this is Richard's fault. And that's something I've worked hard to figure out. That Richard and Sandro and

Charles and Ira are to blame. That they're the fucking assholes who ruined us. Or tried to ruin us. Some days I can't decide if I'm ruined or not. Some days I think this is all behind me, but other days it feels like it's right in front of me, like it's the *only* thing in front of me, and it will be in front of me forever.

I read your story and now I understand why you did what you did at the trial. It took some work and I talked through it with my therapist and I still think it's insane and so fucking shitty, but I can empathize. As you and just about every person with an internet connection knows, I've also done some crazy shit since that summer.

But here's the other thing I figured out: Even though this mess is Richard's fault, I can't blame *him* for the way *I* act. I can't blame Richard and Sandro and Charles and Ira for the shitty things *I* do. Because only *I* am responsible for the shitty things that *I* do. You and Richard and everyone else didn't *make* me have a meth-fueled breakdown in a Denny's parking lot or *make* me act like a fucking asshole to everyone in my life or *make* me take a knife to my wrists when I tried to kill myself. I did all those things myself.

Trauma is like a gift. The shittiest fucking gift in the world. Coal in your motherfucking stocking. But the minute you receive it, it becomes *yours*. And it's your responsibility what you do with it. And you *can* use it as an excuse to destroy your life and destroy the lives of people around you, but you *shouldn't*.

Here's what I kept thinking when I read your letters: You're still walking around with all this trauma. You clearly need to tell your story. But I don't think that this confession, this testimony, is for me. It's for you. And I think you need to tell this all to a professional who can help you. Because if you don't, you'll either keep hurting yourself or keep hurting other people. You gotta stop living in denial and start dealing with your shit. And I'm telling you all this stuff because it's stuff I tell myself every day to go on living.

Believe me when I tell you it's hard. To go on living. But you find a way. After I got out of rehab in New Mexico, I moved into my mom's condo in Albuquerque. She'd gotten sober too and things were good between us. I found a therapist I liked, an outpatient program I liked, a Narcotics Anonymous group I liked, and I didn't know what life in fucking Albuquerque would look like, but hey, I was sure it'd look better than the basement in Burbank where I'd spent the prior year getting fucked out of my skull on meth.

I was safe. I'd escaped all the craziness surrounding the TMZ video. I was feeling hopeful in Albuquerque, of all places, and if you can feel hopeful in Albuquerque, I'm pretty sure you can feel hopeful anywhere. But just when I started to feel hopeful, that article about you came out, the one that "reexamined" my lawsuit against Richard. Suddenly I was back on the news every day, back on the internet every fucking day, back in the public eye. Now the very same people that had eaten me alive after the Denny's incident suddenly gave a shit about me, and, oh, they were *so fucking sorry about how they made fun of me before,* and, oh, *they were ready to reframe the way they told this story in the #MeToo era.* They acted like the story of *my* fucking life was *their* story.

In a way, I guess it *was* their story. That's what hurt so bad. The realization that it wasn't my story anymore. I became a symbol without asking for it.

I *became* my tragedy. It will be a part of my obituary I'm sure. They'll list the film roles right alongside my role as a victim of Richard, Charles, Sandro, and Ira. Which is why I never issued a public statement, never appeared on any talk shows, news shows, or any other sort of shows. Because I wanted no part of it. I wanted to be myself. Not the story of me everyone else was telling. Just *myself.*

But I'm realizing it's impossible to "be myself." I don't know who that is anymore. And I know you can relate. Which is why I forgive you, Jonah. Because I understand you. Because I can't imagine not forgiving anyone who went through what we did. I can't imagine not forgiving anyone who's going through what we're going through now.

Some days I wish I could forgive Richard. And Sandro and Charles and Ira. I wish I could unlock the door to the Land of Healing. A place where we eat fucking gumdrops in the goddamn clouds and laugh and sing and forget.

But it's too hard to forgive them. I don't have it in me.

But I can forgive you, Jonah. And I hope that can bring a little peace to us both.

Go to therapy, you fucking idiot.

Love,

Mace

28

I WAS UP all night. Your e-mail gave me a manic surge of optimism — left me feeling hopeful that we could reconnect in person, even become friends. I attempted to go to sleep around four a.m., failed, and marched back to my laptop to reread your letter again and again. Your words felt like they could save my life.

The news hit at six a.m.

I first saw the story on Twitter: Your mother found you in the bath of her Albuquerque condo. Wrists slit. Constant updates followed all morning. The coroner discovered crystal meth in your system. Your family wants privacy. A funeral is planned for next week.

The online eulogies began around six thirty a.m. As you predicted, the obituaries are effusive. The very news outlets that mocked your TMZ breakdown in October are now celebrating the story of your life. Now that they have their tragic ending, they've returned to the beginning to retell the whole thing. Richard was mentioned in every hot take, every think piece, every tweet and Facebook post. Even the articles that weren't about Richard were about him: "Why We Shouldn't Mention Richard Shriver When We Eulogize Mace Miller" and "Let Mace Miller Be Defined by Something Other Than Abuse." Already, there are two documentaries about your life in development. A hashtag surfaced on Twitter — #YourFaveMaceMemories. People use it when posting stories about the impact you had on their lives through either your films or your role as a public survivor of sexual abuse. You were a meme in life, a meme in death. Created by the internet to fuel the internet.

By eight a.m. I began to feel hopeless. I didn't know what to do. Or, rather, I knew what I *wanted* to do but was too afraid to act on my impulse. Too afraid to pursue a goal so monumental, an act that could forever change the trajectory of my life and your legacy. It was then I did what many anguished Americans faced with crippling anxiety do: I went to Gwyneth Paltrow for advice. I'm normally skeptical of the snake-oil start-up Goop, but desperate times call for dubious lifestyle brands. And God knows religion hadn't worked out for me. I scoured the Goop home page, skipping reports about crystal sales and karmic wounds, until I found what I needed: an article titled "Divide and De-Stress." It argued that the best way to complete any large task is to divide it into smaller, manageable tasks so as to avoid being overwhelmed by the immensity of your goal. I'm writing this to you at a rest stop somewhere along 495 West to say that the technique works. Shatter the impossible and make it a puzzle, something to achieve in pieces.

Step one: Rent a car.

Earlier this morning, I went to Hertz, waited in line, and rented a car. Easy.

Step two: Drive.

My next tiny task was to start driving. I found that if I just focused on the road ahead, I was able to keep my agitation at bay. All I was doing was driving. And I kept driving until I saw a sign for Target somewhere outside of a town literally called Hicksville. I turned off the interstate and pulled into the parking lot. Driving, done.

Step three: Get kerosene.

Two jugs in case one wasn't enough. I put them in my cart but didn't think about what I'd use them for. That was against the rules. I continued through Target, passing Christmas displays of cheap gifts and hideous sweaters, until I found what I needed next.

Step four: Get a ski mask.

I grabbed one off the wall, and as I did, Mariah Carey's "All I Want for Christmas Is You" came over the store's speakers. I burst into tears. Because all I want for Christmas is *you*, Mace. But then I thought of what you'd say if you were still alive and how you'd roll your eyes and make fun of me for breaking down in some random Target because of a *fucking Mariah Carey song* and how you'd laugh at me for being so cheesy. And the minute I thought of you laughing, I could also laugh, and then I was laughing hysterically in the Target aisle, laughing and crying all at once. When the song ended, I settled down and focused.

Step five: Get a screwdriver.

I waited in the checkout line. My heart was a bomb. I placed my items on the conveyor belt, paranoid that the cashier would clock my anxiety and label me a suspicious character. But she barely glanced my way. She stifled a yawn and bagged my items and stared into space as I pushed my cart into the cold, crowded parking lot.

I barreled down the highway, haunted by the cashier and the possibility that she'd wake from her catatonia, realize what I was doing, and call the police. *Something was strange about him, Officer, maybe it was those two giant jugs of kerosene he bought, yeah, that seemed a little odd when paired with the ski mask and the screwdriver.* I started doing ninety on the interstate, almost forgetting my next tiny task.

But I didn't.

I pulled off at another random exit and drove until I found a secluded dirt road that came to a dead end deep in the woods. It was a sort of informal rest stop, hidden by a cluster of cedar trees. I cut the engine.

Step six: Grab my screwdriver.

Step seven: Get out of the car.

Step eight: Unscrew my license plates.

Step nine: Throw them in the trunk.

I got back in my car, where I'm writing this now. One last letter to you, even though you're gone. Maybe this is more of a prayer.

Step ten: Justice.

Things didn't go as planned.

By the time I reached the compound it was late. Past midnight.

Any courage I'd mustered vanished the minute I saw the great iron wall that surrounded Richard's property. I gripped the steering wheel as images, smells, and sounds set my mind on fire. The odor of sex and blood in the basement, the taste of Richard's fingers in my mouth, the faces of the men above me, the burn of the sling on my thighs, a stray laugh from Charles, a slap from Sandro, a shriek from Seb. I pulled over and screamed until my senses deadened.

A strange, adrenalized calm cleared my mind.

I was ready.

I rolled up to the call box outside the gate. You appeared beside me. Suddenly, it was the night you set me free. We were in Richard's BMW. I heard your voice as you told me the code: *Zero, eight, sixteen.* I felt stronger in your presence. I punched the numbers and watched as the gate swung open and the drive appeared before me.

You disappeared.

I sat for a minute outside the gate, hurtling through another flashback. I saw myself running down the road, naked, screaming, crying, laughing, running for my life, and collapsing right there in front of the gate. I collapsed in front of myself.

I disappeared.

I pressed the gas gently and the car crept onto the compound. Each structure I passed was darkened, its inhabitants either elsewhere or asleep. I knew Richard would be home, however. In my compulsive cataloging of his downfall, I read a *Hollywood Reporter* article entitled "Where Is Richard Shriver Now?" The piece said that Richard had "holed up in his Hamptons compound" in order to "escape the public eye" while the "state's investigation of his illicit sex ring gears up." Still, there had been a few moments where he "dared to show his face in town," and the journalist had interviewed local boldface names who'd been scandalized to see him at Nick and Toni's. The outraged Hamptonites wondered how Richard had gotten a reservation and contemplated the etiquette of "running into monsters at dinner in our current climate."

I cut my lights and approached Richard's house at the far end of the property, gravel popping beneath my wheels. I stopped about a hundred yards from my destination, sweating, skull pounding. My breath came in short, irregular gasps. As if I'd forgotten how to breathe.

I put on the ski mask.

I got out of my car.

The cold winter air hit my face, sending a shiver through my body. I felt blank inside. No more sights or sounds or smells to invade my consciousness. Nothing. I walked to the trunk and opened it. I pulled out the jugs of kerosene. I carried one in each arm and walked toward Richard's property.

I stopped when I saw him. Moonlight beamed through the floor-to-ceiling windows of his home, illuminating his sleeping body. He was sprawled on the plush king-size mattress we'd shared for a brief, blissful period. A serene expression spread across his sleeping face.

Fucker, I thought.

I took the kerosene and walked around the perimeter of the house, pouring the liquid. Once I'd made a full circle, I tried the sliding glass door to the kitchen.

It was open.

I trod lightly as I made my way inside carrying the remaining jug of kerosene. I tipped the lid low to the ground and spilled the liquid on the floor. I doused the kitchen and living room but stopped short of the bedroom. I couldn't risk waking Richard.

I lit the shag rug.

I ran out.

I returned to my spot outside the bedroom window to watch the fire do its work. The blaze spread at a rapid rate, and soon the entire left side of the building was engulfed in flames. The bedroom was the last to go. I watched as it filled with smoke. Richard coughed himself awake. He leaped to his feet in panic, struggling to find an exit. He stumbled to his knees, choking on the toxic fumes. And as he retched on the floor, his eyes locked with mine.

I ripped off my ski mask so he could see my face.

Terror contorted his expression. I saw him realize that he was going to die, that I was the reason for his death, that I had finally exacted my revenge—*our* revenge, Mace. Even with this knowledge, he reached out toward me, placed his hand on the glass, and mouthed *Help*. I stood motionless in the field, watching as his eyes fluttered shut and he crumpled to the ground, unconscious.

I waited for relief.

But all I felt was panic. Killing Richard wouldn't make him go away. It would bring him closer. Nothing would be solved. Nothing would be healed. My life would be defined by his death. Defined by the knowledge that I was capable of just as much cruelty as Richard.

I wanted to blame Richard for his own murder—*Look what you made me do, you sick fuck*—but I knew that I couldn't. I remembered what you'd said in your letter, Mace, about trauma being a gift. And a responsibility. The act of killing Richard would only push me deeper into the prison that he'd built for me.

I needed to release him.

I needed to reclaim my own life.

I wished I could reclaim yours too.

I thought of you as I picked up a giant rock. I thought of you as I held its weight in my arms. I thought of you as I threw it at Richard's bedroom window. I thought of you as the glass shattered and the smoke poured out, polluting the cold, clear air. I thought of you as I dragged Richard from his bedroom floor onto the thick grass outside. I thought of you as I pressed my lips to his — an act that triggered memories of his angry kisses, the force of his tongue against my unwilling jaw. I thought of you as I blew air inside his mouth. I thought of you as I pounded on his rib cage, trying to resuscitate his motionless body.

I thought of you as I saved Richard's life.

Suddenly, he coughed and then he coughed again and his whole body shook and his eyes opened and he looked up at me and moaned.

"Jonah?"

And I thought of you as I punched him in the face.

2018

29

December 16, 2018

Dear Mace,

I'm not even sure why I'm writing to you.

Well, that's not entirely true. I'm writing to you at the behest of Jeremy, my therapist. I asked for mood stabilizers, but instead he gave me a writing assignment. In our initial sessions, I struggled to articulate my story aloud, afraid to touch the fire in my belly. Afraid it would burn me up. I needed an easier way to explain what happened. So I shared my writing with him. All my thoughts to you. I told him this document was, at times, my only reason for living.

Which is why he suggested I continue this correspondence. To make peace with you, with myself, with my family, with my own spirit. And I suppose it's no coincidence that I'm writing this on the one-year anniversary of your death.

I miss you, Mace.

—Jonah

30

I'M HEADING HOME for Christmas.

There's a phrase I thought I'd never use again: *heading home for Christmas*. The plane ticket was not an insignificant expense given my limited budget these days. A former colleague recently hooked me up with a gig ghostwriting an advice column for *Cosmopolitan*, a job that appeals to me because of its anonymity and mindlessness, though it pays me much less than my former position at the *Profile*. But this trip home felt like an essential investment, though I don't know if I can describe my father's farm in Illinois as "home." Still, there is a familiar ache in my heart as I sit in the airport and wait for the plane that will take me to the man I miss more than anyone: my father, who art in Kabumfuck, Illinois, hallowed be thy name.

Jeremy said I could call him if there's an emergency. We've been working toward this moment for months. Back when I first hired him, I said that I longed to reestablish a connection with my father. I wanted to apologize for telling the lie that destroyed his life and our family. Despite Jeremy's insistence that I first needed to forgive my-self — that I'd lied to ensure my own survival, to escape conversion therapy — I still felt incredible guilt. I feared that my father would be furious, that he would still believe I was going to hell.

Finally, my need for resolution overwhelmed my fear. With the support of Jeremy, I responded to my father's e-mail — the one he sent back in October of 2017—and requested that we talk on the phone. "I'm so sorry, Jonah." His distant voice was fractured by shitty reception; it sounded like he was calling from the past. "I'm sorry for everything I put you through."

His words shocked me. This was the one possibility I hadn't prepared for, that *he* would feel responsible for what happened. That I was not to blame. Our first call was not productive, as I was barely able to speak through my sobs. But over the ensuing months we were able to sustain a dialogue, offering up stories to explain away the years of silence.

My father told me how he'd wanted to die. He'd wanted to die when he first heard my false accusation. He'd wanted to die right there in the church office, right in front of my weeping mother. He'd wanted to die right in front of the church elders instead of listening as they debated how to "handle" the situation, like my father was a problem to be solved instead of the man who'd held them as they wept in his arms and confessed their sins. He'd wanted to die when no one believed that he wouldn't abuse his son. But suicide was a sin, and so he'd wanted to die but couldn't do anything except pray for a car accident, a lightning bolt, a plummeting piano.

My father told me that when everyone lost their faith in him, he lost his faith in God. After all, what kind of a God would punish *him*, the minister who'd adhered to every last rule and regulation, who'd devoted his entire existence to celebrating God's love? It didn't take long for him to arrive at an answer. He'd made one crucial mistake: me. Somehow, he'd ruined his only child. He'd taken the Lord's blessing—a beautiful baby boy—and turned it into an abomination. A homosexual. And for *this* reason, he concluded, God punished him.

My father told me about how he'd moved home to live with his own father, my grandfather. He told no one of his whereabouts. He became a man without a past, only a future. There was plenty of room on my grandfather's farm. My father's pulse quickened when he saw that familiar stretch of strawberry field outside of Wood-stock, Illinois, and turned into the long dirt driveway that led to the home where he was raised. *This is where I will begin my new life*, he thought as he rolled up to my grandfather's farmhouse. *Thank You, God, for bringing me home.*

But soon, my father told me, the trouble started. My grandfa-ther was not exactly thrilled about the return of his son. He'd al-ways been a stern man, a lifelong evangelical who'd survived a mis-erable Depression-era upbringing due to his rigid asceticism, and he became even more taciturn and judgmental after my grandmother passed. Years of solitude had hardened my grandfather, who had no one to talk to but the men who worked his farm and the chickens that produced eggs for his daily breakfast: an omelet, two pieces of toast, and seven fresh, farm-picked strawberries.

My father told me that my grandfather viewed his return as a sinful flaw in his character. A real man would never leave his wife and child. My father didn't offer the story of how his family had fallen apart, and my grandfather never asked, but still, a painful si-lence swelled between them. Soon, my grandfather's health began to fail. He believed his demise had been precipitated by the presence of sin within his home. As dementia eroded my grandfather's brain, he grew increasingly spiteful, lashed out against my father for the slightest infraction.

My father told me how he started to drink because he began to believe what his father believed: that he was an abomination, that he had brought shame to his family, that he was beyond saving. And so all there was left to do was drink and take care of his father until the day my grandfather died in his sleep—a rare smile on his face. My father viewed this final, peaceful expression as proof my grand-father had made it to heaven, a fact that filled my father with dread, because it meant that my grandfather had been right all along: my father was destined for hell.

His drinking got worse after that. He was searching for oblivion, a way to forget the fate that awaited him in the next world. He drank and drank, and the days disappeared, and the nights blended together, and time collapsed, until one evening he grabbed a bottle of aspirin and did what he'd wanted to do for so long: he consumed the entire bottle. Then he rifled through the medicine cabinet, found another bottle, and downed all the pills in that one too. He stumbled outside, took in the beauty of the landscape one last time, dropped to the earth right outside the chicken coop, and fell asleep on the ground, waiting for the Devil to claim his property.

My father told me he died that night. Or, rather, a version of him died. When he woke the following morning in the hospital — brought there by one of the farmhands who'd discovered his unconscious body on the way to feed the chickens — my father felt an urgent need to speak to me. To tell me he was sorry. To fix the years of brokenness.

My father told me he had a vision that day — he saw his son crying in the strawberry field. He rushed toward me, swept me into his embrace. Our history, healed.

My father told me he'd joined Twitter because he read about a growing online movement of "ex-vangelicals," people who had left evangelicalism due to trauma inflicted on them by the church. They were finding healing in community, attempting to discover a new understanding of God that did not oppress them because of race, gender, or sexuality. Many of these ex-vangelicals were unapologetically queer — freed, for the first time, from the closet, or forced celibacy, or conversion therapy. When my father read these stories, he thought of what he'd put me through and how he wanted to make things right.

My father told me how, through this online community, he found a real-life community, a small support group of ex-vangelicals who met every week in Chicago at the city's LGBTQ community center. He drove an hour and a half each way to attend these meetings, where he'd listen to stories of broken families and broken bodies and broken spirits, where he'd share his own. Gradually, this support group became larger until eventually it took on the qualities of a church, but a new kind of church, a space where everyone was welcome. A space of healing.

My father told me all this over the course of many phone calls, and finally, last month, he asked if I'd like to come visit him. I said yes. And I had been happy with my decision—until today.

It started this morning in the cab to JFK. My gut churned with doubt. Adrenaline surged through my veins. No matter how many times I assured myself that my father had changed, all I could think about was our past—his hands shaking my body, his voice raging toward heaven. The harder I tried to banish these thoughts, the more immediate they became, until they no longer felt like memories. I sat there, lost in this violent time warp, until the car came to a stop and the cabbie barked in my direction and I forced my feet to move.

As I entered the airport, I became convinced that returning home would ruin me. I needed to numb out. Find a bar. But Jeremy had warned me against the dangers of self-medication. It took all my strength to bypass a TGI Friday's in favor of the airport bookstore. I rounded up all the tabloids and junk food my arms could contain and stood in line poring over *Us Weekly,* hoping that news of Candace Cameron Bure's go-karting accident and a pack of jumbo Twizzlers could distract me. I practiced the deep breathing technique Jeremy taught me—inhale for three seconds, exhale for three seconds, hold, repeat. My pulse had nearly settled when I reached the cashier and looked up from my magazine.

Which is when I saw Richard.

There he was, standing behind the register. All the adrenaline came rushing back. I dropped my magazines and screamed, *"Get away from me,"* and ran out of the bookstore. It was only when I looked back and saw the confused face of the cashier that I realized my mistake.

I took an Ativan—I had a few for emergencies—and now, as I

wait to board the plane, I'm starting to feel better. Writing to you also helps. And yet I can't stop thinking about how the men in my life always fail me. How trauma seems to follow me wherever I go. How I find it impossible to trust the embrace of another man, to experience touch as anything other than a precursor to violence. Even so, I keep going back for more. Even so, I'm getting on this plane, hoping this time will be different.

Hoping my father's love won't destroy me.

31

MY ENTIRE BODY tensed when I saw my father through the glass doors of the terminal. He stood sentinel by his white Honda, worry fixed on his face. I was shocked by how much he'd aged—his full brown mane had been replaced by balding patches of white, his formerly robust shoulders had caved. Guilt overwhelmed me. I felt responsible.

I emerged from the arrivals gate. He stared directly at me but didn't see me. It wasn't until I lifted my hand to wave at him that he finally registered my presence. A tentative glimmer appeared on his face as he stretched out his arms. Instantly, my body was torn by two separate impulses: the urge to run into my father's embrace and the urge to run away for good.

But I didn't run away. I took a deep breath like Jeremy taught me—in for three seconds, out for three seconds, hold, repeat—and registered the rhythms of my heart. The pounding lessened. I approached my father and hugged him. We wept for what could have been a minute or an hour.

"It's good to see you," my father said finally, breaking the spell. "Should we go to the farm?"

Snow fell as we drove. By the time we reached my grandfather's strawberry fields, the dead farmland was completely erased by white. Fear seized me; what if I was snowed in, unable to escape my father's farm, trapped where he could torture me, just like Richard trapped and tortured me? My mind knew this thought was irrational, but still, I started sweating and biting the skin around my fingernails. Once again, I practiced Jeremy's breathing exercise—in for three seconds, out for three seconds, hold, repeat. My father filled the ride with nervous chatter about his chickens. I just sat there inhaling, exhaling, hearing my father but not listening.

By the time we rolled into the driveway, I at last felt calm. My father turned to me and put his hand on my shoulder. "I know you're nervous." He sighed. "I am too. But no matter what happens, know that I love you."

I said nothing. I'm desperate to believe in his love but still so afraid to trust.

We e-mailed my mother on that first day. We wanted to speak with her, to explain how we're healing, invite her back into our family. Her response was devastating but not surprising: *I'm sorry, but I don't wish to speak to either of you at this time. You are both living in defiance of God's intention for our lives. I pray that the two of you can once again allow Christ into your hearts. But until that time, I will not engage in any further communication. Your sins have done enough damage to my life.*

We try not to let my mother's e-mail dominate our thoughts. We understand the awful grip of the evangelical church. We hope she finds freedom. We hope she finds us.

I've been on the farm for three days now. Each day is easier than the last. My father has put me up in the Strawberry House, so called because it was once the roadside stand where my grandfather sold his strawberries during the early days of his farm. It has since been converted into a small guesthouse with one room, big enough for a queen bed. If I need an escape (and there are moments when I feel claustrophobic around my father, when I see a flash of Richard's face), I can retreat to my tiny Strawberry House.

Overall, however, I feel strangely at peace. Memories of Richard seem to be fading. He has evaporated from my dreams. I sleep through the night. I feel so far from my life in New York. Here, there is no risk of passing a restaurant or storefront or some stretch of city that brings me back to Richard, which then brings me back to the basement, which brings me back to the night I held Richard's life in my hands.

Fear of being prosecuted for my revenge has prevented me from seeking other forms of justice. Not that I have any faith in the legal system at this point. The state investigation of Richard and his co-hort fell apart. Chase filed a civil suit that was dismissed due to the statute of limitations. Michael—homeless for years—has now vanished, joining Evan in the ether. Only Seb managed to get a settlement—an insulting seventy-five thousand dollars.

No one has been held accountable. Richard still walks free.

Some days I wish I'd killed him. But most days I don't. It was hard enough in the months that followed my final visit to his compound. I lived in constant fear of being arrested. I scanned the headlines daily. The fire was reported, of course. The news provided cathartic justice for so many, and there were countless tweets that celebrated Richard's fate. It was arson, that much was confirmed by the police. Richard claimed that an unidentified man had broken into the compound and set fire to the house. Whether it was guilt, fear, or gratitude that prevented him from reporting me to the authorities, I don't know. And to be honest, I don't want to.

I'm writing this sitting in the Strawberry House. Despite all the injustice I've endured, a fragile optimism has taken root in my mind. I find myself thinking about the possibilities of my future instead of the injuries of my past. I think this feeling is called hope, though it's been so long since I've experienced it that I'm not quite ready to trust it.

Earlier this evening, my father asked me to go to church to hear him preach. I never thought I'd step foot in another church as long as I lived, let alone to hear my father preach. I told him I couldn't handle it. I'm afraid that going back to church will break me. I'm afraid that *not* going back to church will break me.

"But it's Christmas," he pleaded. "Please, just give it a chance. Give *me* a chance."

"Okay." I hesitated. "I'll do it for you."

32

December 26, 2018

Dear Dad,

Do you remember that Christmas Eve when Mom slipped on the ice? I was eleven. I remember her body splayed on the black glaze of our driveway. Her shriek, muffled by snow. Her ankle, which didn't look like an ankle but a jumble of bones threatening to burst through skin. I remember rushing to her side, hugging her with savage force, my embrace twisting her body as she let out another scream and you pulled me off her and she clutched her leg. Her eyes were twin fires. I was certain she would die. Certain my secret had killed her.

And then the dull glare of the hospital. The limp tinsel above Mom's bed. The pathetic cardboard Santa taped to the wall. I ripped his head off at the neck, threw it to the ground. I went back for his body, but you stopped my hand.

Mom sighed. *Why don't you and Daddy go for a little walk?*

Is Mommy gonna die? I whimpered later as you led me through the sterile halls.

Of course not, you whispered.

How do you know?

Because we love her, you said, brushing away my tears. *Because God loves her. And that love is more powerful than death. That love will save us all.*

But you didn't know my secret. Boys like me didn't get God's love. We got His wrath. You said so yourself, in so many sermons.

And then the next morning. Our famous family breakfast. You at the stove. Mom sitting at the table, her crutches propped against the counter, her right leg in a cast. *Reporting for pancake duty,* you said, saluting her. *Filling in for our injured soldier.* You hummed "O Holy Night" as you mixed the batter and the blueberries. Already the crisis was fading, replaced by the rhythms of our favorite ritual. Our family was whole again, but I was not. A tension grew in my body—a tension between what I knew I was and what I knew you and Mom wanted me to be. I felt I didn't deserve to be at that breakfast table—not with my secret sin that triggered God's fury. That almost killed Mom.

And then that Christmas service. Mom standing next to me, crutches under her arms, beaming down. You at the pulpit, telling the story of Christ's birth. Then it was time for Communion. You invited us to the table. Mom took my hand, but I hung back. She tugged at my arm and frowned. I was terrified to approach the altar. Terrified the bread would turn to poison on my tongue. Terrified that this was where God's punishment would claim me. But Mom persisted and we walked to the front and you handed me a piece of bread and smiled and said, *Take and eat, for this is the body of Christ.* I cried as the bread softened in my mouth. You smiled again, mistaking my tears for reverence.

See, I told you, Jonah, you said after the service. *Love saved us after all.*

But love didn't save us, did it? Not in the long run.

I want to love again, Dad. Which is why I'm writing you this letter. Which is why I went to your new church yesterday. Which is why I sat in the back row and stared down at my slush-crusted boots as everyone else stood and sang "O Holy Night." I sat, my body stiff with terror, as the band quieted and you stepped onstage.

Suddenly, I was in two places at once: I was a kid sitting in the pews of my childhood megachurch and I was an adult sitting in a folding chair, holding a lifetime of hurt. The only thing that kept me in my seat—the only thing that kept me from running out, running to the car, leaving forever—was the hope that the present could heal the past.

"Merry Christmas," you said to the room. A warm expression spread across your face. "I'd like to start this service by welcoming everyone. We are all loved by God, loved for exactly who we are, no matter our race, gender, or sexuality. And I also want to acknowledge that this is a difficult message for many of us to hear. So many of us in this community have been hurt by the evangelical church. So many of us have been shunned, shamed, or"—your voice broke, but you continued—"shut out of our own families. And I want to acknowledge that pain and remind us why we're here: to reclaim our faith."

Your words were addressed to everyone but felt like they were meant just for me.

You began your sermon.

You told the story of a family. A desert journey, a couple desperate for shelter. A woman pregnant, about to give birth. Her life and the life of her child at stake. Mother and father pushed through burning sand, suffocating heat. Finally, one innkeeper took pity, allowed them to take refuge in his stable. They joined the animals, fashioned a bed from hay and manure. The stench was heavy. The woman screamed.

The child was coming. The mother's cries agitated the livestock. Oxen kicked and paced. The man sweat through his garments, clutched the woman's hand. Prayed she would survive. And there, in the muck and grass, in the lowliest place imaginable, a miracle occurred. She gave birth to a beautiful boy.

The embodiment of God's love. New hope for the world.

As you finished, you said that God didn't stop with the birth of Jesus. That God continues to birth new love, new light in each of us every day. But you reminded us that birth is painful. That renewal takes time. Yet on the other side of suffering, there can be growth and joy.

You said that as you talked about birth, it was impossible not to think of your own son. Your broken family. For so long, you missed your boy. For so long, you were angry, lost. But out of that pain, a new love had been born. Your son had returned home.

I had returned home.

I am home.

You explained how our reunion brought healing. Hope. You prayed I felt the same.

Then it was time for Communion. You invited us to join you at the table. One by one, people took hunks of bread from your hands and dipped them in wine. I was reluctant to join the group. I remembered the awful Christmas service from my childhood, the terror I'd felt approaching the altar, the certainty that God would strike me dead. My mind knew that this time was different. But I couldn't do it—the pain was too much, the ritual too loaded. Then I caught your gaze from across the room. It was a look I'd never seen before: humble, pleading, hopeful. *You have your father's eyes,* Mom told me once, picking me up from conversion therapy. *If only you saw the world the same way.*

I stood from my seat and you stumbled back, surprise contorting your face. I had the strange sensation that our bodies were connected; I could feel your blood pounding in my skull, your heart thudding in my chest, your muscles pushing me forward.

I had no idea what I was about to do.

I arrived at the altar. I looked down at those empty symbols
—the stale bread, the sour wine—then up at your face. And I
don't know if I believe in Jesus, or God, or the scriptures, or any
of it. But at that moment, it didn't matter. Because I believed
in the tilt of your smile as you lifted your arms. I believed in the
warmth of your embrace as you held me, weeping, and told me
you were sorry. And I believed you when you whispered in my
ear: "I love you, son."

I love you too, Dad. I wasn't able to say it in the moment.
Wasn't sure I believed it. But now, as I sit and write this letter,
I know it's true. From my desk, through the frosted pane, I can
see Grandpa's house. A light glimmers in the kitchen. Your
silhouette passes a window. For a moment, Mom's there too.
My heart pounds faster. But no, it's just a curtain, playing
tricks. A ghost. Mom vanishes, but you stay. Your shadow
flickers and my pulse steadies. My body relaxes. You emerge
from the house. A smile ignites your face. You step off the
porch and into the fresh snow. You walk toward the Strawberry
House.

You're coming to get me.

You're knocking at the door.

You're calling my name.

"Jonah," you sing. "I made breakfast."

"Coming," I say.

—Jonah

ACKNOWLEDGMENTS

This book would not exist without PJ Mark. I am forever grateful to him for his passion, humor, insight, and unwavering belief in both me and my work. I feel so unbelievably lucky to have found such an incredible agent. Thanks to Ian Bonaparte, who provided crucial support throughout the publishing process, Allison Hunter, and everyone at Janklow and Nesbit.

Pilar Garcia-Brown understood this novel from the very beginning. I am truly blessed to have such a brilliant, passionate, funny, and kind editor. Her perspective and input made this book better than I ever could've imagined. To everyone at Houghton Mifflin Harcourt—I am so, so thrilled to have found such a wonderful home for my work. I'm lucky to have Emma Gordon on the publicity front and Lisa McAuliffe leading the charge on marketing. Kelly Winton designed such a stunning cover. And I'm incredibly thankful for Tracy Roe and her copyediting superpowers.

For their generosity and support of this book, I am forever grateful to Kristen Arnett, Alexander Chee, Garrard Conley, Samantha Hunt, Alex Marzano-Lesnevich, De'Shawn Charles Winslow, Taymour Soomro, Jennifer Tseng, Maud Casey, Noah Bogdonoff, Benjamin Schaefer, Jonathan Freeman-Coppadge, Jordan Rossen, and Diana Wagman. Sam Lansky was among the first to lay eyes on this manuscript, and I cannot thank him enough for his early support.

I workshopped chapters of this book at the Bread Loaf Writers' Conference. My experience during my two summers there profoundly shaped the writer I am today. Thank you to everyone I encountered there—the artists who inspired me, challenged me, and made me laugh.

I'm grateful to Marla Mindelle, Matthew Risch, Connor Gallagher, Philip Drennan, Danny Visconti, Da Sul Kim, Adam Roberts, Craig Johnson, and Kyle Buchanan for the years of laughter and support.

I'm blessed to have such a talented team working on the television adaptation of this book—Stephen Dunn, Patrick Moran, Ari Lubet, and everyone at PKM productions and Amazon Studios.

New Abbey in Pasadena, California, has been the source of so much spiritual healing for me. I'm fortunate to be part of a community that provides a safe space for so many queer and trans people to reclaim their faith.

Kelsey Miller has always supported me over the course of our friendship, but her new role as my anxious-debut-author therapist is one I am particularly grateful for. Chrissy Angliker and Deborah Siegel have also been there since high school, and I'm so thankful for their friendship.

Thanks to my family for a lifetime of love.

Henry Slavens—you inspire me with your incredible intellect, depth of compassion, and sparkling wit.

Finally, to Ryan—your love is the greatest gift.